THE
RARE

DIANE ANTHONY

AUTHORS 4 AUTHORS PUBLISHING
Marysville, WA, USA

Second Edition

Published by Authors 4 Authors Publishing
1214 6th St
Marysville, WA 98270
www.authors4authorspublishing.com

E-book ISBN: 978-1-64477-139-6
Paperback ISBN: 978-1-64477-140-2
Audiobook ISBN: 978-1-64477-141-9

Edited by Rebecca Mikkelson
Copyedited by Brandi Spencer

Cover design ©2022 Practically Perfect Covers. All rights reserved.
Interior design by Brandi Spencer

Authors 4 Authors Publishing branding is set in Bavire. Title and headings are set in Pirulen. Author name and chapter numbers are set in Perfect Thoughts. Correspondence text is set in Segoe Print. All other text is set in Garamond.

THE
RARE

DIANE ANTHONY

Authors 4 Authors Content Rating

This title has been rated 14+, suitable for teens, and contains:

- moderate language
- intense violence
- brief implied sexual violence
- negative mild tabacco, illicit, and fantasy drug use
- suicide and mental illness
- governmental conspiracy

Please, keep the following in mind when using our rating system:

1. A content rating is not a measure of quality.

Great stories can be found for every audience. One book with many content warnings and another with none at all may be of equal depth and sophistication. Our ratings can work both ways: to avoid content or to find it.

2. Ratings are merely a tool.

For our young adult (YA) and children's titles, age ratings are generalized suggestions. For parents, our descriptive ratings can help you make informed decisions, but at the end of the day, only you know what kinds of content are appropriate for your individual child. This is why we provide details in addition to the general age rating.

For more information on our rating system, please, visit our Content Guide at: www.authors4authorspublishing.com/books/ratings

DEDICATION

To Sage and my Three Kings.

WORKS BY
DIANE ANTHONY

Supernova

The Rare Trilogy

The Rare
The Remnant
The Return (July 2022)

TABLE OF CONTENTS

TABLE OF CONTENTS

1

A continuous, rhythmic beeping pulls me out of my dreamless slumber.

Crap! I'm not dead.

This is the third time I've tried but failed to free myself from this dismal existence. I keep my eyes closed, hoping not to bring unwanted attention to my awakening. I don't need the looks of disappointment, the words of false concern, or the endless questions about why I would do such a thing.

I wince in pain as I try to swallow. My throat is raw and swollen. They must have pumped my stomach again. The first time I tried to end my life was with a whole bottle of my Zoloft prescription. I thought the irony of killing myself with a bottle of antidepressants was amusing. This time, it was a container of aspirin washed down with a bottle of Benadryl. It seemed like a better way to go than my last attempt. Let me tell you, drowning is not as poetic of a way to go as you might think. The burning in my lungs, the pain and dizziness in my head from lack of oxygen, and the subsequent retching and coughing of water after being pulled from my moment of death were so unpleasant it made me vow to never try it again.

I crack my eyelids open just enough to peer through my eyelashes. I want to see if I can spot my mother. I can make out a blurry form in the corner. I open my eyes just a bit more. I'm not wearing my glasses, but I can tell by the way her head is leaning off to the side that she is asleep in the rocking chair.

Good.

I have an itch on my nose that has been driving me mad since I woke up. I try to lift my hand as slowly and silently as I can, so as not to wake her, but something pulls on my wrist, and my hand stops only inches off the bed.

What the...?

I try to lift my other hand, but it, too, is strapped down. My heart races, causing the beeping of my heart monitor to quicken. I start hyperventilating as a panic attack sets in. All I can think about is freeing myself from this newest prison.

I start to thrash around as everything fades to black. It's as though I'm looking through a narrow tunnel, seeing nothing but the painting hanging on the wall across the room. My hyperventilating turns into a full-blown

1

asthma attack. So much for being inconspicuous. My mom is awake now and rushes over to the call button to get a nurse in here.

"What's going on? Why am I strapped down?" I squeak between shallow breaths.

"Calm down. You need to just calm down," my mom says.

I squeeze my eyes shut, tears leaking down my cheeks, and I try to hold still. My chest is heaving as I struggle to take an adequate breath. I know the drill. I have had so many asthma attacks in my life it seems as though I spend more time using my inhaler than I do breathing on my own. My muscles tremble from the adrenaline that is coursing through my body.

Why couldn't I have just died this time? I hate my life!

My mom grabs my inhaler from her purse and holds it up to my mouth.

"Ready? One, two, three, breathe," she says as she squeezes the medicine down my throat. I try hard to hold my breath for the ten seconds before exhaling, but my lungs burn from a desire to cough.

Hold it...hold it...

I let my breath out with a chest-wrenching cough. My already sore throat feels like it's about to rip out of my neck.

"What's going on in here?" asks a plump nurse as she makes her way to my bed, followed closely by a man dressed in white.

"She's having a panic attack, which triggered an asthma attack," my mom answers.

"Give her another dose of her inhaler while I go get something for the panic attack," the nurse says, turning around and waddling back out of the room. The man stands at the foot of my bed, watching me closely.

Every muscle in my body is shaking now. I'm still not breathing well enough, and my face starts tingling from the insufficient amount of air.

"Here you go. One, two, three, breathe," Mom says again.

I breathe in the medicine, and I'm able to hold my breath this time. My mom puts my glasses on me so I can see again.

"Where am I?" I eye the man who hasn't moved an inch since coming in. My heart is still racing. I wish I could run away right now.

"You're in the psychiatric ward of St. Mary's hospital, Olivia."

I shudder at the thought. I'm in the looney bin? Great. I pull at my restraints again, hoping they will break so I can fight my way out of here.

The nurse makes her way back into the room holding a syringe.

"Orderly, I need you to expose her backside."

I start yelling incomprehensibly. Every word I utter dies in my injured throat.

"Hold still, please," the nurse says, annoyingly calm but firm. "I'm giving you a dose of diazepam. It will help you calm down. It'll take a little bit to kick in, though. I suggest you try to relax until then."

There's a pinch in my butt where she injects the medicine, and then the orderly lets me go. I stop pulling at my restraints, but my heart is still pounding, and my head is fuzzy.

"How..." I try to clear my throat so I can spit out my question. "How much longer do I have to be tied down?"

"Until we feel that you will not try to run away or injure yourself again," the nurse answers. "You will be staying here in the hospital wing until you're healed. Once you no longer need medical attention, we'll move you to a different room in the psychiatric ward, but until then, you need to stay in this bed and rest. I'll be back to check on you in a little while to make sure the medicine has taken effect."

"Maybe if you remove the restraints, I'll be able to calm down better," I plead. "I promise I won't run away," I say as innocently as possible. I have every intention of getting out of here once no one is looking. A psychiatric ward? I don't think so!

"Nice try. The medicine should kick in soon, and then we'll have a chat," the nurse says, turning to walk out of the room. The orderly follows.

I huff in frustration. I lay my head back down on the pillow and focus on a crack in the opposite wall. I try to do my breathing exercises to settle myself down.

"You did this to yourself you know," my mom says accusingly.

"No, I didn't. I planned on dying, not being thrown in a mental hospital and strapped to a bed."

"Olivia! Why do you want to die so badly?"

"My life is hell, Mom! You of all people should know this! I'm in and out of hospitals constantly; I have such severe asthma that I need to have at least two inhalers with me at all times, in case one of them should run out during the day and leave me unable to breathe; I'm practically blind without these coke bottle glasses; I have no friends—"

"You have David," my mom interrupts.

"Yes. I have David. Another human who happens to be in the same boat as me." I roll my eyes. "If you recall, we met in a hospital."

"Well, you can't expect to make friends if you don't try."

"Mom, everyone at school thinks I'm a weakling and an idiot. I'm failing most of my classes because I'm not smart enough. I get picked last in gym all the time, which I guess I don't blame them. I would pick me last too."

"You're struggling in school because your hospital visits set you back. You'll catch on eventually if you would stop trying to do this..." she says, gesturing at me.

I roll my eyes. There is no talking to this woman. She will never understand the hell I have to live with. I'm not sure I have ever seen my mother sick in all my life. I, on the other hand, spend more time in and out of hospitals with illnesses than should be humanly possible. I just want it to end.

"Once you get home, I think you should invite Susan over again. You seemed to have a nice time together the last time she was over," my mom offers.

"Yeah, maybe," I agree, trying to dodge the topic.

Susan is my next-door neighbor in the apartment complex we live in. What Mom doesn't know is that I made a deal with Susan that day. If she pretended to be having a good time whenever my mother was around, I would give her my week's allowance. She was a surprisingly great actress. When my mom would walk in the room, Susan would put on a big smile and laugh extra loud, as though I said something profoundly hilarious. Once my mother would leave, we would go back to stony silence, and Susan would sit, texting anyone and everyone she could. Susan isn't one of the popular girls in my class, but she has enough friends to keep her texting fingers busy and her big blue eyes glued to the phone screen. I'm not sure why she isn't popular. Must be by choice or something. She has beautiful long black hair, a pretty face complete with long lashes and pouty lips, and a toned athletic frame. A great deal different from my short blonde hair, plain face, and sickly, thin body. I can't seem to put on any weight between hospital visits. Most of the illnesses leave me with no appetite.

Now that I've calmed down, my muscles start to release tension. My breathing slows, and the tingling stops. My mom has returned to the rocking chair and keeps glancing at me. I know she's trying hard to hold her tongue and not lecture me some more like the last time I was in the hospital after trying to commit suicide. She went on and on about how foolish I was and how I have my whole life ahead of me and whether I know how expensive these hospital stays are. I finally screamed at her to just get out, and she left me for a couple of days before returning to apologize. And that's our relationship in a nutshell ever since I can remember: fighting, accusations, arguing, and then apologies and tolerance until the next fight. I don't think my mom was ready to be a mom when she got pregnant with me, and with my Dad gone, she's had to do it all alone. She tries to be a good mom sometimes, but I'm pretty sure she resents my existence.

I take a deep breath in and close my eyes. My muscles are relaxed enough now that I slowly start to fade into the state of waking dreams, that is, until the city's air raid sirens start blaring. I get sucked out of my dream and reflexively try to sit up, but the restraints tug at my wrists, and I flop back into the pillow.

My mom is at the door, peeking her head out.

"Nurse? Nurse!" she calls out, trying to get somebody's attention.

The hospital emergency system starts going off to match the sirens. The cacophony makes me want to cover my ears, but of course, I can't.

"Excuse me! What's going on?" I hear my mom yelling out the door now.

"This is not a drill. All patients and personnel are required to stay inside until further notice. This facility is in a lockdown. I repeat this is not a drill. All patients and personnel..." repeats an unnervingly calm voice over the P.A. system.

I look over at the door to see my mom reach out and grab a nurse's arm as she hustles by.

"What's going on? Are we being attacked?"

"No, ma'am. It's raining," the nurse answers as she pulls her arm out of my mother's grip and quickly walks away.

5

2

I instinctively glance out the window, but I can't see anything in this unceasing fog. I sure hope they gave enough warning this time. The last time it rained, eleven people died because they didn't get out of the rain fast enough. Scientists call it "poison rain," but everyone I talk to calls it "death rain." It's different from acid rain, which destroys buildings. This just destroys humans.

Scientists tried to come up with umbrellas that can handle the rain, but they are rudimentary, at best. I have seen higher quality rain protection gear, but it's only for the rich. Not many people can afford it.

My mom is always paranoid that the sirens mean there is another attack happening like the one that got our country in the mess it's in now. But it is always just the rain.

The sirens continue to blare for a couple more minutes, but they shut it off once the lockdown is complete. I lay my head back onto the pillow and start to fall back to sleep.

Everything is green. The sunlight dances through the trees as the wind gently sends them swaying. The breeze is cool on my face, cutting through the intense heat of the day. I take a deep breath of the sweet smelling air and find that my lungs fill without protest from my asthma. I take a good look around. Everything is so green!

I'm in the woods. At least, I assume it's the woods. I have only ever seen them on TV or in pictures in books. What am I doing here? I need to get back home before some wild beast gets me! I glance around, hoping to find a trail that will take me back to the city. I stumble over branches and undergrowth that seem to grab at my feet. I pass between two giant boulders draped with soft green moss, and I stop short. There is a black figure up ahead in the shadows about forty feet away. I can't seem to make out what it is. I slowly start to back up, hoping to hide behind one of the boulders until it leaves. Is it looking in this direction? I make my movements slow and calculated. It seems to be hunched over something. I'm almost back to the boulder when my foot steps down on a branch with a resounding crack.

The dark figure spins around to face me. Just as it does, the wind picks up, and a beam of sunlight lands on its dark mottled fur. Its eyes are pools of inky black. Its long snout is crimson and wet. It bares its teeth, revealing needle-sharp fangs, dripping with blood. It looks as though it had once been a wolf, but its stature is larger and disfigured. It lets out an unearthly growl and starts bounding toward me. There is no way I'm going to get away from this thing! I turn around to run, but a pair of hands grab me and pulls me behind a boulder. I hear a twang sound, and then a loud whine comes from the direction of the beast. I look up and see a man standing on the boulder, nocking another arrow. He lets it loose, and I hear a loud thud accompanied by the breaking of branches and then silence. He must have killed it.

The man jumps down from the boulder to make sure the beast is dead. I turn around to get a look at the person who pulled me out of harm's way. He looks to be in his early twenties, although it's hard to tell with his face covered in a thick beard. His brown hair is long and tied back with a strip of cloth. His clothes look worn and dirty. His eyes are a crystal clear blue that seems to hold my gaze and won't let go. The hunter comes back around the boulder and breaks this guy's scrutiny of me. He turns from me and gives his friend a slap on the back.

The man who killed the beast looks remarkably like the young guy who pulled me behind the boulder, only older, maybe in his late forties. His brown hair is cut short in odd angles, as though he did it with a knife. A thick brown beard with streaks of gray grows on his face, and he has green eyes. His clothes are also in a state of disrepair but are covered by a garment made of animal fur. Black fur. A lot like the beast he just killed.

"Thank you for saving me. I don't even know how I got here." I look back and forth between the two men.

"You're welcome, Olivia," the older man says.

"Olivia!" my mom shouts.

I awake with a start. My legs are twisted up in the sheets, and I'm drenched with sweat.

"Are you okay? You were thrashing around in your bed, moaning. I've been trying to wake you up for a couple of minutes now."

"Um...yeah. I'm fine...I think," I mumble, trying to make sense of what's going on. That dream. It seemed so real. Who were those people?

My mom helps me straighten out the sheets and gets me comfortable again. I try to fix my hair, but then remember that I'm still tied down to the bed. She hesitantly strokes some strands of hair out of my face. She bends down and picks my glasses up off the floor and puts them back on me.

"How're you feeling?"

"How do I look?" I snap back. My mom looks down at the floor, dejected. Oh jeez. Now I hurt her feelings.

"I'm sorry, Mom. I shouldn't have snapped at you. I feel like crap, and it's making me moody."

There's a quiet knock at the door, followed by a head with greasy black hair.

"David? What're you doing here?" I croak out.

"I was having a follow-up appointment to make sure the pneumonia was cleared up this time. I heard you were here and thought I would come visit," he says, finishing off with a deep chest cough.

"You sound like garbage," I say.

"You look like garbage," he replies, putting his hand up to his ear and fiddling with his hearing aid.

"Stop it, you two. David, is your mother here with you? I would like to talk to her," my mom says.

"Yes, Mrs. Sloane. She's waiting for me in the hallway."

My mom heads out to the hallway, quietly closing the door behind her.

"What'd you do this time?" David asks.

"Tried to kill myself with aspirin and Benadryl."

"Looks like you failed," David says with a hint of a smirk playing at his lips.

"No crap," I roll my eyes.

"So, when do you get out?" He pushes my legs over so he can sit on my bed.

"No idea. Looks like they're sending me to the psychiatric ward after I'm healed."

"Yikes. I almost got locked up once in the padded room for throwing a chair at the window."

"Why'd you throw a chair at the window? Trying to prove that you belonged there or something?" I ask, watching him pick at a huge zit on his chin. I turn my head away before I throw up.

"I was playing truth or dare with Bartholomew. He dared me to do it."

"You idiot. Bartholomew isn't real. I think they should put you in the loony bin permanently."

"Yeah, whatever. I told you before, Bartholomew shows up right before I'm about to get sick. It's like he's my guardian angel or something..."

"Right. A guardian angel who dares you to throw a chair at a window in the psychiatric ward."

"He said he was sorry. He got carried away."

David stops looking at me and stares up at the ceiling.

"What? Do you see him?" I roll my eyes.

He doesn't reply and continues staring. He's having a seizure again. I sigh, waiting for it to end.

After a few seconds, David looks back at me. "What were we talking about?"

"You just had another seizure."

"Damn it. This medicine isn't working either," David says with tears welling up in his muddy brown eyes.

"I'm sorry. I'm sure they'll figure something out," I offer gently.

"Maybe I should be like you and just try to end this sad excuse of a life. I could just run out into the rain and let my flesh melt off my bones." He stops to think about it and then shudders, shaking his head. "Who am I kidding? I could never do it."

"Me neither. Once you're dead, it wouldn't matter, but what a crappy way to go."

"Maybe we should run away into the woods."

"Ugh. Not this again. What is your obsession with running off into the wilderness? Do you want to be eaten?"

"No...yes...I don't know. I have this strange feeling that there's something else out there."

"I had a dream about the woods. I have no idea how I got there, but I was trying to get back to the city, and there was a beast that tried to kill me. I was saved by these two guys who, I swear, seemed really familiar."

"Maybe it's a sign."

"No, David. Look at me! Does it look like I'm in any condition to go traipsing out into the woods? And what about you and your epilepsy? You wouldn't last two minutes out there."

"Fine," David huffs, looking away.

We fall into an awkward silence. I hate it when he starts going on and on about the woods. I have no idea what he thinks is out there that's so important. We aren't even allowed to leave city limits unless it's on a train. The woods are a dangerous place full of numerous ways to die. I've heard stories. If you manage to not get eaten by any animals, the plants themselves will kill you. I just read an article a year or so ago about a group of botanists who went to the woods to document the plant life. Some of the foliage looked different, and they wanted to take samples. Their bodies were found just outside of the fence. The doctors still weren't sure what plants could cause this. Little barbs were found inside of the scientists' skin, and their internal organs had been decomposed to mush.

"So, are you headed back to school tomorrow?" I ask, trying to break the silence.

"Yeah, they gave me the all clear. I can gather some of your homework and try to bring it to you if you want."

I rattle my restraints in response.

"I suppose you won't be able to get much done with your hands tied down."

"There's no way I'm ever going to catch up on my school work. I will probably have to do junior year again."

"I'm sure it won't be that bad. I can tutor you once you get out of the loony bin," David offers with a wide smile that exposes his crooked yellow teeth. I glance away again.

"Yeah, maybe."

We hear my mom come back into the room.

"David, the rain has stopped, and it's time for you to head home," my mom says.

"See you later, Liv."

"See ya," I mumble as David steps out the door.

My mom walks over to me, holding a bottle of vitamins, and shakes a large red pill out into her hand. I have to take two extra drinks to get the vitamin to finally slide down my throat. I cringe at the pain as well as the taste. I wish we had some of our bottled water here. I hate the way the tap water tastes. The government has a filtration system put in so everyone can have drinking water and not get poisoned by the rain, but I don't like it, so my mom buys bottled water for us to drink.

The next couple of days I spend quietly lying in bed, staring off into nowhere, earning the fat nurse's trust so she will take my restraints off. Once she finally does, she makes me promise that I won't try to run away.

I wait for my mom to fall asleep that night and slip my way out of the hospital bed. I peek my head out of the door, and there's no one in the hall. I make it about three rooms away before I hear someone coming and try to scramble into the closest room, but I'm caught and strapped back into my bed by none other than Nurse Tubby. I finally realize that there is no way I am going to sneak my way out of here.

I try to apologize to the nurse, but she's skeptical of me now. We don't get along well. I'm pretty sure she has ordered unnecessary tests to be done just so she can take extra vials of my blood. She's not too gentle with that needle either. I guess I might deserve it, though. I lied about running away. Just to get back at her, I wet my bed on purpose once, after a particularly nasty blood draw. I'm confident she missed my vein intentionally. She made me stand cuffed to the bed in my wet hospital gown while she changed the sheets, cursing under her breath and giving me death glares. My mom chewed me out and seemed so worked up that I decided to lay off Nurse Chunk. It's probably better that way anyway since I'm not getting out of this hospital anytime soon.

My mom has to go to work every day, but she comes back and stays with me at the hospital at night. I usually allow myself to cry while she's gone. It's easier to hold it in and let it all out when I don't have an audience. Our relationship is tense as it is, and I don't want to stress her out more with my depression. My mom and David are the only people in the world who actually seem to like me.

A couple more days pass, and I can finally eat and take my vitamin without pain now. The last time Nurse Fatso was in here, she asked me to rate my pain between one and ten. I hate it when they ask me that. I mean, I get it; they want an indication of how bad your pain is, but pain can be so different for so many people. I just have a swollen throat and asthma attacks. How can I compare that to someone who has their legs chopped off or a broken bone protruding out of their skin? I feel I can't say over a five without looking like a complete doofus.

I hear a tapping on the door.

"Well, girly," says Nurse Pudge, "looks like you're all healed up. It's time to move to your new quarters."

"Will I be getting my own room?" I ask hopefully. I don't want to be stuck with some psycho.

After the nurse finally stops laughing so hard that her rotund belly shakes violently under her scrubs, she answers, "This ain't no five-star hotel, deary. Don't worry. I picked out someone perfect to be your roommate."

That evil look in her eyes makes my stomach drop. I'm in trouble!

3

I shuffle behind the nurse, following her down the bleached white hallway, passing room after room before I make it to my new living space. I hear a few screams coming from behind some of the doors. I hope my roommate isn't a screamer.

Luckily the room is empty when I arrive, so I can get settled in before they show up. I wonder what kind of nut job the nurse put me with.

"I've been told you have a half hour before mandatory group time. They run a tight ship around here. Be on time or else," the nurse warns as she turns around to head back to the hospital wing. Once she closes the door behind her, I flip her the bird. I shouldn't have done that. They probably have cameras in the rooms to monitor the patients. My eyes drift around the room, looking for cameras. I can't spot one, but I should be a little more careful, just in case.

My room is plain. There are two twin beds with gray metal frames on opposite sides of the room. I sit down on one and find that the beds are adorned with scratchy white sheets and a threadbare light blue blanket. There are two waist-high dressers for our clothes next to the beds and a window in between the dressers. The floors and ceiling are stark white, which is quite the contrast to the walls: a faded yellow color that makes me think the last resident was a chain smoker. I walk over to the barred window to get a look at the view from this room. We are four stories up, which makes it challenging to see anything on the ground through the fog. I can make out the outlines of a few people, hurrying off to do important things with their freedom. How nice that must be.

"Get away from the window!" A high-pitched voice squeals at me.

I turn around and see a short girl standing in the doorway, staring at me wide-eyed. She looks to be about twelve years old, her black hair pulled back into a ponytail.

"Why? What's wrong with the window?" I look back and forth between the window and the girl.

"They'll see you!"

"Who?" I step slowly away from the window and back over to my bed.

"The monsters. They're always watching. Waiting. We're never alone. Just stay away from the window. I don't want to lose another roommate." She keeps her back to the wall as she sidesteps her way to her bed.

I am officially freaked out.

"What happened to your roommate?" I ask, not really wanting to hear her answer.

She responds with an ear-piercing scream. I cover my ears so she doesn't bust my eardrums. Moments later, a nurse comes bounding into our room with a syringe. The girl starts swatting at the nurse, trying to knock the syringe out of her hand, but the girl is no match for the large, muscular nurse. Once the medicine has been injected, the girl lies still on her bed, panting.

"What happened?" the nurse asks.

"I don't know. She told me to stay away from the window and mentioned something about her roommate. I asked her what happened, and she started screaming..."

"Do us both a favor, and never ask about her roommate again. Got it?"

"Yeah...sure." I agree. Holy crap! What have I gotten myself into?

The nurse leaves the room, closing the door with a resounding thump. I sit on my bed, glancing at the girl now and again. After about five awkward minutes of silence, she sits up, letting her legs dangle over the edge of the bed. She holds her head down in her hands as though she has an intense headache. Suddenly, she looks up and locks eyes with me. The pale blue color of her eyes is kind of creeping me out. They are so pale they almost look white.

"My name's Cindy," she says innocently.

"I'm Olivia."

She smiles wide, the corner of her lips curling up, making her look like a female Joker.

"I think we are going to be best friends, Olivia. I got this place figured out. I can give you tips."

"Um. Okay. Tips for what, exactly?"

"Scoring extra drugs like I just demonstrated, which nurses let you get away with certain stuff, how to say just the right things to the other patients to get them to have an episode to end group time...you know. Stuff like that."

What a brat!

"How long have you been here?" I ask.

"Pretty much my whole life." Cindy kicks her feet back and forth with her toes brushing the floor. "Why're you here?"

"I tried to kill myself."

"How fun! I've done that too." She shows me the insides of her arms. Thick scars run down her wrists.

"How old are you? You seem too young to want to die."

"Oh, you're too kind! I'm older than I look. I'm twenty-five."

"Twenty-five? No offense, but I thought you were, like, twelve when you first came in."

"Twelve?" She says, laughing hysterically. "I'll admit, I'm a little short for my age, but damn. You really thought I looked twelve? You sure you don't need to have your eyes checked?"

I've had enough of this chick already.

"I'm kinda tired. I think I'll lie down for a little bit before group time."

"Yeah, sure thing." Cindy scooches her back to the wall.

I lie down facing toward her. I'm not sure I trust her enough to turn my back to her. As soon as I close my eyes, I hear her clicking her tongue like a clock. I sigh loudly, hoping it will make her stop. She does, but then she starts humming "The Itsy-Bitsy Spider" slowly and ominously. I open my eyes to glare at her and find that she is doing the motions to go along with the song.

"Cindy, do you mind being a little quieter so I can sleep."

"Oh. Sorry." She brings a finger to her lips.

Silence. I'm starting to relax when I hear the squeak of her bed. What is she doing now? I open my eyes just a bit, but I don't see her. I hear the click of the bathroom door. She's just using the bathroom. I take a deep calming breath, filling my lungs as full as I can, and let it out slowly. These beds are pretty comfy. I might actually get some sleep. After I let all the air out of my lungs, I start to take my next breath, and my nose is filled with the stench of rancid milk and candy. I open my eyes and find Cindy's face inches away from mine. I scramble to sit up.

"You're pretty when you sleep."

"Don't do that! You need to stay on your side of the room! I get panic attacks really easily." I feel my chest tightening. I probably shouldn't have told her that.

"You do? Well, I'll just have to keep that in mind." She bounces her way back to her bed.

I take a dose of my inhaler and glare at Cindy.

"Group time, girls," a nurse says, standing in the doorway.

I stand up and follow the nurse, hoping they have separate groups. I don't want to be around Cindy anymore.

"Where should I go?" I ask the nurse.

"Your group time will be held in the room next to the cafeteria down that way," she says, pointing down the hallway behind us. She turns back around to continue informing the rest of the patients about group time.

I make it to the room I'm supposed to be in and see a circle of people already there. Cindy is nowhere in sight. What a relief.

My group time is boring. The nurse tries to coax people out of their shells. Nobody seems to want to share much, though. People say their name and how they're feeling. A lot of "fines" and "tireds." We had one exciting part when a patient started punching the catatonic guy in the leg because he thought he saw a spider. I don't know why I thought it was funny, but I had to hide my chuckle behind a coughing fit.

After group time is lunch time. Sitting next to the cafeteria made me hungry. Once I have my tray of food, though, I am sorely disappointed. I'm not sure I can identify most of it. Gray mush, green slimy stuff, a stale dinner roll, and a pile of canned fruit I think must be pears. Yum, yum.

I see Cindy walk through the door, so I scan for a place to sit where she won't be able to sit by me. I find a spot between two people from my group, spider guy and an old lady named Gretchen who rocks back and forth continuously. We all eat in silence. I can handle this.

I finally make it back to my room after hours of grueling group sessions and "free time," which just means I can watch the TV that is playing old black and white movies, I can make a craft, or I can stare out the window. Meds were handed out right after supper. I looked in my little cup to see if I could identify what they're trying to give. Luckily, it was only my daily vitamin. I don't know what I would have done if they tried to give me some random medication. Now it's lights out in an hour. I sit down on my bed, exhausted for some reason, and notice that Cindy isn't back yet. I wonder what kind of trouble she's getting into.

I stare out the window for a little while, watching the hazy daylight fade away to darkness. I decide that my best bet is to just comply, and maybe I'll be released sooner. I whip around when I hear a startled intake of breath.

"Who're you?" Cindy asks, eyes filled with fear.

"Olivia, your roommate," I say, confused.

"Oh. Nice to meet you. I'm Joselyn." She offers her hand for a handshake.

"Joselyn? You told me your name was Cindy."

"No! No, no, no, no!" Joselyn screams, pounding her fists against her head. "Not again! Cindy's trying to kill me!"

4

"Nurse!" I yell. "We need a nurse in here!"

She continues punching her head with her fists, screaming, "Get away from me! I hate you!"

"Hey, this isn't just a show, is it?" I ask, remembering her last plot to get more drugs. I suddenly feel guilty for even asking. If she is faking it, she is an astounding actress.

The same nurse as before comes into our room, carrying a syringe. She injects the medicine and then holds the girl's hands in a tight grip so she stops punching at her head. The look of terror slowly fades off Cindy's face. The nurse lets her go and takes a few steps back, watching as she falls over on the bed and appears to be sleeping.

"You okay?" The nurse asks. It isn't until I look at her that I realize she was talking to me.

"Um...yeah. What's wrong with her?" I take a dose of my inhaler. "She just told me her name is Joselyn. Is she a pathological liar or something?"

"No. She has dissociative identity disorder. So far, you have met two of her personalities, Cindy and Joselyn."

"You mean, there are more?" I ask incredulously.

"Unfortunately, yes. We've found a medicine that seems to help, but it only works if she actually takes it. I think she cheeks the medicine and spits it out later, but we haven't figured out how she does it."

"Why would she do that if the medicine works?"

"She complains about feeling stupid while on the medicine. I tend to think that Cindy is a much stronger personality than we care to believe. She doesn't like the idea of being erased, and so she tends to take over more often."

"Cindy told me she fakes episodes so she can get more drugs."

"We'll look into it. I need to get back to the nurse's station. You need anything else?"

"A new room?" I plead.

"No can do. Nighty-night!"

I let out a big huff and sit down on my bed. I hate you Nurse Chubs! Why did they have to stick me with her?

"I heard you talking about me."

16

I look over at Joselyn and see her slowly opening her eyes, and although they are still the creepy pale blue color, they seem to have a childlike innocence to them. She seems more scared than anything.

"Yeah. Sorry."

"I hate Cindy. She's ruining my life," Joselyn says, starting to cry.

I stand up and make my way over to the foot of her bed. I slowly sit, cautiously waiting for her to start freaking out again. She just lies there sobbing instead.

"She said the medicine helps. Maybe you should take it."

"I can't," Joselyn says between sobs. "I feel dumb when I'm on them. I can't finish a sentence or even a thought."

"If you hate Cindy so much, isn't it worth feeling a little dumb if it means getting rid of her?" I offer.

"Yeah, maybe," she says, calming down a bit. "I hate that these are my options! I either live with a bunch of personalities where I don't know who I'm going to wake up as and have no memory of what happened while I was someone else, or I can take medicine that makes me feel like an idiot. I lose no matter what."

"It sounds like it sucks." I pat her leg again. "I'm sorry you have to deal with this."

"It could be worse, I guess. I have a guy in my group who believes he's a squirrel. He's hilarious to watch eat. He nibbles his food and sometimes shoves things in his cheeks until they puff out like this." She blows her cheeks up.

We both laugh for a moment. This Joselyn kid isn't so bad.

"Cindy told me she's twenty-five. How old are you really?"

"I'm twelve."

I knew it!

"So, how long have you been here?" I ask.

"As long as I can remember. My dad died when I was real little, and that's when Cindy showed up. So, my mom sent me here and never came back to see me." Fresh tears roll down her cheeks. "Cindy tried to kill herself—I mean, us, and that's when other personalities came. I just don't know what to do," Joselyn says, sobbing.

I sit by her for a little while, patting her leg while she cries. After a few minutes, I realize she's quiet. She fell asleep. I make my way back over to my bed just before the lights shut out. I hope I can get out of here soon.

5

In the morning, I awake with a start when something brushes against my cheek. It would appear Cindy has come back to visit. She's sitting on the edge of my bed, staring at me with those creepy pale eyes boring into my soul.

"Who's David?" She asks with a smirk.

"He's a friend." I rub the sleep out of my eyes. "Why?"

"You were calling out his name while you slept. 'David...David...no, don't go there!' Where was he trying to go? Your panties?" She finishes with a wicked laugh.

"No! You're sick!" I say, disgusted.

"Correct you are, Dr. Olivia." Cindy titters, standing back up and twirling in circles to her bed.

I sit up, knowing that I will not be getting any more sleep with psycho girl over there. After sitting for a couple of minutes, watching her twirl her ponytail and hum "Pop Goes the Weasel," I decide to play at her level and stir up the bees' nest a bit.

"So, why did the nurse tell me not to ask about your roommate? What happened?"

"Cassandra was my first roommate. She was an annoying wench who kept trying to help Joselyn make me go away permanently, so I took it upon myself to make her life a living hell. I pulled pranks on her every chance I could get. I made her wet the bed with the fingers-in-warm-water trick; tied individual strands of her long hair to the bedpost bars while she slept so when she got up, it would rip them out; I left bugs in her bed that I would find around the joint. I even made myself throw up on her favorite shoes once, pretending I was sick," Cindy says, eyes glistening as she reminisces about her evil ploys. "Anyway, she couldn't prove I was behind any of it, and nobody would believe her when she blamed me. That didn't sit so well with her bipolar disorder. Nope, nope, nope! She got more and more depressed until finally, she stole a knife from the kitchen one day and killed herself over by that window," Cindy finishes with a slight giggle as she mimics stabbing herself in the heart.

I stare at her, horrified.

"Oh, don't worry, Olivia! I would never do those things to you. I want us to be best friends! Don't you?" Cindy's eyes bulge slightly as she smiles.

I try to smile, but my muscles just spasm a few times. I swallow hard and find that my mouth has gone completely dry. I need to try to stay on her good side. I just nod my head a little. That seems to appease her, and she goes back to twirling her hair and humming to herself.

The rest of the day was uneventful after that. We have to have blood drawn every morning. They say it's so they can analyze it to know how much medication to give. I think they just like sticking us with needles. We had to go through another hospital lockdown because it's raining again today, but nobody seemed to notice; it happens so frequently. I try extra hard at group time to participate and appear happier so I can get myself home sooner.

I return to my room that evening and lie down, waiting for Cindy to return, hoping it will be Joselyn instead. Before I know it, the lights are turned out, and she hasn't come back. I'm afraid to go to sleep, wondering what horrors Cindy has in store for me, but exhaustion wins out.

I wake up in the morning and find that her bed is still empty. I wonder where they are—I mean, where she is.

I ask a nurse, and I'm told that Cindy got herself thrown into solitary confinement after being caught whispering in the ear of a patient with severe paranoia. Once they calmed the patient down, she informed them that Cindy threatened to smother her with a pillow while she was asleep. Looks like I will get the room to myself for a while.

■■■■■

"Well, Olivia. I think you've made some real progress here," says Dr. Regan Hughes, the head of the department. It's been three days since Cindy was taken to solitary confinement. Three days that I have busted my butt to participate in any way that I could. I was rewarded with good behavior yesterday after I helped calm the spider guy down when he saw a spider on the windowsill. They let me choose what to watch on the TV during free time. There wasn't a whole lot to choose from, but a movie from this century was a far cry better than the boring crap they usually played.

Dr. Hughes continually pushes his large round glasses back up his oily nose as he studies my file. I stare at his bald head reflecting the lamplight, wondering if he polishes it in the morning before he comes to work. He looks up at me, and I quickly meet his eye line. His dark brown eyes stare at me expectantly, waiting for a response.

"Oh, uh, I have made progress. I feel a lot better. I know now that it was silly of me to try to kill myself. I have so much to live for," I say, laying it on thick.

"Yes, well, I think with a few more sessions you should be able to go home."

"A few more? Can't I just go home now? I promise I'm better," I plead.

"Slow down, Olivia. We need to make sure you are completely rehabilitated."

"I am. I won't ever try to kill myself again. I promise! Please, just let me go home to my mom."

He looks at me with his bushy eyebrows furrowed, scrutinizing me. How can he possibly have that much hair above his eyes when his entire head is as bald as a cue ball?

"No. There's something else going on here. I don't think it's because you miss your mom." He glances back at my file. "There are no notes about you saying you miss your mom in any of the sessions. So, tell me: why do you want to leave so badly?"

"Fine. My roommate Cindy is being released from confinement, and I would rather not be here when she gets back," I say sheepishly. "I really do feel better, though."

"Ah...Cindy. Yes, she is a hard one to handle." Dr. Hughes sighs, clicking his pen a few times, thinking. "All right, I'll make a deal with you. Go to today's sessions, and we'll talk tomorrow."

"Really?"

"Yes, well, as I said, you have made some real progress. I believe you will be ready to return home tomorrow."

I would rather have gone home today, but I'll take what I can get.

Dr. Hughes dismisses me to head to my session. I can't seem to wipe the smile off my face, knowing I'll be going home tomorrow. That is until I walk into my session and see Cindy sitting there. She's staring down at the floor. I don't think she notices me sit down.

"Hello," she says in a deadpan tone. I look over at her, and she is glaring at me through her long black hair, which is usually pulled up in a high ponytail. Her long bangs drape over her face, obscuring one of her eyes.

"Hi, Cindy," I say cautiously.

"I'm not Cindy," she says with the same emotionless tone.

"Sorry, Joselyn?"

"Nope. The name's Landon."

"Landon? Isn't that a guy's name?"

"Yeah?" She gives me a weird look like I'm an idiot.

I decide to just stop talking. A dude? One of Joselyn's personalities is a dude? Weird.

"Who're you?" Landon asks.

"I'm Olivia. Your roommate," I say slowly. That's right. *Landon* wouldn't know that.

She nods her head and goes back to brooding. I feel horrible for Joselyn. I can't figure out why she would want to deal with all these personalities instead of taking her medicine and making them go away.

During the session, they only get one-word responses from Landon. He—I mean she— Oh, this is so confusing! He just stares at the floor, only looking up at me once in a while. I'm not sure if I'm imagining it, but the malice I usually see in Cindy's eyes has been replaced with a look of pain in Landon's.

Once it's lunchtime, I seek Landon out to sit with. Perhaps if I tell him there's a way to make the pain and suffering go away, he'll try taking the medicine Joselyn needs to get better.

"Hey, Landon. Do you mind if I sit with you?"

"Go for it." He stabs his fork at what looks like a pile of mashed potatoes. I take the seat across from him.

"If you don't mind me asking, what are you in here for?" I ask, curious as to what his response might be.

He brushes his bangs out of his eyes to look at me quizzically. I give a little smile to let him know I'm not being a jerk.

"I've been told that I'm just a personality inside of a girl named Joselyn. Pretty effed up, if you ask me," he says, continuing to smoosh around his food.

"Yeah. That's gotta be hard."

When he doesn't respond, I try to continue as gently as I can.

"Look, Landon, I can tell this is not an easy position to be in. The little girl that you are stuck inside could really use your help. She has another personality that is bad news—"

"Cindy. I know about her." He looks up at me abruptly. "I've been told all of this before. What do you want me to do about it?"

"If you could take the medicine that will make Joselyn better, you wouldn't have to be in pain anymore. You know... knowing you're not..." I stop and clear my throat, not sure if I should continue. I see that he is looking at me, almost as though he's wondering if I have the guts to finish my sentence. I take a deep breath and try to say it quick, like ripping a band-aid off. "Knowing you're not a real person. She's a sweet kid who's got a tough life."

"So, you want me to take medicine to make myself go away?"

"Well...yeah. I guess that's what I'm asking. I'm sorry, Landon. I'm just trying to help Joselyn out. You seem to be unhappy. I thought maybe you would like to have a way to escape the pain of knowing you're just a personality inside of a twelve-year-old girl's body. You would be sacrificing yourself to save someone," I finish.

He sighs and lets his head hang, his hair almost falling into his food.

"You're right. I don't belong here. I never have," he agrees. "I'll take the medicine, but I can't control what Cindy does. Nobody can."

We eat the rest of our lunch in silence and continue on with our day. Once medication time comes, I look around the room to see if I can spot Landon. He's standing a couple of places behind me in line. I take my vitamin and stand off to the side to encourage him. Once it's his turn, he grabs the little cup and dumps it in his mouth, washing it down with the water. I give him a big smile and two thumbs up. He gives me a strange look and shakes his head vigorously as though trying to shake a bug away. He looks at the little cup in his hand, and his eyes go wide. "Damn it!" he yells and runs off to the bathroom. I follow quickly behind and stand outside of the door, listening to what's going on. Suddenly, I hear vomiting.

I start banging on the door. "Don't do that!" I yell. "Nurse!"

"What are you yelling about?" a nurse scolds in hushed tones. "You're going to get the other patients worked up."

"I convinced Landon to take the medicine that will help Joselyn out, but he started acting weird, and now he's in there throwing up!"

"Ah, yes. This has happened before. That seems to be the trigger for Cindy. Why don't you head back to your room? I'll take care of this."

I go back to the room and change into my pajamas. Only moments after I lie down, Cindy comes barging into the room.

"You're trying to get rid of me, aren't you?" Cindy glares at me.

"I was just trying to help Joselyn out. She seems like a good kid," I say defensively.

"You're trying to recruit that weak-minded moron, Landon, to get rid of me? You're gonna have to try harder than that." Cindy flops down on the bed.

"Why do you want to stick around so badly when you know you don't belong? You're a twenty-five-year-old personality trapped inside a twelve-year-old. Doesn't that seem wrong to you?"

"No. The alternative is that I don't exist at all. Stay out of it, Olivia, or I swear, I'll kill you," she threatens.

I huff and lie my head back down on the pillow. I'm afraid to go to sleep. I lie awake for hours that night, continually checking to see if Cindy is going to do something to me.

I finally fall asleep sometime around two o'clock. After a few hours, I wake up to find Cindy sitting on her bed, back against the wall, staring at me again.

"Heard you're going home today," she says.

"Hopefully."

"We'll see about that. I may have told Dr. Hughes that you talked about killing yourself again last night."

"You *what?*"

"Consider it a little payback for trying to get rid of me."

6

I race down to Dr. Hughes' office. I knock on the door, shifting my weight back and forth, waiting for a response. Come on, come on, come on! I put my ear against the door. Nothing. I squat down to look through the keyhole. I can almost see his desk...

"What are you doing, Olivia?"

I jump so hard, I smack my head against the doorknob. Rubbing the sore spot, I stand up and see that Dr. Hughes is back with a steaming cup of coffee.

"Cindy just told me that she told you that I told her that I was thinking about killing myself." I shake my head at my inability to form proper sentences when I'm upset. I take a deep breath. "I just wanted to come down here to let you know that Cindy lied. I never talked about killing myself. You have to believe me!"

"Of course, I do. Come into my office," he says, opening the door.

I follow him in and have a seat. It is only then that I realize I'm still in my pajamas. I wonder if he notices me blushing.

"I was told that you tried to help Joselyn out by means of Landon. I'm really impressed by the way you want to help people, Olivia. Keep that up. I believe helping others out can really help lift your own spirits when you're feeling down."

I nod my head in agreement. "So, does this mean...I can go home?" I ask quietly, afraid he is going to say no.

"Yes. I've already called your mother. She's on her way."

"Oh, thank you, thank you, thank you!" I clap my hands. He gives me a big smile.

"You can head back to your room and gather your things together. Don't take this the wrong way, but I hope I never see you again," Dr. Hughes says with a wink.

I smile and skip back to my room. Cindy isn't there when I return. Good! I pack my things up and wait for my mom. Suddenly, the sirens start going off. I race to the window and see rain sliding down the pane of glass. No! It's raining again.

I make my way to breakfast, hoping the rain stops soon so I can go home. I sit down at a table to eat with spider guy and Charlotte, a girl who believes she has magical powers. I've only ever seen her around here once or twice. She's quiet and keeps to herself most of the time. I'm hoping to have a peaceful breakfast.

"Stop taking it, Olivia," Charlotte says through a mouthful of food.

"What? Stop taking what?"

"It takes your powers away so you can't use the magic within."

"What magic? Charlotte, we have no magic. There is no such thing as magic."

"You're wrong!" Charlotte yells, standing up and storming off to another table. I sigh, hoping I didn't just ruin my chance to get out of here. What in the world was she talking about?

I lean over to take a bite of food when I feel hair being ripped out of the back of my head. I turn around and see Cindy holding a few strands of my hair.

"Oops. Sorry. It was an accident." Cindy drops my hair on the floor. She just turns around and walks away. I hate her. I can't wait to get out of here. I really want to stand up and punch her right in her stupid face, but my desire to get home keeps me in my seat.

Finally, after two hours of sitting around staring at the window, waiting for the rain to stop, I see my mother walk through the door. Out of relief, I run over and give her a big hug.

"I'm so glad to see you. Let's get out of here, Mom."

She awkwardly hugs me in return. We don't usually show big signs of affection; in fact, this might be one of the first genuine hugs I've given her in years.

I hear shouts of "goodbye" and "hope to never see you again." I stop by my room and grab my stuff. As I'm finally walking down the sidewalk outside, I feel like I'm being watched. I turn around to look up at the fourth floor and can just barely make out Cindy standing at the window, watching me walk away. I give her a little wave, and she gives me the middle finger. I will definitely not miss you, Cindy.

Once I'm home, I walk into my apartment and take a deep calming breath. The welcoming scent of familiarity hits my nose. The hospital always smelled like bleach and other assorted chemicals. Our apartment smells like the lilac potpourri my mom always has lying around and the woody smell of the cedar chest my mom keeps extra blankets in.

"Welcome home, Olivia. I'm going to make you your favorite supper tonight..."

"Tacos?" I ask excitedly. "I miss tacos so much. That hospital food was terrible!"

My mom smiles, and I head off to my room to get unpacked. As I'm pulling out the few changes of clothes I had, the phone rings, and my mother shouts, "Got it!" I finish setting my hairbrush on my dresser and head to the kitchen to get a snack. I hear my mom talking on the phone in the living room in almost a whisper. I stand against the wall next to the doorway and listen, curious to know why she would be whispering.

"Hey, this isn't my fault. She was in your care... She didn't mention anything to me about her... Yes, I know it is important that we stay on task... I will keep giving it to her and report to you should anything change... Yes, thank you, Doctor. Mmm-hmm. Yup, goodbye."

I race to the dining room table with my snack and wait for my mom to come in.

"Who called?" I ask in what I hope is a nonchalant tone.

"Oh...um...just your doctor checking in to see how everything is going."

"That seems a little soon. We just got home."

"Yes, well, they want to be thorough. Anyway, there's your homework." She points to the end of the table that is stacked with about a foot of paper and textbooks. "Why don't you get started on it and get some done before supper?"

Mom is acting weird. I wonder what she's up to.

I sit down and grab the first folder of homework. I'll be lucky if I can ever get this done.

By the time my mom announces that the tacos are done, my hand is cramped, and I have a killer headache.

The tacos are so delicious that I scarf down three before I realize I should slow down, or they might be making a reappearance. We eat in silence. My mom keeps looking at me as though she's about to say something, but she stays quiet. I don't mind the silence. There was always someone chattering at the hospital. It's nice to have some peace.

After I've finally had my fill of tacos, I help my mom clean up the table and get back to my homework. As I'm staring at my trigonometry worksheet, trying to make heads and tails of it, my mom calls from the other room, "Olivia, David is on the phone." I am so grateful for the break, I run to my room to take the call.

"Hey!"

"Hi, Olivia. Glad to hear you're back home. Are you coming to school tomorrow?"

"Yeah, I think I'll give it a try. I'm taking a crack at my homework, but I think I might have to take you up on your offer to tutor me. I can't figure out what I'm supposed to be doing on my trigonometry."

"Not sure I will be much help to you with trigonometry, but I can give it a try."

"So, what have I missed at school? I mean, besides classes. Give me the dirty details."

"Let's see, Victoria broke up with Eddie and is now dating Preston."

"Tramp," I interject, rolling my eyes. "How long did that relationship last? Two weeks this time?"

"Yeah, well, she caught him making out with Rose at some party."

"Rose? Why Rose? She's not even part of 'The Group.'"

"Hey, don't pick on Rose. She's a nice girl."

"Oh yeah, sorry. I forgot you had a *thing* for her."

"Well, maybe if you would finally go out with me..."

"We're getting off topic here," I say, trying to dodge yet another advance from David. He has wanted to date me since the seventh grade.

"Fine. Um, let's see. I guess I haven't really been paying that much attention to the drama at school. I've been more worried about you and my battle with pneumonia."

"Olivia! You need to get off the phone and get some homework done!" my mom yells from the other room.

"I gotta go, David. I'll see you tomorrow at school."

I change into my pajamas and drag myself back to the table to get more work done. So much for my mother's sympathy.

7

My alarm wakes me from my fitful sleep. I was dreaming about the woods again. Why I keep dreaming about somewhere I've never been, I have no idea. This time it wasn't as realistic. Just a nightmare. I was running through the woods with Cindy chasing me.

She kept yelling in a sing-songy voice, "Olivia, I'm coming to get you. Come out, come out, wherever you are! I want to be your best friend!"

I ran as fast as my legs would let me.

I do *not* miss Cindy.

I try to look at the time, but the clock is just blurry light, thanks to my poor eyesight. I grab my glasses and begrudgingly leave my warm bed. After taking a dose of my control inhaler, I get myself dressed in my school uniform: a tan A-line skirt that hangs just below my knees, a white blouse that's way too big on me because they didn't have anything smaller than a large, a tan and black striped tie, and black dress shoes. Some girls try to fancy up their outfits with brightly colored socks, which I don't think they're supposed to do, but they get away with it. I just wear the standard issue white dress socks. I don't want to stand out. It's not my thing.

Just as I sit down to eat my bowl of cereal, my mom starts lecturing me while she gets herself ready for work.

"Now remember, Olivia, you don't have to tell anyone where you were or why you were in the hospital. It's none of their business." She drops my vitamin on the table as she walks past me to head to her room.

"Mmm-hmm."

"And pay close attention in class. You might be able to catch up on what you've missed. You're going to have to work hard to keep up!" she shouts from her room.

"Yup," I grunt, staring down into my bowl of cereal as I shovel another bite into my mouth.

"Remember to ask Susan if she would like to come over sometime. I think it would be good for you to spend time with friends," she says, walking to the bathroom while trying to get her earring into her ear.

I roll my eyes in response. She's not really paying attention to me anyway. After a couple of minutes of silence, she's back at it.

"Don't forget to grab your extra inhaler on your way out. And make sure you eat all the lunch I packed for you. You need to be getting enough nutrition."

"Mom! I'll be fine!" I snap.

She stops and looks at me. "You're right. I'm being overbearing."

She goes back to getting ready for work, and I stuff my homework back into my bag. I'm feeling pretty nervous. I hope David will be there.

My mom drops me off and gives me one last look of concern, but she keeps her mouth shut. I wave goodbye and walk through the hazy fog to head into school. So far, nobody has even given me a second glance. Good. I open my locker, and a piece of paper falls to the ground by my feet. I pick it up and see bubbly handwriting with a heart dotting the i.

"Try harder next time."

I know who wrote this. That stupid tramp, Victoria. I glance around the hallway to see if I can spot her. There she is standing with her minions down the hall, giggling with each other. I'm not sure if they saw me read it or not, and I don't care. I crumple the note up and throw it on the bottom of my locker.

My chest is tight at the moment, but I don't want to take my inhaler in front of anyone. I slip into the bathroom and find a stall to hide in. I can't help but think about how much nicer it would have been if I had just died with my last suicide attempt. I don't need this bullcrap.

As I'm finishing up, I hear a group of girls come into the bathroom, laughing about something. I stand as still as possible, hoping they don't know I'm here.

"Did you see her? She looks even uglier than before, all pale and skeletal," Victoria says.

"I didn't even think that was possible." Her best friend Marcy giggles.

"She could have done us all a favor and just finished the job. Sometimes I'm worried I'm going to lose my lunch when I look at that butch hair and flat chest." Victoria pretends to gag. The group of girls starts laughing and even though their words hurt, I can't help but picture them as a bunch of slack-jawed hyenas. I stifle a giggle.

The bell rings, and the preppy girls shuffle their way out. I wait until I hear the door close and make my way to the sink. I look at myself in the mirror and sigh. I have dark circles under my eyes, and my hair is slightly bed-headish. I guess I didn't put too much effort into my looks this morning. I wet my hands and try to flatten it out before heading off to class.

I head back to my locker to grab my books for first period. As I shut my locker and turn around, Victoria slams into me, knocking my books out of my arms.

"Watch where you're going, freak!" Victoria sneers.

I glare at her and start picking my papers up off the floor. A hand suddenly appears holding some papers out for me. I look up and see that David is helping me.

"Thanks, David," I say, relieved to see him.

"Don't let them get to you, Olivia. They're just jealous."

I start laughing so hard, I think I might need my inhaler again. "What are you talking about? What could they possibly be jealous of?"

"Me! They want me bad and can't have all this," David smirks, gesturing to his gangly body. "I'm your best friend, and they're jealous."

I punch him in the arm, and we walk to class, laughing. David always seems to know how to make me laugh.

By the time it's lunch hour, I am exhausted, physically and mentally. There is no way I'm ever going to catch up on school. I came close to having a panic attack when Mr. Schuller, the chemistry teacher, paired Victoria and me together at the lab table. I tried my hardest to keep a civil tongue when she almost dripped the sulfuric acid on my arm. Luckily, Mr. Schuller was coming around to our table, and Victoria had to abandon her efforts to burn my arm. She repeatedly reminded me that she hated me under her breath, though. Nothing I'm not used to.

When I see David sitting alone in the corner of the cafeteria, I quicken my pace to join him. I sit down beside him and stare at my food. A tear rolls down my cheek.

"Hey. What's the matter, Olivia?" David asks, concerned. "Wait—hold on second—let me turn up my hearing."

He likes to turn his hearing aid down when he's in the cafeteria to block out some of the excess noise. I wish I could do the same.

"I can't do this, David. I can't... I can't do any of it," I say, allowing myself to have a moment of grief.

"What can't you do?"

"I am never going to catch up in school; I feel so physically drained that I could collapse right now, and I'm not sure I would be able to get back up, and if Victoria tells me that she hates me one more time...I think I might rip her stupid hair out of her stupid head!"

David is quiet for a moment, staring down at his tray of food.

"What?" I ask, suddenly worried that he's having another seizure.

"Let's leave," David mumbles.

"You mean, leave school? I'm not sure that's going to help."

"No," David says, suddenly looking into my eyes intensely. "I mean run away. Stop rolling your eyes for a second and listen to me. Our lives suck enough as it is. We don't need the constant bullying from these losers at school. I say we pack up our stuff and see what's out there!"

"Out where, David? There is nothing outside of the fences but death! That's why there are fences. To keep all the bad stuff out."

"Or is it to keep us all in here? How do we know what's out there? We only know what they tell us. I would rather die going on an adventure and seeking truths than die inside a hospital never having lived. I want you to come with me," David pleads. He then whispers, "You just tried to kill yourself, Olivia. If you are fine with dying, then why not die trying to find answers. It's been bothering me. What if there is more out there? What if we are being lied to?"

I just stare down at my food and don't respond to him because I honestly don't know what to say.

He huffs, "Think about it," and then leaves me alone in the cafeteria.

I spend the rest of the day barely holding on. Maybe a full day of school wasn't the best idea. Once I finally get home, I collapse on the couch, unable to move. My body aches everywhere. Before I know it, my mom is calling me to eat supper. I push myself off the couch onto the floor and struggle to stand up, my muscles protesting from the effort. I shuffle my way slowly to the table and flop down, glad to be off my feet again.

"How was your first day back?" She scoops a heaping pile of mashed potatoes onto my plate.

"Sucked," I mumble.

My mom lets out a huge sigh. "You'll get there. Just keep trying." Clearly, she thinks I'm talking about the school work. I have no energy to tell her otherwise. Besides, she'll just rattle on and on about how I need to make an effort to get to know people if I really want to have friends.

She finishes dishing up my plate and encourages me to "eat up." I have no appetite. I just shove the food around my plate with my fork and take bites only when my mom says something about me needing to eat.

After supper, I plod off to my room to do some homework. I open my history book and land on a page that has pictures of The Vietnam War. I stop on the page and stare. Not at the people but at the jungle behind them. There is something about the trees and all the green that intrigues me. We don't have trees here in the part of the city where I live. The only park we have has a sad group of trees that don't get enough light from the sun in this unending fog. Their sickly yellow-green leaves are the only indication that the trees are still alive.

Suddenly, something clicks in my head. I remember seeing the pictures they took of the woods when those two scientists died while trying to take samples from outside of the city. The leaves were all green. How? Every plant in the city is a pale chartreuse color. Farmers struggle to grow enough food to feed everyone because the fog never lets enough sunlight in. How are the woods outside the city so green? Plus, how come we were even able to see the trees in the picture. Shouldn't there have been a backdrop of fog? Maybe David is on to something. Maybe there is something more out there that we're missing.

8

I wake up to the sounds of my mother pounding on the door, yelling that I'm going to be late if I don't get up *now*. I put my glasses on and see that it's 7:25. I must have dismissed my alarm by accident. I sit up, but my entire body aches, and I fall back down on the bed. I can't do it. Call it laziness if you must, but I have no desire to try to go to school today.

"I can't, Mom," I half yell back.

She opens the door and stares at me with her hands on her hips.

"And what's the matter now?" She asks skeptically.

"I can't sit up. My whole body hurts."

"Well, I'm sorry to hear that. You need to get your butt to school."

"Why can't I just stay home and rest, Mom? I feel like crap."

"Honestly, I think you're just trying to use your recent hospital visit as an excuse to stay home from school. Need I remind you that you were the one who did this to yourself?"

"Nope. No need to remind me. Thank you." I roll my eyes.

"Good. Now get out of bed and hurry up. We have very little time to get you to school, and I'm going to be late for a very important meeting!"

My mom works for the United World Coalition for Peace, which is the government that was set into place after the war was over. She won't tell me what she does exactly, but that her job is "very important." I bet she's just a secretary or something.

"I'm not going!" I pout, covering my head up with my blankets. Not sure what I hope to accomplish by acting childish.

"Oh yes, you are!" my mom says, on the verge of yelling. She storms over to my bed and rips my blankets off.

"Ugh! What is wrong with you? Why are you being so mean?"

She heaves a big sigh and pinches the bridge of her nose. "I'm sorry, Olivia. I'm just so stressed out over this meeting. I didn't get much sleep, and now we're running late. Please get ready for school. I don't think you should miss any more of your classes," she pleads.

I huff and sit up on the edge of the bed.

"Thank you. Now, I'll go get something for you to eat on the way to school. You've got five minutes," she says, hurrying out to the kitchen.

I reluctantly get myself ready. I don't say much on the ride. I just eat my granola bar and take my vitamin and my painkillers. Technically I'm not supposed to have any painkillers because of my recent stunt, but I snuck some anyway. There is no way I'm going to make it through this morning without them. I chance a look at my mom to see if she noticed me pop the pills, but she didn't. The way she keeps chewing at her fingernails, and her eyes keep darting to the clock every few seconds, tells me she's pretty tense about today. I'm not sure she would even notice if I opened the car door and fell out right now.

"So, what's your meeting about?" I finally ask once we're about a half mile from school.

She starts at my voice breaking the silence. "I can't tell you that," she says, half-laughing.

"Why not? It's not like I have a lot of friends to tell."

"Doesn't matter. I'm not allowed to speak about what we're doing with anyone," she says resolutely.

"Whatever," I mumble. I'm about to fall back into stony silence, but a question keeps needling me. "Mom, last night, I was flipping through my history book and saw a picture of a jungle, and then I remembered the picture of the scientists who died while trying to get a sample from the woods..."

"Yeah?"

"The trees were so green. How come the trees in that picture were so green when all the trees and plants in the city are yellow and sickly? You work for President Turk. Is there something going on that they're not telling us?"

Her eyes narrow, and her cheeks flush a bit, but then she smiles at me with a smile that doesn't quite reach her eyes. "Of course not! I'm sure that photograph was just doctored up on someone's computer to make it seem more colorful."

"I suppose..."

"And why would President Turk be trying to hide anything?" she says, her eyes getting all misty when she says the president's name. "The government is here to help people. If it weren't for the vitamins they hand out, everyone would be suffering from a severe lack of vitamin D."

"Okay, Mom..." I say as we pull into the school parking lot.

"Not to mention how they're protecting us from getting attacked by not only animals but humans too. The war your grandparents had to go through was terrible! The world was out of control, and the war wiped half of the human race off the face of Earth! The damage those nuclear bombs did..." She pauses, tears welling up in her eyes. "I, for one, am glad we have President Turk and the Coalition working around the clock to keep the rest of us safe so something like that doesn't happen again."

"Sorry I asked..." I mumble, opening the car door to head into school. I turn around and see my mom wiping a tear off her cheek as she drives away. She's so touchy about this subject.

"Hey, Liv!" David yells.

I turn around and see him quickly limping his way toward me.

"What happened to you?" I ask once he's caught up.

"Ah, nothing. I twisted my ankle getting off the bus. It was the humiliation from everyone laughing that hurt more, though."

"Aw. Does your ego need a hug?" I joke. He gives me a playful shove as we walk into the school.

"Hey, you wanna come over to my house to study tonight?" he asks.

"Study? Study for what?" I push my backpack into my locker.

"For our history test," he says.

"We have a test? I don't remember him mentioning a test. I've only been back for a day. I'm nowhere near being up to speed on what I've missed. Mr. Carlyle has to give me more time to catch up with everyone."

"I don't know, Liv. He's pretty tough."

"I'll ask him about it. If he's going to be an ass, then sure, I'll come over to study."

The bell rings, and we head off to our first-period class. The morning drags on as usual, and Victoria has plenty of insults to hurl at me during science class. I just keep my head down and try hard to control my tongue.

By lunchtime, my painkillers have worn off, and I'm just about ready to keel over. I find a table in the corner and plop down with my super-nutritious vending-machine lunch of potato chips, a Milky Way, and a Mountain Dew. I didn't have enough time to pack myself a lunch, so Mom gave me a couple bucks to get hot lunch. After taking a good look at the wilty salads, mystery meat, and shriveled baked potatoes that are being served for lunch, I decided this might be a safer route. At least, I know I won't get food poisoning. Soon David joins me.

"Jeez, Liv! You look like you just climbed Mt. Everest or something. You feeling okay?"

"Not really, but I'll survive. By the way, it was a no-go with Mr. Carlyle. Apparently, he doesn't really care that I've missed school and have four other classes to catch up on. What a jerk. So, I guess I'll come over to study after supper. I'm sure my mom won't mind giving me a ride to your place."

A huge smile spreads across his face. "Great! I'll get some snacks for us and plenty of Mountain Dew to keep you awake."

"Good plan." I rest my head on the table, wishing I was still in my warm bed sleeping.

At the end of the day, I stand by the parking lot, waiting for my mom to come and get me. I pace back and forth as I watch car after car pull out, leaving only a few stragglers behind. No sign of my mom. After twenty minutes of standing there looking stupid, I turn to head back inside to the office to see if I can give her a call at work. It's so embarrassing to have to use the phone in the office when everyone in the whole school has a cell phone, except me. My mom doesn't believe I should own a cell phone until I'm an adult. Cheapskate. I stop dead in my tracks when I hear a quick honk of a horn and turn around to see my mom pull in.

"It's about time!" I slam the door.

"Sorry. The meeting went late, and I couldn't leave to call the school."

"I was standing there for almost half an hour! I was hoping to take a nap when I got home."

"I said I was sorry, Olivia," she says testily.

I roll my eyes and rest my head against the back of the seat, keeping my eyes closed in hopes that she won't talk to me.

Once home, I storm up to our second-floor apartment and flop down on the couch.

"Don't you have homework to do?" she says, putting her keys in the basket by the door and sorting through the day's mail. She hands me a letter, and I just grab it without looking at it, fold it, and shove it in my pants pocket.

"Yeah. But I have a nap to take too." I turn on my side to face toward the back of the couch.

"Olivia, you need to get to work on your homework. You will not be flunking out of junior year."

"And what difference does it make if I do junior year over again or not?" I yawn.

"It makes a pretty big difference because you're moving out once you turn eighteen! I can only protect you for so long."

"Protect me? What are you talking about?" I turn to face her. She has her hand clapped over her mouth.

"Nothing. Now go to your room, and get going on your homework..."

"No. What are you talking about 'protecting me'? From what? If it's from getting sick or from having a terrible life, you're really doing a bang-up job, Mom."

I can tell I hit a nerve as I watch her face turn a dark shade of maroon and her eyes narrow until they are almost closed. I'm on my feet, shaking from either exhaustion or anger, I can't tell.

"I am trying my hardest, Olivia! I have done nothing but provide for you. I cook; I clean; I work hard to try to pay the medical bills you've racked up."

"I'm sorry I'm such a problem!" I yell. "I wish Dad were still alive!"

"Don't you *dare* bring up your father!" She points her finger at me.

"Why? You never talk about him."

"I can't! It hurts too much!" Tears leak down her cheeks, leaving tracks of black eyeliner.

"I want to know what happened to Dad! I deserve that much! I have spent my entire life without a father, and my mother won't tell me anything about him!"

She glares at me with an intensity that makes me back up a few steps and sit down on the armrest of the couch.

"Fine. You wanna know?" She asks me with a quiet, dangerous tone. "He joined the military and was sent overseas to fight in a war we shouldn't even be a part of. I was young, pregnant with you, and terrified. I pleaded with him to stay with me, but he signed up anyway. And he never returned. No body. Nothing. They say a bomb fell where he was stationed, and they found nothing left of him to return to me."

I stare down at the floor, tears starting to form in my eyes.

"What? You got nothing more to say? Nothing to throw in my face to make me feel even worse? I have been nothing but patient with you through all your suicidal attempts, psychiatric stays, bad attitudes, and rudeness. But if you keep treating me like this...like your enemy...you can just get the hell out of here. I have put up with enough for today. Now, go to your room."

Huh. I've never seen my mom get so pissed at me before. I oblige and head to my room, giving the door a good slam in defiance. That must have been one hell of a meeting to put her in such a mood.

9

I lie on my bed, with my feet up on my wall, trying to make up my mind about what I'm going to do. She wants me gone? Fine. I decide that I'm going to go over to David's house, but I want to wait until my mom won't see me leave. Something is poking my thigh, and then I remember that I had shoved a letter in my pocket. I sit up and look for whom it's from. There is no return address.

> Dear Olivia,
> I miss you being here. I can't stand what Cindy is doing to me. I just woke up in solitary confinement again. It's so cold and dark in there. Please, help me!
> Joselyn

I stare at the words "help me" until my eyes blur. Poor Joselyn. I wish there were something I could do. I grab a piece of paper and write back.

> Joselyn,
> I'm so sorry. Stay strong! You need to keep taking your medicine. Cindy can be controlled if you just take it. I hope to someday see you outside of the hospital, Cindy-free. Until then, keep fighting!
> Olivia

I search online to find the address for the hospital. After I finish the letter, I stay in my room for about half an hour and finally get the nerve to crack my door open and peek out to see where my mom is. The door of her bedroom is open slightly, and I can hear her snoring. So much for supper. Oh well. This is my chance.

I pull my door open just enough to squeeze through it, hoping the door doesn't creak and wake her up. I slide my sneakers on and make my way as quietly out the front door as possible. I see the keys in the basket beside the door but decide that I'll just walk. I don't want to give her a reason to call the cops on me, saying I stole her car or something. I drop the letter I wrote to Joselyn into the mailbox on my way out.

The fog gives me a feeling of being enclosed that I don't like. I quicken my pace, hoping I can make it the five blocks to David's house. By the time I get there, my legs are like jelly, and I stop outside of his door to take a dose of my inhaler. I ring the doorbell and see David's ruddy face look through the curtain of the side window before opening the door.

"Hey! You made it."

"Barely." I lean against the doorframe, breathing heavily.

"What'd you do? Walk here?" he asks, closing the door behind me.

"I had to. I had a big fight with my mom. She doesn't know I'm here." He leads me through the kitchen.

"Hi, Olivia. How're you?" David's mother asks me from the stove. She's a portly woman with long brown hair and a kind face. She looks up from the stove and gives me a friendly smile.

"I'm doing okay, Mrs. Beckett."

"Did you eat? We're having spaghetti and meatballs. There's enough if you want some."

"Um...sure. Thank you."

"Mom, we're going to go to my room and start studying. Let us know when supper's done." David takes my arm and pulls me to his room.

"Remember to keep the door open, David." Mr. Beckett calls after us from the living room, reminding him of their house rules. Like I would ever do anything with him that would require the door to be closed.

I walk into his surprisingly clean room and have a seat on his bed. He closes the door until there is a sliver of light shining through, just enough to be able to say he's following the rules.

"Wow. Your room looks so clean."

"I knew you were coming over, so I tidied up a bit," he says, sitting in a chair across from me. "So, what did you and your mom fight about this time?"

"She was being a total witch and wouldn't let me lie down to take a nap, so I told her I wish Dad were still alive, and she snapped. I finally got her to tell me what happened to him, though..."

"Oh yeah? Do tell."

"He signed up with the military and was shipped overseas. I guess a bomb dropped on his location, and there was nothing left of him to deliver home."

"They didn't find his body?" David asks with a faraway look in his eyes.

"That's what she said. Anyway, she told me she was tired of my attitude and said I should leave if I wasn't going to stop being this way. I went to my room, waited for her to cool off, and after a while, I found she was sleeping, so I snuck over here."

"Great! Now she's going to come looking for you and get mad at me."

"Nah, I think she's going to sleep until morning. She didn't get a lot of sleep last night because of the 'big, important meeting' she had today."

David looks up at me abruptly. "A big important meeting? Did she say what it was about?"

David is always intrigued by what my mom could be doing at the government building. He's working his way into being a full-fledged conspiracy theorist. Like a lot of people, he neither likes nor trusts President Reginald Turk. David believes Turk is a sleazy, smooth-talking viper of a man who has no business being our president. He was appointed by the UN, instead of being voted in like things were done in the United States before the war.

"No. She said it was classified and wouldn't tell me anything. The meeting ran late, and she picked me up half an hour after school let out. Then she was all cranky and short-tempered. She did say something that seemed odd, though."

"What?" David's eyes glisten.

"She told me that I needed to finish school because I have to move out when I'm eighteen because she can only protect me for so long."

"What? What does that mean?"

"I know, right! I asked her, but she started telling me to go do my homework."

"Hmm...interesting." David strokes his chin in a conspiratorial way.

"You're not going to go all tinfoil-hat on me now, are you?"

"Well, there's obviously something your mom is hiding."

I start to huff at him but then remember the conversation I had with her on my way to school.

"Actually...you know what? It was kind of weird when I asked her if the Coalition was hiding something about the woods and why they are so green when everything in the city is half dead, she started getting all defensive. 'Why would the Coalition try to hide anything from us? The government is here to protect us from uncertain doom' and crap like that."

"Of course, someone working for the government is going to defend what they're doing. They've probably been told by *President Turk*," David says with as much disdain as he can muster into saying the president's name, "to not speak to anyone about their lying and manipulation. There probably isn't anything actually wrong with the woods. Like I said before: what if they are just trying to keep us in the city like sheep in a pen."

"For what purpose?"

"Control. Power. Fear is a good motivator for compliance. If they have everyone inside of the city, they can keep tabs on what everybody is doing. And everyone will continue living like good little robots."

"Is that a bad thing? Sounds to me like they just want to make sure everyone is safe."

"I don't know, Liv. As long as you aren't hurting other people or their property, who cares what you do? Why does the president care so much about people leaving the city? If I want to leave the city, knowing the risks involved, I should be able to, but they have the entrance so heavily guarded you can't just leave."

"David! It's time for supper!" Mrs. Beckett calls from the kitchen.

"Did you just say something?" David looks around.

"No, turn up your hearing aid," I say with a playful eye roll. "Food's ready."

"To be continued." David fiddles with his ear.

As I sit at the table, eating the delicious supper—*I wish my mother cooked this well*—I keep replaying what David said. He's right. The president has no right to lock us up in the city. The fence is there to keep animals out, and the guards are there to keep enemies out, but what about us? What if we want to take the risk to leave? Is keeping us contained like prisoners really a good way to protect us?

"Liv...*Liv*!" David shouts, snapping his fingers in front of my face.

"What? I'm sorry. I was lost in thought."

"My mom asked if you would like a ride home after we're done studying."

"Oh, sure. That would be great." I give her a small smile.

We help clean up the dishes and then head back to David's room.

"What was up with you at supper?" David asks, closing his door most of the way again. "It's like you went all zombie on me."

"Sorry. I was thinking hard about what you were saying."

"Really?" David smiles wide. "So, are you finally going to agree to run away with me?"

"Shhh!" I hush, glancing at the door. "Just hold on. Say we did decide to go see what's out there. How are we even going to get out?"

"I've thought a lot about this." David scoots his chair closer to me so we can keep our voices down.

"Don't tell me you want to try to sneak through the bad part of town," I say nervously.

After the war, there was only a part of the city that was still standing and livable. To the east of us is the rundown part of the city, where criminals and homeless people live. The Coalition put up a fence around that part of town too to keep wild animals out, but they don't station guards there anymore. After a few guards were killed by druggies, they stopped caring what happened to the people in that area and left them to fend for themselves.

"No, of course not. We wait until it's dark, pick a section of the fence between guard towers, and use my dad's bolt cutters to cut a hole in the fence. It doesn't have to be big—I mean, look at us," he continues, gesturing to his scrawny body. I nod my head in agreement. "The fog will help conceal us as we make a break for it."

"But our parents will know we're missing, the hole will be discovered, and they'll come find us. We're not exactly top physical specimens able to outrun anyone."

"That's why we leave in the middle of the night, and by the time they realize we're missing, we'll be hours ahead of them out in the woods," David says, excitement lighting up his face.

"I still don't know, David. A part of me wants to know what's out there, but I'm scared. How are we going to protect ourselves if there are monsters in the woods?"

"With this." David leans down and grabs a shoebox from under his bed. He glances at the door before opening the box, making sure his parents aren't standing out there, peeking at us through the crack. He grabs a sock from inside it and slides whatever is in the sock out. A small black handgun rests on his palm.

"Where did you get that?" I say a little too loudly.

"Shh!" David warns, glancing at the door again. He quickly shoves the gun back into the sock and puts it all back.

"David, where did you get that? All the guns were supposed to have been turned in after the war. Only military are allowed to use them."

"I know. My grandpa gave this to me before he died. He told me he kept it because 'if you don't have the freedom to defend yourself, then you might as well be dead.' It was small enough that he hid it under a loose floorboard when soldiers came through to search people's houses for guns. My parents don't know I have it. Grandpa told me to keep it a secret."

"Do you know how to use it?" I ask, unsure of this whole idea.

"Well...no. Not really. I mean, I understand the concept. You point and shoot. But I can't exactly go outside and practice with it."

I take a deep breath. This talking about running away has me on edge.

"What about if it rains? The umbrellas we have are pretty much worthless."

"We won't go if it's raining, and once we are out of the city and in the woods, the trees should be able to block a lot of it. We'll take a couple of extra umbrellas with us and make a little shelter for ourselves if it does rain. We might be able to find a cave or something to hide in too."

"All right, say we do get out, and there aren't any threats... Then what?"

"I don't know. We explore. We discover. We'll pack food and clothes and matches, things we need for survival, and we go find answers. Why are Turk and the Coalition keeping us in here? What else is out there? Are we being lied to?"

I stare at the floor in thought. A sense of excitement is welling up in my chest. Maybe this kind of adventure is what I need. Maybe I need to get away from my mother and the bullies at school for a while.

"Okay, David. I'll go with you," I say, keeping my eyes on the floor. *What am I getting myself into?*

David jumps up out of his seat and fist-pumps the air.

"But I need time to get ready. How about we go next week sometime? Give me an opportunity to pack and maybe get some extra inhalers stockpiled. I'll just tell mom that I've been having a harder time with my asthma and that I need refills."

"Good idea. That'll give me time to sneak some more food," David says. "I can't believe we're doing this! I have been dreaming about this for a long time now."

I'm glad he's excited about it. I'm just hoping we don't die a horrible, painful death.

10

"You're a nice girl, Olivia," Mrs. Beckett says as we pull onto my road.

"Thank you, Mrs. Beckett," I reply, knowing where this is headed.

"David thinks very highly of you. He's a good boy. Maybe you should give him a chance and go on a date with him."

I really wish David had decided to ride with us. This is so freaking awkward.

"I know. I'm just not really interested in dating anyone right now, what with all of my sicknesses and being so behind in school."

"I understand. Just...give it some thought, okay?" she says, pulling up to my apartment.

I nod my head and thank her for the ride as I get out of the car. I think she's worried that David will never find someone to love him with all his physical needs. She's hoping that since I suffer from a long list of problems too, that maybe we would be able to take care of each other and be understanding to each other. But who's going to take care of both of us should we get sick at the same time?

I head up to the apartment, hoping that my mom is still asleep. I need some time to think about this plan I made with David. Just as my hand is on the knob, the door swings open.

"*Where have you been?*"

Crap. She's awake.

"I went over to David's to study for the history test I have tomorrow," I answer, trying to sidestep to get past her. She blocks my way.

"I wake up, and there's no note or anything! You're supposed to tell me where you're going. How would I know where to start looking for you if you hadn't come back?"

"I'm fine! I didn't realize you cared so much. You certainly didn't seem to give a crap about me a few hours ago...you know, when you told me to stop acting bratty or leave?" I duck under her arm and head to my room.

She grabs my wrist and spins me around to face her. She takes a moment to check her anger, and finally, her face softens. "I'm sorry about that, Olivia. I know I'm not the greatest mom in the world. I say things I don't mean sometimes."

Looks like we're back to the apologetic/tolerant part of our relationship again. I was actually okay with her being angry with me. I could leave without feeling guilty.

I sigh. "It's okay, Mom. I'm sorry for being so cranky lately."

"We both have. I'll try harder if you promise to do the same."

"Sure," I agree, hoping she'll let me go to my room.

She holds my wrist a little longer, staring at my face. I look at the floor, slightly uncomfortable with this moment of...affection? She's got my wrist held pretty tightly, almost threateningly.

"I never told you this, but you have your father's eyes," she says quietly. My eyes are an emerald green, while hers are a dark brown.

"That's because you never talk about him," I say, trying to keep my tone light.

"Yes, well, you got me thinking about him again. It was easier to just not think about him, and the pain would numb. But I guess that's not really fair to you." She lets go of my wrist.

"That's okay. We don't have to talk about him right now," I offer. "I was hoping to go over my notes once more for the history test before going to bed."

She nods her head. "That's a good idea."

I head to my room and close my door gently. I really do need to go over my notes since David and I didn't do any studying whatsoever because we were too busy working on our plans. I sit on my bed with my back against the wall and stare at the notes without seeing them.

Are we really going to do this? What if we get caught? What is my mom going to say when she finds out I ran away? She'll probably put me back in the looney bin, making sure I share a room with Cindy. Oh god!

After about an hour of getting nowhere on my studying, I get up and pace around the room. I stop by my door when I hear my mother's muffled voice coming from her bedroom. I crack the door open slightly to let her voice in clearer. She must have called someone, because I didn't hear the phone ring.

"I can't do it. You know how I feel..." She pauses, listening to the other end of the line. "No. We will not go forward with the original plan. She's back home, and she's fine... You don't know that! Look, we will continue doing things this way until I say we're done! Yes...okay...talk to you soon."

Who was she talking to? I don't have a lot of time to think about it, though, because my mom is headed toward my room. I quickly run and hop onto my bed, adjusting myself up against the wall just in time for her to open my door. I wonder if she will notice my heavy breathing.

"Hey. I just wanted to check to see how you're doing. Need any snacks or anything?"

"Nope. I'm fine."

"Okay. Well, I'm going to go take a shower and then head to bed," she says, stifling a yawn. "It's been one hell of a day."

I nod my head as she closes my door. I slip off my bed and listen at the door for the shower to turn on. Once I hear the water running, I slide out of my room and tiptoe my way into her room, looking for her cell phone. I want to know who she was talking to about me.

I find it on the bedside table and start searching immediately. My mom doesn't take long showers, so I need to make this quick. Huh. It says that she hasn't made or received any calls for days. I pick up our cordless landline, and there aren't any calls on there either. Who was she talking to? My curiosity is eating away at me. I hear the bathroom door open, and I make a mad dash to leave, but she meets me in the doorway of her bedroom.

"What are you doing in here?" She jumps a little when she sees me.

"Oh, um, I was just looking to see if you had any extra inhalers in here..." I say lamely. "I've been going through mine like crazy, and I just wanted to check for spares."

"No, I don't keep any in here," she says, eyeing me up skeptically, as she adjusts the towel tighter around her chest.

"Okay, well, would you mind picking up a couple extra ones for me?"

"Sure." She steps past me, leaving the scent of her shampoo lingering in her wake.

"Close the door behind you, please. Goodnight."

I close the door and hurry back to my room. That was too close. My mother likes her secrets, and I don't want to find out what she would do if she found me snooping around on her phone.

‖ 1 ‖ 1

By the time it's the weekend, I'm ready to do nothing but lie around and eat ludicrous amounts of junk food. My mom seems to have cooled off a bit from our last fight and lets me binge watch my favorite movies. She spends most of her time working on her laptop at the kitchen table. I can hear the keys clacking away while I get up to put *The Lord of the Rings* in the DVD player. She occasionally reminds me that I need to do some homework this weekend—pretty much whenever she walks past me to go to the bathroom. I reassure her by grunting, "Maybe after this movie."

I talk to David a few times to finalize our plans. We're going to leave Wednesday night because my mom has a meeting on Thursday morning, and she always tries to get extra sleep the night before meetings.

Before I know it, it's Sunday night, and I got absolutely nothing accomplished this weekend. My mom finally finishes whatever it is she has been working on and is now hassling me to do my homework.

"It's not a big deal! I worked on some of it last night before I went to bed," I lie. "I'll go work on some more of it now."

"You'd better," she says, yawing big. "I'm going to go to bed. 'Night."

I go to my room, but instead of working on homework, I start packing some things I'm going to need for Wednesday. I grab a couple changes of clothes, extra socks, a spare toothbrush and toothpaste, shampoo, the couple of extra inhalers I have, a blanket, bottles of water, some dried fruit and beef jerky, my jacket, some matches, hand sanitizer, and a roll of toilet paper—a girl has needs! I slip the bag on my back and take a look at myself in the mirror. A wave of excitement hits me, closely followed by terror. Are we really going to be able to survive out there? Is my life really so bad that I am willing to run off into the wilderness with David, leaving behind a relatively comfortable existence...or at least a life with shelter and food?

I close my eyes and imagine what it's going to be like out there. Do I have what it takes? I remember the dream I had of me being in the woods. There was something about all that green and life around me that intrigued me. The woods seemed so wild yet comforting. It's silly to base my judgment of whether this is a good plan or not on a dream, but I can't shake the feeling that there was something more to it than just a dream.

I slide the bag off and shove it as far under my bed as I can. I can't wait to talk to David tomorrow.

■■■■■

I make my way through the thicker-than-usual fog toward the school. The fog is so bad today, you almost run into people before you see them. Once inside, I start scanning for David. I don't spot him before I get to my locker. Victoria stands on the other side of the hallway, laughing. I ignore her while I put my things away. I feel so vulnerable without David standing by my side. After an outburst of roaring laughter, I turn around and see Victoria holding her fingers in circles around her eyes, slumping her shoulders forward, and making a ridiculously stupid face. Clearly, she's trying to impersonate me. I give her as mean of a death glare as I can and then head off to my first-period class in hopes that I can get inside and just sit at my desk until school starts.

I see no signs of David between classes, and by the time lunch comes around, I conclude that he must not be in school today. I hope he's all right. I spend the rest of the day worrying about him instead of paying attention in my classes. There is no doubt that I'm going to fail every single one of them.

I call him as soon as I get home.

"Hello?"

"Hi, Mr. Beckett. Can I speak to David, please?"

"I'm afraid not. He's in the hospital."

"Oh no! What is it this time?"

"He had a severe seizure last night and hit his head on the edge of the kitchen table as he fell down. He cracked his head open pretty good. The doctors say he'll live, but he's got to stay in the hospital for a while so they can find out what kind of damage he did."

"That's terrible! Is there a good time for me to come see him?"

"Uh, I would give it a couple days, Olivia. They are doing some extensive tests to see why his medicine hasn't been working."

"Is there anything I can do?" I ask feebly.

"Just keep him in your prayers and maybe pick up some of his school work for him if you can. You can drop it off here. I'll be stopping at home after work each day to clean up before I go see him."

"Sure. Please let me know if anything changes. I'm so worried about him."

"Of course."

I hang up the phone, bury my face into the pillow, and cry. There is no way we should be running off into the wilderness together. I have no idea how to take care of him if he were to have a seizure! This is a terrible plan. I cry for a while longer and try to compose myself when I hear a light knock on my bedroom door.

"Is everything, okay?" my mom asks.

"No, not really, but come in."

She opens the door slowly, and her face falls when she sees me wiping away a tear.

"What's the matter, Olivia?"

"David is in the hospital again," I sniff.

"Oh, dear. What's it this time?"

"His seizure medication isn't working, and he had a bad seizure while standing. He fell and hit his head on the table. Mr. Beckett said that I should wait a couple of days before I go to see him," I say, tears flowing freely again.

My mom tentatively walks over to my bed, sits on the edge, and stiffly places her hand on my shoulder.

"I'm so sorry, Olivia."

"I just don't understand why David and I have to keep dealing with all of this crap! It's not fair! I just wish we were healthy, normal teenagers. I wish Victoria had to walk in my shoes for a day. Maybe she would stop picking on me all the time."

"Who's Victoria?"

"Victoria is a popular girl in school. She's always telling me she hates me and making fun of me. I actually overheard her say that she wishes I would have succeeded in killing myself."

"That's terrible!" My mom says, aghast.

"Yeah, it is. Sorry, I guess I never told you about it. I just try to ignore her most of the time."

"Well, maybe you need to stand up for yourself. Maybe you need to confront this Victoria and let her know you don't like her treating you that way."

"What would I say? 'Stop it! You're hurting my feelings.' Yeah, that will go over real well." I roll my eyes.

"I don't know, but you need to say something. Tell a teacher. Or the principal. Maybe I should see if I can talk to her parents…"

"No! No, Mom. That would only make things worse. I can handle it myself."

"Okay," she pauses awkwardly. "Well, I guess I'm going to go start making supper. Unless…you needed me to stay and talk a little while longer?" she offers, almost looking worried that I was going to say yes. I can tell she's uncomfortable.

"No, that's okay. I think I need to be alone for a little while."

She exits the room, and I fall back onto my pillow and stare at the wall. It's going to be a rough couple of days.

12

I can already tell that today is going to suck. My mom lectures me all the way to school about having a talk with Victoria. How "being civil and talking through problems can really strengthen a relationship." I quietly stare out the window, watching the endless white haze pass by. I don't think she understands just how much Victoria and I hate each other. She finally forces me to agree to give it a shot. She thinks she's being diplomatic or something, a true employee of the United World Coalition of Peace, just trying to make the world a better place. I think she's being a relentless nag, full of crap and bad ideas.

As I walk into school, I'm more on edge than normal, as if my mother is watching me to see if I follow through with my promise. I really don't need this kind of pressure. I'm guessing that she is just trying to take my mind off from David for a while, but this is definitely not what I want to do instead.

I can see Victoria standing at Marcy's locker down the hall. My chest starts tightening just looking at her. I start to walk over by her when the bell rings. Oh, thank God! Maybe I'll confront her in science class. I have a few hours to think about what I might say.

I make it to science class, where Victoria sits behind me. She has a lovely habit of shooting spitwads at the back of my head when Mr. Schuller is facing the whiteboard. And sure enough, while he writes today's lesson up on the board, I feel something hit me. I turn around to face her, and she gives me a look of disgust.

"What do you want, loser?"

"Stop shooting spitwads at me."

"And why would I do that?" She smirks.

"Why do you hate me so much?" I whisper. My heart is pounding out of my chest.

"Where do I begin? Take a look at yourself! Better yet, don't. We wouldn't want to crack any mirrors."

"Care to share with the rest of the class, ladies?" Mr. Schuller calls out from the front of the classroom.

I turn around and face forward, shaking my head no. Great plan, Mom.

Mr. Schuller gets back to teaching his lesson on atomic mass numbers, and every time he turns around to refer to the periodic table, Victoria shoots a spitwad at me. I start breathing heavy as I fill with rage. I try hard to calm myself down. Only twenty more minutes of class left. After the seventh time, though, I've finally had enough.

"Mr. Schuller! Victoria is shooting spitwads at my head when you aren't looking."

"Is that true, Ms. Campbell?"

"No! Of course not!" Victoria says, placing a hand on her chest and giving him a look of shock.

"She's lying. Look at the floor if you don't believe me."

Mr. Schuller makes his way back to my desk and looks at the small scattering of spitwads on the floor.

"Those were there when we got here, Mr. Schuller. I swear, it wasn't me."

"I think you can collect your things and sit in the principal's office for the rest of the hour, Ms. Campbell." He turns around and makes his way back to the front of the class again. He picks up the phone on his desk to call the office and tell them that Victoria is on the way.

"I'll get you for this. You're dead," Victoria hisses as she gathers up her stuff.

This is not at all what I wanted. Why did I listen to my mom?

I try to keep my eyes on Mr. Schuller, but Marcy keeps turning her head over her shoulder and glaring at me from the corner of her eye, giving me the evilest look she can muster. I will be lucky to make it home in one piece. There's not a lot a toothpick like me can do to defend myself against these girls. Especially if they gang up on me. I wish David were here. He's not exactly built either, but at least he would be there to try to defend me.

Once the bell rings, I slip into the bathroom to use my inhaler and hope that I can hide from Victoria. Once I'm in the stall, I hear someone else come into the bathroom. I can see their shoes as they stop in front of the stall I'm hiding in. Long blonde hair comes into view too as the person outside bends down to look under the stall door. They step away, and suddenly, I hear the bathroom door open again and Marcy yell out, "Victoria! She's in here!"

Crap! I stand at the back of the stall with my legs crammed between the toilet and the wall. The door on the stall next to mine squeaks, and suddenly, Victoria's head pops over the wall.

"Well, well, well. You're going to have to come out of there eventually, and when you do, you're going to pay for getting me in trouble. Principal

Meadows called my parents, and now I'm grounded for the weekend. I had plans to go to a party, and now I can't because of you, you freak."

Just then, the bell rings for the next period.

"To be continued." Victoria sneers.

I wait until I hear both girls leave the bathroom before I start breathing again. Crap! Crap, crap, crap! Now, what am I going to do?

By the end of the day, I am shaking from fear. I wish I had never said anything to her. I wish I would have just left it alone. I wish I weren't here anymore. I grab my stuff from my locker and try to walk quickly out of the school before they find me. Hopefully, my mom will be waiting for me in the parking lot. I step outside, and suddenly, a hand grabs me around the waist, and another hand covers my mouth. They drag me around the corner of the school, where nobody will see us, not that anyone could see us through the fog anyway. They let go, and I see that it's Victoria's boyfriend, Preston. He keeps his forearm pressed against my chest and neck, holding me against the wall.

"Victoria, we're over here," Preston calls out in a loud whisper.

Victoria steps out of the fog and stands so close, I can smell the mint gum she's chewing. Without warning, her hand comes flying up and slaps me hard against my cheek. If it weren't for Preston holding me against the wall, I probably would have fallen over.

"That's what you get, loser," Victoria says, curling her lip.

"I'm sorry, Victoria. I didn't mean to get you in trouble—"

Before I know it, she slaps me again, even harder. I can feel a welt rising on my stinging cheek. My heart is beating out of my chest, and adrenaline starts coursing through my body. The fight or flight response starts kicking in, and I can't think of anything right now but running the hell away.

"Don't talk to me, you little skank. You have no right to even look at me. You disgust me. I wish you were dead."

"Come on, Victoria. We better get going before someone finds us." Preston looks nervous as he keeps watch.

"You go ahead, Pres. Wait for me in the car. I have one last thing to do, and I'll catch up."

Preston pulls his arm off my chest, and I slump over, rubbing my stinging cheek. I hear him walk away, and suddenly, Victoria has a handful of my hair and pulls my head backward.

"If you tell anyone about this, I will do more than slap you."

It feels like my scalp is about to rip open. Rage starts bubbling up inside me, and before I know it, the bones in Victoria's nose are crunching under my fist. Blood gushes down her blouse, and she screams as her hands fly up to her face. She falls to the ground, and I run as fast as I can to the parking lot. I find my mom's car and quickly climb in.

"What happened to you? Why is your face all red?" my mom asks.

"Drive!" I yell.

13

My mom doesn't hesitate and takes off.

"Are you going to tell me what's going on?"

"Can we wait until we get home? My face hurts too much to talk." I gingerly touch my welt.

She huffs but stays quiet for the rest of the drive. Once home, she grabs an ice pack for me and then has a seat on the couch, looking at me with a raised eyebrow, waiting for an explanation.

"Well, I did what you told me to do. I confronted Victoria, but she didn't really have a reason for why she hates me...just that she hates me. Then she kept shooting spit wads at me, and I told the teacher. He sent her to the principal's office, and she got grounded by her parents. So, she had her stupid jock boyfriend grab me when I was trying to leave school, and she confronted me, slapping my face a couple of times, and pulling my hair—"

Just then, my mom's cell phone rings, and she holds a finger up to stop me from talking.

"Hello?... Yes, this is Mrs. Sloane... She did what?" My mom's eyes grow wide, and then she turns her head to glare at me. "I see. Yes, of course. I understand you can't allow that to happen... Did you talk to Victoria's parents about her bullying my daughter?... You did. Okay. I'm very sorry about this, Principal Meadows. I will have a talk with Olivia... Thank you. You too."

My mom hangs up the phone and sets it on the coffee table with a shaky hand. She sits still for a moment, staring down at her phone.

"What were you thinking?" She finally yells, causing a vein to bulge in her neck. "You punched the girl and broke her nose? I told you to talk to her, not get into a fist fight!"

"She was ripping my hair out of my head! What was I supposed to do?" I yell back.

"Well, I certainly don't want you breaking people's noses!" She yells, jumping up on her feet, bearing down on me. "You got yourself suspended for your little stunt! I hope you're happy! You might as well kiss senior year goodbye! You're never going to catch up now!"

"What is wrong with you!" I shout, jumping to my feet to match my mother. She's taller than me, but I want to show her that I'm not going to back down. "She slapped me twice and had my hair in her fist, pulling so hard I felt like my scalp was about to give way! But you don't care about that! No! You only care that I got suspended and might not graduate next year!"

"Of course that's what I'm mad about! If you're going to continue to be so damn reckless, you are *never* going to graduate! You are never going to get a decent paying job and move out on your own! Do you have any idea how all of your suicide attempts and childish antics make me look?"

"Oh, gee! I guess I should have stopped myself from wanting to die because of how it might make *you* look. Mom! You are so selfish!"

"I've had it with you! *Go to your room!*" She screams.

I turn around and storm off to my room, slamming the door hard enough that a picture falls off the wall in the hallway, and I hear the glass shatter.

"Great! Thanks a lot, you little brat!" she yells.

I flop onto my bed, expecting to cry, but I am so angry, I can't. My chest is tight, so I take a dose of my inhaler, cursing my life as I do.

I hear my mother cleaning up the glass and secretly hope that she cuts herself. It'll serve her right. I can't live with her anymore. I hope David gets better soon because I want to run away more than anything right now, with his seizures and all. I hate my life. I hate Victoria. And as of this moment, I hate my own mother.

In the morning, I sneak out to use the bathroom and find a note laying on the floor outside my door.

> Since you got yourself suspended, you also got yourself grounded. Stay in the apartment, and you are not allowed to watch TV. You can use this time to work on catching up on your homework. I will be late for supper. Make it yourself.

I crumple up her note and throw it in the trash. How is she going to stop me from watching TV? I walk straight into the living room to turn it on just to spite her, but the TV isn't there. Where did it go? I see a little slip of paper where it usually sits.

> I told you no TV.

Holy crap! She *literally* took the TV away.

I walk past the dining room and see all my homework spread out. She was certainly busy last night. I keep walking and decide that I'm just going to stick it to her by pigging out on junk food for breakfast. I open the fridge to grab a Mountain Dew. It's gone! I slam the fridge and look in the cupboards, only to find all the candy and sweets gone. There's another note on the counter.

You can forget about sweets and junk too. Have a nice day!

I'm a prisoner in my own house because I fought back? This isn't fair!

I run back to my room and start punching my pillow. Once exhausted, I lie down and think longingly about my plans with David. I dig my backpack out from under the bed and go over the things I've packed. I add a couple more articles of clothing and some more food. I can't think of anything else to add, so I shove it back under the bed.

What am I going to do for the next few days? As I pace my room, trying to think of something, I grab the necklace I once found in a box of my Grandpa's old stuff. I like to fidget with it when I'm bored. I didn't show it to Mom when I found it because I knew she wouldn't let me keep it. I was snooping around the apartment one day when I found a box labeled "Dad's stuff," and there it was, rolled up in a pair of socks.

It's a crystal cylinder about two inches long. It has five separate sections that spin. Each section has the same seven weird symbols on them. I like to hold it and spin them around and around, staring at the different symbols, pretending it's some sort of secret key or alien relic.

Suddenly, I get an idea. I put the pendant back in my jewelry box, and I step out of my room. I look down the hallway even though I know she isn't here. I sneak into my mom's room and start looking through her drawers. She likes to keep her secrets? Well, let's just see if we can find some of them.

I search through her end table drawers and find nothing but the usual boring stuff: books, pads of paper, pens. Next, I start at the bottom drawer of her dresser and work my way up. I'm about to call it quits, but then I see something in the top drawer. I move her bras off to the side, and there's a photograph lying on the bottom of the drawer. It's a picture of my mom looking young, beautiful, and pregnant. She's standing next to a man who has his arm wrapped around her. My breath catches in my chest. I think it's my dad!

I rush over to the lamp and turn it on so I can see the photo better. I study his face, and notice that I do, indeed, have the same eyes. Other than that, I look mostly like my mother. He has shaggy brown hair slicked back from his face, a sharp straight nose, full lips, and a broad chin. I can see why my mom was smitten. He's quite handsome. I wish I had gotten to know him.

Even though my dad died before I was born, there is something familiar about him. But it can't be, because this is the first time I have ever seen him.

I hold it with reverence, knowing this is our only family picture, even though I'm technically not in it. I turn it over and stare at what's written.

It's dated five years before I was born.

1|4

I place the picture back in the drawer and try to arrange her bras back over it just like it was when I found it. I race back to my room and lie down to process what I just saw.

What is going on? Is there a chance that she is just messing with me? Maybe she just wrote the wrong date down, thinking that I might snoop around and find it, and she wanted to screw with my head.

By lunchtime, I decide that I'm going to work on homework to try to take my mind off the mysterious picture. I'm working so hard that I don't realize what time it is until I hear the front door open and see my mom step in.

"Glad to see you doing your work," she says, attempting to sound nice. I yawn, nodding my head.

"Did you make supper?" She drops the mail on the table next to the door.

"No. I got so busy working on my homework since there was nothing else to do, thanks to you. I lost track of time and forgot to make supper."

"Well, I have to say, I'm surprised you did what I asked you to do. Keep working, and I'll go make us some supper. Oh, and you got a letter."

She hands it to me as she walks to the kitchen. No return address again. I rip it open hoping to hear from Joselyn.

> Olivia,
> Once I'm out of this damn hospital, I'm going to find you, and I'm going to kill you. Stop trying to help Joselyn. You can't. I'm here to stay, and there's nothing you can do about it.
>
> Cindy

I shudder. I'm so glad that Cindy is locked up. I hope they can figure out a way to make her disappear for good. Joselyn deserves a better life.

I get back to work on the last few problems of trigonometry, and I can smell that my mom is making tacos again. She's probably hoping to apologize to me by using my favorite supper.

I clear my homework off the table, and my mom starts bringing the food in, giving me a smile as she sets the taco meat in front of me. I roll my eyes as she walks back into the kitchen.

As I dig into my first taco, my mom already starts in on her apology.

"Look, Olivia. I got a check-in call from Dr. Hughes to see how you're doing. I told him about your run-in with Victoria, and he seemed to think that you responded the correct way. That you tried to be civil first and then did what you had to do to defend yourself," she says. "I'm sorry I overreacted. He's right. You shouldn't let people hurt you. I got angry that you were suspended, and I couldn't think about anything other than that. I'm glad she didn't hurt you worse than she did."

I give my head a little nod to acknowledge her. "It's okay, Mom. I'm sorry I broke her nose. I was just trying to get away from her by any means necessary and was shocked when I realized I had punched her."

"Good arm." She winks. We go back to eating, and I can't stop thinking about the photo I found. I really want to know what it means. Maybe she will keep herself from yelling at me since she's trying to be nice again. I decide to take the risk.

"Mom, I have a confession to make."

She sits back and gives me her full attention.

"Go ahead."

"Well...I got bored today and was mad that you took away the TV and everything I enjoy eating, and I decided to look through your stuff. I found a picture in your dresser of you. You were pregnant and standing with a man who, I'm guessing, was Dad? But the date was five years before I was born. Why is the date wrong?"

Her expression is deadpan as she stares at me.

"You snooped through my stuff?" She asks, dangerously quiet.

"Yeah. I'm sorry. I know I shouldn't have. But I did. So, what is up with that picture? I can't stop thinking about it."

"Well. Aren't you a sneaky little urchin. You had no right to go through my stuff, Olivia. Do you ever think before you act?"

"Save me the lecture, please. I know what I did was wrong. I said I was sorry. But you have a lot of explaining to do. Did you write the wrong date on the back just to screw with me?"

"You keep trying to reopen old wounds that I have taken years to heal from. First, you throw your father's death in my face, and now this," she huffs. "Fine, since you brought it up, I'll tell you. I was pregnant before you. I was only seventeen at the time. He was stillborn. I was too young to be pregnant, but I didn't want my baby to die either. It was one of the hardest times in my life. That picture was private, and you had no right seeing it. Now, if you'll excuse me, I need to be alone." she says, a single tear running down her cheek. She stands up, drops her napkin on her plate, and walks back to her room, closing the door with a resounding thud.

Well, now I feel like crap. I had no idea.

I clean up the table as I let it sink in that my mom lost a child before me. That had to be difficult. I guess maybe I mean more to my mother than she lets on.

Morning comes, and my mother doesn't speak a word to me. She goes through the motions of getting ready for her day. I keep trying to apologize, but every apology that gets to the tip of my tongue is evaporated by my mother's icy glare. I'm not sure I'm going to get out of this one too easily. It looks like I have finally hit her last nerve. She leaves for work without a goodbye, and I'm left to figure out what to do with myself for the day.

I grab the phone book and search for the hospital number. I need to see how David is doing.

"St. Mary's hospital. How can I help you?"

"I would like to speak to David Beckett, please."

"I'm sorry. He's not ready to talk to anyone yet. Why don't you try again tomorrow afternoon? Let him rest up some more."

"'Kay. Thanks," I grumble.

I hang up the phone and sigh. Looks like it's homework for me again today. I continue plugging away at it in hopes that maybe I will actually catch up. I keep a close eye on the clock so I can surprise my mom with supper. I make spaghetti and meat sauce, and when she comes home, I stand at the dining room table with our places set, but she just puts her stuff away and heads to her bedroom.

I chance it and knock on her door.

"Mom, I made spaghetti for supper. Want some?"

"No, thanks," she answers. And those are the only words I hear her say for the rest of the night. I really screwed up bad.

By the next afternoon, I'm going stir crazy. I make myself wait until two and then call the hospital again. I get transferred to David's room.

"David!" I yell.

"Ouch, my ear! Hold on while I turn my hearing aid down."

It's quiet for a moment, and I'm almost worried that he hung up on me.

"Hey. How's it going?" he asks weakly.

"Oh man, David, I have missed you so much! I was going crazy waiting to talk to you. I got myself into tons of trouble while you were gone."

"Sounds about right," he says, chuckling a bit. "What did you do now?"

"I punched Victoria and broke her nose, and I got suspended. Then I got mad at my mom and searched through her stuff and found a picture in her dresser that was dated years before I was born, but my mom was pregnant. I asked her about it, and she got totally pissed! Now she won't talk to me! I can't wait for you to come home. Do you know how long you have to be in there?"

"Whoa, whoa, whoa! Back up. You *punched* Victoria? You need to start from the beginning and tell me the whole story."

I take a deep breath and start from the beginning. I try to make sure I tell him every little detail to bring him up to speed.

"Well, sounds like you were busy. You always seem to get yourself into trouble when I'm not there."

"When do you get to come home?"

"They need to run a few more tests, but I should get to come home tomorrow afternoon. I'm feeling miserable, though. They have me on a medicine right now that makes me throw up. Hoping they take me off this one soon."

"I'm sorry, David."

"No worries. Hey, my mom's in the bathroom right now, so I just wanted to apologize quick for ruining our plans. We would be out there right now if it weren't for my stupid sickness. I still want to run away with you once I'm outta here."

"I don't know, David. Are you sure we should even try this? I have no idea how I would take care of you if you had a seizure while we were out there. Maybe we need to reconsider."

"Yeah...maybe..." he says, deflated.

"Hey! Don't you get mad at me now too! I just care about you," I plead.

"I know," he says. "I should probably go. Talk to you later, Liv."

Great! Now he's mad at me too. I can't do anything right!

1|5

It's Friday, and I get to return to school today, but I would really rather not. I want David to be there, but he's not being released from the hospital until this afternoon, and he needs more rest. My mom gives me a ride to school but keeps her cold disposition the whole way, not uttering a single word to me. I try to say goodbye, but she just ignores me, staring straight ahead, and pulls away as soon as I close the door.

I walk to the school, keeping my head down, hoping nobody is staring at me. The fog isn't as thick today, so it's fairly easy to see. I quicken my pace and make it into the school without incident, but as I work on my locker combination, Victoria whispers, "You're dead," behind me. I turn to see her bandaged face glaring at me. Angry bruises leak out from under the bandages and surround the bottoms of her eyes.

"Leave me alone, Victoria," I say vehemently.

"Oh, I'll leave you alone...for now. Wouldn't want to get suspended again. You ruined my life, and I'm going to get you for it. You better watch your back."

I roll my eyes as she walks away. I can just punch her broken nose if she tries to mess with me again. Maybe I shouldn't feel too cocky, though. Next time she tries something, I'm sure she will have her entire entourage with her, and there's no way I will be able to fight a group of people.

My day is going surprisingly well. My classes go more smoothly now that I am almost caught up, and Mr. Schuller moved me away from Victoria in science class too. Now I'm in the front right corner, and she's in the back-left corner. We couldn't be further away. What a relief!

I'm not a people person, but I hang out in the busy cafeteria all lunch period to try to avoid being alone and giving Victoria a chance to attack me. If I'm around a bunch of witnesses, it's less likely that she will try to get me. I take the same approach when leaving school too. I ease myself into the middle of the flow of students leaving for the day. I spot my mom's car and jog over to her.

"How was your day?" I ask.

She shrugs her shoulders in response.

"You can't give me the silent treatment forever, Mom. You're going to have to start talking to me again sometime."

"It's better for us both if I just stay quiet. I have nothing more to say to you."

Yikes. She's still pissed.

I just stay quiet for the remainder of the car ride. Once home, I drop my backpack on the floor and race to the phone.

"Is it all right if I call David?"

"Sure." A fleeting look of compassion softens her demeanor. "Tell him I hope he gets well soon." And with that, she heads to her bedroom to ignore me once again.

"Hey, Liv," David answers after the first ring.

"How'd you know it was me?" I ask, surprised.

"I've been watching the clock all afternoon, waiting for you to call."

"How're you feeling?"

"Still not a hundred percent but better. How about you? Did you go back to school today?"

"Yeah. Nothing to report. Victoria gave me her daily death threat, but other than that, not much. You should see how hideous Miss Perfect looks!" I gush. "Bandages all over her nose and bruises under her eyes. It's fantastic!" We both start laughing hard.

"Ow! My head. Stop making me laugh!" he says, still chuckling.

"Sorry." I pause as I wipe a tear from my cheek. I take a deep breath to try to get serious again. "Look, David. About the not wanting to run away..."

"I understand, Liv. I'm not sure what I would do if the roles were reversed, but I still want to go. I can't live every day in fear of a seizure happening again. What kind of a life is that? I'm not sure how much longer you and I have left to live, to be honest. It's a miracle that either of us is still alive, considering how many times we're hospitalized. And that's why I want to go. Think of it as a major bucket list item. I need to know what's out there."

"You make a good point, but..."

"Don't answer me now. Just take some time to think about it. I know I'm asking a lot of you, to be willing to deal with any of my seizures, but please, just think about it," he pauses a moment. "Ugh! My head is really throbbing right now. I should probably go."

"I'll call you tomorrow."

Once I hang up, I fall over onto my pillow. I just don't know what to do.

At supper, I try to talk to my mom again, hoping I will be able to smooth things over a bit.

"Look, Mom. I'm sorry I snooped through your stuff. It was a bad mix of boredom, anger, and curiosity. I know I shouldn't have done it. Please, just talk to me."

"I don't know what you want me to say, Olivia. You invaded my privacy. How would you like it if I searched through your room?"

"I wouldn't care. I have nothing to hide," I say, but then my cheeks burn as I remember the bag I have stashed under my bed.

"Doesn't matter. I wouldn't do it anyway. I believe in a person having the right to keep some things private. You need to respect that and stay out of my stuff."

We go back to eating in silence. After supper, as I'm cleaning up the table, she drops a paper bag in front of me.

"Here's the extra inhalers you asked for," she says, and then walks off to her bedroom.

"Thanks!" I call out. I go straight to my backpack and stuff them in. She might be mad at me, but I take the extra inhalers I asked for as a sign that she still loves me.

Early Saturday morning, I wake up to my mom knocking on the door. "I have to go into work to get things prepared for a big meeting on Monday. You're on your own. Behave," she says as she leaves.

I lie back down and sleep for a couple more hours. I finally get myself out of bed and see that my mom put the TV back in the living room. I turn it to the Discovery channel to see if there are any old survival shows on that might give me tips on how to survive if David and I do decide to run away. They like to play reruns of old shows that used to be popular before the big war. It's interesting to see what the world was like before: people went into the woods whenever they wanted; they could stand out in the rain and not die; and man, what I wouldn't give to stand in that glorious sunlight that isn't diluted by the fog. I'm just glad that we still have TVs, phones, radios, and stuff like that. The world would be so boring if there weren't any electronics. What did people do before they were invented?

There's nothing good on TV, so I call David.

"Whatcha up to?" I ask as I eat a bowl of cereal.

"About five eleven."

"Har...har."

"Nothing really. My headache went away. I feel pretty good considering, but my mom is making me stay in bed. I'm so bored!"

"I have a pile of homework for you that your dad asked me to grab. Want me to bring that over?" I ask around my mouthful of cereal.

"You can't. Look outside."

I look over and see raindrops sliding down the glass.

"Shoot. I was supposed to drop it off for you earlier. Sorry."

"Not a problem. School won't matter soon. Once we are off on our adventure, homework will be a thing of the past."

"David, I'm torn. I want to go now more than ever since my fight with Victoria and my mom being so cold and distant, but you just got out of the hospital. Shouldn't we take it easy and wait?"

"Wait for what? The next seizure? The next illness? The next cracked skull? We hardly ever have much time between yours or my sicknesses. I say we go while we can still move."

I don't say anything as I think it over.

"Did you hear the news this morning?"

"No. You know I don't watch the news."

"You should," he scolds. "Anyway, our great and wonderful president has decided that 'for the good of the people' everyone is going to get microchips implanted in their arms."

"What? Why?"

"He claims it's a chip that will alert you when the rain is coming, so we can have fewer casualties. Apparently, the government will release a warning signal that will cause the chips to start glowing and grow warm in your arm. They want to put it inside people, so nobody has any chance of losing it, and everyone will have one. That way, there will be no excuse to end up in the rain."

"Hmm...I suppose that might be a good plan..."

"No, it's not, Olivia!"

"What? What's wrong with wanting fewer deaths?"

"They couldn't care less about people dying in the rain! All they care about is controlling people. And what better way to control people than to have every single person microchipped so they can keep track of everyone's whereabouts? They are just trying to come up with a sneaky way to do it so people like you—no offense—will think it's a great and wonderful plan that was set up to protect and save people. But the truth is they are trying to take away our privacy."

"You don't know that that's what they're doing," I say, trying to brush it off. "I think you like to come up with worst-case scenarios and try to make the Coalition look like they are always up to something."

"They are!"

"Whatever."

"Mark my words, Liv. The Coalition is full of bad people, and one day, we will all be brainwashed puppets doing their bidding. I, for one, will not let them put that chip in my arm, even if it means fighting to my death!"

And with that, he hangs up on me.

16

David refuses to answer my calls now, and my mom still won't talk to me. Could I be any more of a screwup? On Sunday, I sulk around the apartment in my pajamas, eating peanut butter out of the jar with a spoon, and watching mind-numbing amounts of TV.

As I'm flipping through stations, I stop on a news report talking about the chip implants David was telling me about. President Turk is standing in front of the Coalition flag, which is a new take on the old United States flag with the original thirteen stripes, but instead of fifty stars, there's ten in a circle—signifying the ten cities that are left—surrounding an olive branch. Kind of lame, if you ask me.

President Turk is encouraging people to "not resist it," that "it is for the good of mankind." What a slimeball. Even his appearance seems greasy: long black hair slicked back, shifty brown eyes adorned with thick, bushy eyebrows, a long hawk nose, and a thin-lipped smile revealing teeth that are so abnormally straight and shiny, I wonder if they're real. I change the channel to old game shows and leave it on that the rest of the afternoon.

I throw a pizza in the oven just as my mom gets home. She walks in the door and gives me a look of disgust.

"What?"

Finally, my schlubby appearance breaks her silent treatment. "What have you been doing all day? You didn't even get dressed?"

"No. Why bother? You're still mad at me, and now David won't answer my calls."

"And why's that?"

Crap! I can't tell her the real reason, so I make something up quick. "Oh, he um...didn't agree with me on which Lord of the Rings movie was better, and I told him he was an idiot, so he hung up on me and won't take my phone calls." Wow, that was a stupid excuse! I hope she buys it.

"Huh. Well, that's not a good way to treat your friend. Doesn't surprise me, though," she finishes with a mumble and walks off to the kitchen to get plates for supper. I flip her the middle finger when her back is turned.

We eat supper in silence, and my mom returns to her room. I don't understand why she is still punishing me over finding a dumb picture.

You know what? I'm done. I'm sick of this! I'm sick of my mom treating me this way. I'm sick of getting death threats from Victoria, not to mention the ones from Cindy too. I'm leaving as soon as she goes to bed. I just hope David isn't so mad at me that he won't carry out our plan.

I wait until her bedroom light goes off around midnight. Taking one last look at the apartment, I secure my backpack on my shoulders and close the door, locking it behind me. The streets are empty as I make my way to David's house. The president has made it clear that it would be best for people to stay inside when it's dark, and like good little sheep, people listen. I sneak around behind David's house and peek through his window. He's lying on his bed, reading a book. I tap on the glass to get his attention, and he starts when he sees me looking at him. I drop my black hood and give him a smile.

"What do you want?" he asks after opening his window.

I lift my backpack up in response. His eyes widen, and a big grin spreads across his face.

"Unless you've changed your mind?" I say playfully.

"No! Nope. Not at all." He walks over to his closet and wrestles a large black bag out. He then pulls an envelope out of the side pocket and carefully places it on his pillow. It reads, "To: Mom and Dad."

Once he has his shoes, a couple of extra layers of shirts, and a coat on, he climbs out of the window and pulls the pane down to hide that we left this way. Excitement is coursing through my body. I feel like I could run all the way there. But we don't run. We walk, carefully staying within the shadows, keeping our heads down. It's going to take a few hours to get to the edge of the city this way, but I don't care. I can already feel a sense of freedom that I have never felt before.

We keep our talking to a minimum so we don't expose our whereabouts. We see a couple of people on the other side of the road, drunk and stumbling their way home. After about an hour, we leave the downtown area, and there are no more streetlights. We can walk freely now, no longer needing to hide in the shadows. The full moon lights up the fog and gives us just enough visibility to not run into anything directly in front of us, but that's about it. David tries to hold my hand, but I give a light squeeze and drop it, sticking my hands in my pockets, pretending I'm cold. I don't know if he thinks I'm suddenly going to start liking him that way since I was willing to run away with him, but I'm not. Ever.

I take to following behind David after I start zoning out and walk into a car parked on the street. Thank God, the alarm doesn't start going off, or we would be done for.

It is eerily quiet out here, which makes me even more nervous. I feel like my footsteps—hell, even my *breathing* is too loud, and someone is going to catch us, but we don't see anyone. After hours of walking, I'm afraid that we are going in circles and will never find our way to the fence. My feet are killing me, and I've needed to take my inhaler every fifteen minutes or so. At this rate, I will be out of inhalers before we even make it to the woods.

Suddenly, David stops short, and I almost walk into him.

"We're here." He slings his backpack to the ground.

I look around him and see the chain link fence looming ahead. I listen intently for guards or anyone who might catch us, but all I hear is David searching his pack for the bolt cutters he brought.

I stand back and keep a lookout while David starts cutting the fence close to the ground. I can't believe we are actually doing this! I cringe with each loud snap of the tool cutting through the wire. I keep glancing over my shoulder to see if anyone is coming, but all I see is poorly lit fog.

"Shh!" I shush nervously. "We're gonna get caught."

"Done," David whispers, pushing the fence to widen the hole. "Ready?"

I nod my head in response.

"I'll go first." He pushes his large bag through the hole. He lies down on his belly and wriggles back and forth until he gets through. He stands up and brushes the dirt off.

"Push your bag through, and then I'll help pull you out."

I shove my bag under the fence and lie down in the dirt.

"Wait! Did you hear that?" David asks.

I freeze. Then I hear it. Footsteps.

"Quick! Pull me through!" I whisper, panicking. I lie down on my stomach and start kicking and wiggling until I'm halfway through, but my pants get caught on the bottom wires of the hole.

"Stop!" someone shouts. I chance a look behind me and see a guard holding a large black gun pointed toward me. I start kicking my legs faster and reach my hands out for David to grab. He takes hold of my wrists and pulls, but at the same time, the guard drops his gun and jumps on my legs, wrapping his arms around them tightly. I feel as though I am going to rip in two.

"Get off me! Let go!" I scream, thrashing around as hard as I can, trying to shake him off. But instead of the guard letting go, David lets go of my hands. I scream as the guard starts pulling me back under the fence.

"David!" I grab onto the fence as the guard pulls me out of the hole and back into the city side.

"Let her go!" David yells, and to my surprise, the guard lets go of my legs. I have only seconds to understand what's happening. I look at David, and he has his gun out, pointing through the fence. I look back at the guard.

"Cute gun, kid," he sneers, and I see his eyes go toward his rifle lying on the ground about four feet away. "Do you even know how to use that thing?"

A strange instinct kicks in, and I lunge for the gun, getting to it before the guard does. I pick it up and smash the butt of the gun into the guard's face. He stumbles backward, and I hear a shot ring out. The guard slumps to the ground, holding his hand over the blood gushing out of his chest, right under the Coalition flag patch—a symbol of peace.

"David! What did you do?"

"I didn't mean to!" David says frantically, a pained look on his face as he messes with his ear. "C'mon, Olivia! Hurry up, and get over here before another guard comes to investigate the noise!"

"Shouldn't we help him? David, you just shot him! He's dying!"

"Look, we can talk about this later. Get over here!"

I stand between the guard and David, looking back and forth at them. We are in so much trouble! I finally make my decision and scramble to crawl under the fence as fast as I can to get away from what we just did. What David just did. Just as I pick up my bag and secure it on my back, I hear footsteps running toward the fallen guard. At least, he will be getting help. I turn around and start running behind David, taking cover in the strange, unknown woods. What a great start we're off to.

17

"Just keep running!" David shouts back to me, pointing his flashlight in my direction. The moon no longer lights our way once we're in the woods. Everything is dark. It's risky using a flashlight, but we need to move quickly.

"I can't!" I wheeze, taking another dose of my inhaler.

He walks back to me, grabs my wrist, slings my arm around his neck, and wraps his arm around my waist. Half-dragging me, we continue on. We've been running from the fence for a solid forty-five minutes now, stopping frequently for inhalers. My legs are about to give out, and the stitch in my side feels like I have a knife lodged in my ribcage. I have never run so far in my life. But we have to keep going. If that guard survives, we're done for. He saw our faces, and it's only a matter of time before they start searching for us.

I keep moving my feet, taking step after step, disconnecting my mind from my repetitious movements. I find that I can keep going as long as David continues to help me, but finally, David has had enough, and we have to stop. We fall to the ground, panting. I blindly dig inside my bag until I find a water bottle, and we both take turns emptying its contents. We lie on the ground, quietly catching our breath.

I finally break the silence. "David, why did you shoot that guard in the chest? He's probably dead now."

"I wasn't aiming for his chest. I was aiming for his leg. I told you, I've never shot a gun before," he says, sniffing.

"We're in so much trouble..." I fret.

"Look, it's pitch-black, and we're out in the middle of the woods. We've put a lot of distance between us and the city. We'll be fine. That guard will be fine," David adds with a quiver in his voice. "We need to keep going for a little while longer. The sun will be coming up soon."

We stand up, strap our backpacks back on, and continue trudging along. I follow behind David. He keeps his flashlight shining down at the ground. I keep close watch of where he steps, hoping I don't trip. If I fall down, I'm not sure I will be able to stand back up. Weariness starts to take over, so I mentally go over what I packed for survival to keep my mind occupied. I stop short.

"Shoot! David, please tell me you packed vitamins..."

He drops his bag on the ground and starts digging through it.

"No. I didn't," he says with worry in his voice.

"What are we going to do? I knew this was a bad idea, and now we're going to die out here. We need those vitamins, David!"

"I'm sorry, Liv..."

"We need to go back!"

"Are you serious? We can't go back there. Especially now!"

"David, we are in the middle of the woods that we've been told will kill us, running for our lives because you killed a guard, and now we don't have the vitamins that helped keep us alive when we were home. We're doomed!" My chest tightens as a panic attack rears its ugly head. I can't deal with one of those right now! I take slow deep breaths, trying hard to control it.

"For one, we've been in the woods for a couple of hours now, and we haven't seen or heard a thing, other than one squirrel we startled. Two: that guard might not have died, like I already said. We don't know what happened to him. And three: the vitamin thing is bad luck, but we can't go back to get them. That would be stupid. We'll just have to take it easy and try to survive without them."

I close my eyes for a moment and try to calm down. He's right of course. We can't go back for them.

"Fine." I take one last inhaler dose, and we move on. David scans the area with his flashlight, looking for somewhere safe we can hide in for sleeping. We are both shuffling our feet, barely able to lift them off the ground.

"Look over there!" David shines his light on a pile of rocks.

I step closer and can see a hole in the pile.

"I don't know, David. What if something is living in there? We're going to get eaten."

"Stay here, and I'll check it out." David drops his bag next to my feet. He gets down on his hands and knees and shines his flashlight into the opening. He slowly crawls through the hole, and I lose sight of him and the light. I suddenly feel exposed without his presence. I look around me, trying to keep an eye out, but it's too dark. The silence is heavy in my ears, and I jump about a foot when David calls out my name.

"Olivia! Grab the bags, and come over here. This is a perfect spot," he says excitedly from the mouth of the cave.

I hand the bags to David, and he helps me crawl through a short tunnel that leads to a cave big enough for the two of us to fit in comfortably: tall enough to sit up in and long enough to lie down. We unpack our blankets and start making our beds. I lie in the back of the cave, and David takes the spot closest to the entrance. I am so exhausted, but I lie awake worrying about what kind of creatures are going to crawl on me while I sleep. Maybe this wasn't such a great plan. What were we thinking? I'm already missing my warm bed and indoor plumbing. I sure hope David has a plan or, at least, an idea of what he's looking for.

The mustiness of the cave makes me take a couple extra doses of my inhaler, and David's smell doesn't help. His presence is comforting, but I really wish he would wear deodorant a little more often. After such a long journey, he reeks of BO. Hopefully, he has some packed.

"David?" I whisper. I sigh when he doesn't answer me.

"David," I say louder.

He snores in response.

Great. Guess I'm just going to have to suffer through. I roll onto my side, away from him and bring the blanket to my nose. I breathe in deep and smile. It smells like the cedar chest at home.

"Goodnight, Mom. I hope you enjoy your life without me," I whisper out loud. Before I know it, I fall asleep.

1 8

I wake up to the sound of birds singing. More birds than I ever heard in the city. We get the occasional pigeon looking for food, but they don't sing like this. I sit up and reach for my glasses.

"David! Wake up!" I shout.

He wakes up with a jolt, fists up and ready to face whatever threat there is that made me shout.

"What! What is it?"

"I can't see! My eyes are blurry!" I say in a panic, moving my glasses around, trying to see if adjusting them will help.

"Take them off, and see if they're dirty," he says. He lies back down now that he knows there is no danger.

I take them off to clean with my shirt. I glance my eyes toward David and realize that I can see parts of his face. It's still blurry, but I can actually see his nose and lips. I look out the mouth of the cave and can see tree trunks and rocks.

I shove my glasses on my face ,and the world becomes a blur again. I turn toward David, and I can no longer see the distinct shapes of his face. I slide my glasses down my nose, and his face comes into focus better.

"What the hell is going on?" I ask out loud. I take a deep breath in to try to center myself, and my lungs fill with air without any pain. In fact, I take a breath deeper than any I have ever taken, and it feels *good*. I have gotten used to taking shallow breaths so I don't hurt my airways, never allowing my lungs to fill completely like this.

"David!" I shake his shoulder. "Wake up!"

David grunts and rubs his eyes. "What now?"

"I can breathe!"

"Good for you."

I slap his arm. "Seriously, I can take a deep breath, and my lungs feel great. Try it."

David sits up and inhales deeply. "Holy cow! Mine too." He takes another deep breath and smiles.

"I don't know what I'm going to do about my glasses, though. I can see better without them, but even then, I can't see great. How am I going to make it out there?"

"We'll take it slow."

We eat a quick breakfast of dried fruit and a little jerky. I ask David to leave the cave so I can change out of my dirty clothes. Once he's outside, I hear him call for me.

"What?" I huff, wanting to freshen up.

"Come out here!"

I crawl out of the cave and gasp. Although my vision is still blurry, I can see trees. The fog is gone. I look around and see sunlight, pure, bright sunlight streaming through the woods. Lush green leaves are everywhere. All the trees look so healthy and alive. Tears spring to my eyes. This is big. Why would the government be trying to keep us in the city when this gloriousness is out here?

"It's beautiful," I say.

"Where's the fog? See! I told you something amazing was out here!" David says gleefully.

I join him in gazing at the surroundings, but my smile slowly fades.

"Wait a minute, David. We don't have the cover of fog to protect us anymore. If they come looking for us, they are going to be able to find us better now!"

"You're right. Quick, go change and get your stuff packed up. We need to keep moving."

Once we both have all our belongings, we continue our journey further into the woods. I walk behind David and keep my eyes on his feet, glancing up now and again to take in the bright sunlight shining through the leaves. I have never seen pure sunlight before.

"David, can we go over there?"

"Where?"

"See where there is a big spotlight of sun? I want to see what it feels like."

We walk to our right a little and step out of the shade and into the sunlight. I close my eyes and turn my face toward the sky. The warmth of the sun is like a hug for my whole body. I instantly become relaxed and want to lie right down and take a nap in it.

"This is amazing. I have never felt something so beautiful before," David says.

We both stand there for a minute or two, soaking up the sun. I open my eyes to gaze up at it and see its glory. Ow! I cast my eyes to the ground and blink a few times to try to get the bright spot out of my vision. Note to self: don't look directly at the sun.

"Wow, the sun is warm! I'm starting to sweat," David comments.

"Isn't it great?"

"Yes, but we really do need to keep moving, Liv."

I take a deep breath, stretching out my arms as though to embrace everything around me, and let it out with a big sigh.

We continue on our way. With all of this fresh air, I begin to feel clearer-headed and positive. Maybe we are going to be okay. Maybe this is what I needed after all. I continue following behind David, and we walk for a few more hours. The sunshine has done its job of heating up the day, and we are both stripped of all extra clothing by the time we stop for lunch. My t-shirt is drenched with sweat from my backpack holding the heat against my back.

I drop my pack on the ground and rummage through it to find something to eat. I grab a granola bar and pick a spot in the sun to sit.

"How're you doing, Liv? Do we need to find somewhere to camp soon?"

"I'm doing surprisingly well, actually. I have never felt better," I say with a smile.

"Shh! Keep your voice down. You don't need to yell." He looks around.

"I wasn't yelling, David," I snap.

"Okay, maybe not yelling, but you need to be quieter."

"And maybe you need to turn your hearing aid down a little bit," I say.

He takes his hearing aid out of his ear, looking closely at the volume setting.

"It's turned down as low as it will go. I've never had it turned down all the way before. Maybe it's malfunctioning out here."

I shrug my shoulders in response.

We eat in silence for a little while, and I try to strike up a conversation while I'm in such a good mood.

"David, are you scared at all? Being out here in the woods?"

"Well, sure. I have no idea what we are going to find, but I feel good about things. The fog being gone, getting some real sunlight, and fresh air... I think we made the right choice."

"I would feel better about it if my eyesight wasn't freaking out. Everything is still blurry."

David nods his head and continues eating. We share a bottle of water and rest just a bit more before we strap our packs back on and continue.

We walk until the sky turns brilliant shades of orange and pink. I can catch glimpses of the beautiful hues between tree branches, but after I stumble for the third time, I tear my eyes from the sky and keep my focus on David's back. Even though the sky still looks bright, it's dark in the woods, and I have a hard time seeing my surroundings. Everything feels a bit more sinister when you can't see well. I start at every noise and decide I've had enough.

"David, I'm ready to stop for today."

"Me too. I don't see a cave around here this time, but I did bring a tarp and some ropes. I'll set up a shelter for us."

By the time he's done, the sun is gone, and the nightly sound of crickets fills our ears. We eat a small supper, and I fall asleep almost instantly.

I wake up to the sweet sounds of birds again and smile. Stretching out my sore muscles, I sit up and look around, hoping my eyes aren't any worse. To my surprise, they are slightly improved from yesterday. They're still blurry, but I'll take what I can get.

After breakfast, we clean up and continue on our way. I let David lead once again since my eyesight is still poor. As we walk, I watch the sunlight dance through the trees, which are swaying gently in the wind. The cool breeze feels like a soft kiss on the cheek. Suddenly, David holds his arm out to stop me.

"What's up?" I ask.

"I just found a print in the mud," David whispers, staring down at the ground.

"Could it be ours? Are we retracing our steps?"

David kneels on the ground to get a closer look. I would join him, but I wouldn't be able to see it clearly anyway.

"No. These are definitely different. We have on sneakers, and this looks like a boot print." David stands up to look around the forest.

"Crap! How could they have found us already?" I whisper loudly.

We keep trudging along. I glance over my shoulder every thirty seconds to see if someone is following us. David does the same. My feelings of peace have been replaced with paranoia. There's no way they could have found us already.

We keep walking and pass between two boulders covered with a thick layer of moss. I reach my hand out to feel it and smile at the softness of it under my fingers. As we step past the boulders, I look around, and a sense of déjà vu hits me. Since I can't see that well, I'm not really sure why, but I feel like I've been here before.

"David, have we walked this area already?" I whisper.

"No, why?"

"I feel like I've been here before. It seems so familiar."

My instinct tells me to stop moving. I grab David's backpack to stop him.

"Don't move," I whisper with a shaky voice. A chill crawls up my spine.

"What?" David whispers back.

"Tell me, is there a dark figure ahead of us? I can't see," I ask, hoping hard that he says no.

"Holy crap, there is!" David whispers. "What is that?"

My heart starts racing. This is the woods from my dream in the hospital.

"Back up slowly, and try not to step on any branches," I answer.

I grab David's arm as we back up carefully, watching the direction of the beast. Just as we get to the boulder, I step on a stick.

"It's looking at us!" David yells. "*Run!*"

I can see a large black figure start barreling our direction before we turn to run behind the boulders. Before I know it, someone grabs our wrists and pulls us out of the way. A man on the boulder shoots an arrow at the beast. It whines, and he shoots another arrow. There's a crash as the beast falls to the ground. I turn to look at who grabbed us and pulled us to safety, and they are the same startling blue eyes as the guy I saw in my dream.

The other man jumps off the boulder to see if the creature is dead. After a minute or two, he comes back over by us. He pulls a length of rope out of his coat.

"Thank you so much for saving us. You know, it's funny: this happened before in a dream, and I am curious to know who you are..." I say excitedly, and at that moment, the hunter and his young friend who had saved us grab our arms and forcefully push us belly first against the giant boulders.

"Hey! What do you think you're doing?" David yells.

The men get to work binding us with their ropes until we can't move our arms. Then, with strips of cloth, they gag and blindfold us. This is not at all how it went in my dream!

The men proceed to pull us along in a tight grip for what feels like hours. They don't talk, not even to each other. What are they going to do to us? Do they work for the Coalition? Do they know who we are and what we've done? I start to cry. This isn't how things were supposed to go.

Even though we walk at a fast clip, my lungs still feel good. At least, I can be thankful for that. Our pace starts to slow down, and my nose fills with the scent of smoke. I hear some chattering coming closer. The man lets go of my arm and pushes me down until I'm sitting. He unties one of my wrists momentarily, slips my backpack off, and then ties my hands around a post. I don't struggle. Although he is firm with me, he never actually hurts me. I can hear them tying David to a post next to me. We both stay quiet.

Since I can't see anything, I try as hard as I can to listen to my surroundings to see if I can figure out where we are. All I hear are our captors' feet walking over stones and leaves as they move away from us, the crackling of the fire that is far enough away that I can't feel its warmth, the breeze blowing through the trees, and birds singing. Nothing significant. And then I hear a quiet conversation begin, and I will myself to breathe shallowly so I can hear every word.

"Where did you find them?" a woman asks.

"'Bout four miles from here. We tracked a Havoc and killed it, but we had to save their sorry asses."

"Are they dangerous?"

"Look at 'em. Do they look dangerous?"

"You never know. They could be spies."

"That's what I'm gonna find out. Fetch me some water, will ya?"

I hear footsteps making their way back toward us. He takes the gag out of my mouth but leaves the blindfold on. I take a moment to try to get saliva back in my uncomfortably dry mouth.

"Who are ya?" the man asks with a gruff voice.

"Olivia. Can you please take the blindfold off too?" I ask innocently.

"Who do ya work for?" he asks, ignoring my request.

"Nobody."

"Likely story. I'm not gonna ask again. You'll answer my questions, or you can forget about the drink of water I have for you."

My mouth is so dry that my tongue feels like sandpaper. I would kill for a drink of water right now.

"I don't work for anybody. I'm a junior in high school."

"Lies!" he bellows.

"Why would I lie?" I ask, trying hard to keep my tone mellow.

"You want me to believe that two scrawny teenagers are trompin' around in the woods on their own? Do ya think I'm stupid?"

"It's true! I-I swear! David and I ran away to the woods because we wanted to see what was out here...what the Coalition was hiding that they didn't want people to see," I finish, biting my lips together. I shouldn't be revealing so much. What if *they* work for the Coalition?

"I see. So, you and your friend here are suspicious of the government, eh? Why?"

I stay quiet, trying to decide how much to give away.

"Speak!" he yells again, kicking the bottom of my shoe.

"W-well, how do I know you guys don't work for the Coalition?" I ask as boldly as I dare.

Laughter fills the camp. After it finally quiets down, he continues. "You don't need to worry about who we are right now, but I can tell ya, we don't associate with the Coalition. Now, answer my question. Why are *you*, a couple of clueless teenagers, suspicious of the Coalition?"

"Well, we were noticing strange things here and there. Like, why are the trees so green in the woods outside of the fence when all the trees inside of the city are sickly yellow? Why are we not allowed to leave the city if we want to? Are the guards stationed at the fence to keep us safe or to keep us inside the city?"

I can hear a low-level buzz of people murmuring about us. It's starting to annoy me. I wish he would take this blindfold off so I could see them.

"What were ya hopin' to accomplish out here? Ya plannin' on runnin' back home when things got tough? Runnin' back to your mommies and hope that nobody noticed ya ran away in the first place?"

"What difference does it make to you?" I ask, trying to keep my attitude in check.

"Makes a big damn difference that you two idiots probably have people lookin' for ya! Within a day or two, we're gonna have Turk's puppet soldiers out here searchin', and we can't let 'em find us."

Suddenly, someone shouts, "Take 'em back out where you found 'em, tie 'em up, and leave 'em for dead! You never shoulda brought 'em here!"

"I brought 'em here to question 'em. What we do with 'em once I'm done, isn't clear yet!" he yells.

My heart is racing. What did we get ourselves into?

I start to speak, my voice trembling, "Look. I don't know what you want us to say that will make you believe we aren't here trying to cause trouble. We don't want to get caught either. If you just let us go, we'll continue on, and you won't have to worry about us anymore."

"I'm not done with you yet," the man says.

I hear his boots crunch on the gravel toward David.

"Well, boy. You got anythin' to add? What're ya two doin' out here that's so important you had to leave the city?"

"Why should I talk? You're not going to believe me anyway."

Suddenly, I hear a hard slap and a groan from David.

"Stop it! What are you doing to him?" I scream, frantically wriggling around to try to break my bonds.

"Henry! Stand down!"

"What? I'm tired of them giving you lip, Pop. Maybe they'll talk if we slap them around a little," I hear a different male voice say.

"I'm the leader here! Go back by the rest of 'em, and let me handle this."

I hear a huff and then footsteps walking away.

"Look now, boy. You need to answer my question quickly, or we're gonna have a problem. Hear me?"

When David doesn't respond, I hope with all my might that he shook his head yes. This is no time to be difficult.

"Did anyone see you leave the city?"

A feeling of dread washes over me as I remember what happened at the fence.

"Sort of," David responds, heavily.

"Sort of? What do you mean, 'sort of'?"

"We shot a guard. And that should answer your question as to whether we work for the Coalition or not."

I hear some low murmurings and a long whistle come from the crowd.

"Well, well. That would change my mind if I thought it were true."

"It is true!" I shout before I can stop myself.

"This is a story we would all love to hear." He chuckles a bit. "Go on. Let's hear this heroic tale of yours."

David doesn't speak right away, so I begin to tell it. "Well, we made it to the fence, and David cut a hole with his dad's bolt cutters. I tried to get under the fence, but my pants got stuck, and a guard found us. He jumped on my legs and started pulling me back. That's when David pulled out his gun, and the guard let go of me. I grabbed the guard's rifle he dropped and smashed his nose with the butt of the gun, and David shot him. I scrambled back under the fence, and we heard someone running toward the fallen guard as we ran into the woods."

Silence. I wish I could see whether he believed me or not.

"Henry!" the man shouts, causing me to jump. "Check their bags for a gun. If we find one, maybe we'll believe this cock and bull story."

I hear the zipper of our bags open and then all the contents get dumped onto the ground.

"It's tucked in a sock," David finally adds. I hear more shuffling of stuff.

"Yup. Yup, here it is, Pop!" Henry shouts.

"Well, well. Looks like maybe you're tellin' the truth about that little pea shooter there. Where'd you get the gun, kid?"

"From my Grandpa before he died."

"That so?"

"Yeah. He didn't trust the Coalition either and hid the gun under a floorboard when they came to search his house. He passed it on to me, and I've kept it secret ever since."

"Okay, say I do believe this story. Ya think you're a tough guy now because ya shot a man? Show your strength, kid. Henry!" he yells out, his voice turning back to the crowd. "Untie him. Let's see what he's got."

Are they expecting him to fight? David doesn't know how to fight. This is bad. This is very bad.

20

I hear him untie David next to me. "You can watch," he says, taking my blindfold off.

I don't want to watch David get his butt kicked. The sudden brightness of the sun blinds me momentarily. After my eyes adjust, I realize that my vision has improved even more. Now I can see things far away, but everything up close is still a tad blurry. What is happening to me?

I watch worriedly as David stands up, rubs his sore wrists, and follows Henry with shuffling steps into an open area. If they are planning on fighting, David is going to lose. Maybe they're trying to embarrass him for fun.

I take a glance at the people standing off to the side. It's an odd conglomeration of people. There is a small group of young children. Their faces are dirty, and their clothes are worn and ratty, but they are smiling away as they scribble in the dirt with each other. Their mothers stand guard next to them, all wearing a look of maternal defiance, daring us to try to harm their little ones. A group of about fifteen men and women sit by the fire, watching us closely. There is an elderly man, sitting on a stump whittling a stick as though nothing strange is happening whatsoever. A tall, scrawny teenaged boy and a beautiful pre-teen girl with wild, bushy hair stand in front of one of the crude shelters, watching David and Henry with wide eyes, not wanting to miss a thing. Standing next to the leader is an attractive middle-aged woman; her skin is darker than any I have ever seen in my life, and she is staring daggers at me. I avert my gaze, feeling extremely uncomfortable with her scrutiny of me.

David stands in the middle of the clearing, keeping his eyes on Henry, who's walking circles around David, sizing him up. After a moment, he stands in front of David and brings his hands up into a fighting stance. David looks scared like he would much rather turn tail and run, but he brings his hands up to match Henry's. Quick as lightning, Henry pushes David's hand down with his left hand, and in one fluid motion, his right is backhand punching him across his face. David drops to the ground with a thump. After a few seconds, he slowly stands up, moving his jaw back and forth. The odd thing is, Henry doesn't goad him. Nobody does. As a matter of fact, the group of people stays oddly silent, watching with reverence and curiosity.

David puts his hands back up in the fighting stance. His jaw is red from the hit. He never takes his eyes off Henry. They stand still for a few seconds before Henry throws a punch just as quick as the last one and hits David in the stomach. David doubles over with a groan. Henry stands back with a slight smirk on his face but waits until David stands up again and faces off. Henry sends his fist flying toward David's nose, but this time, David brings his arm up and blocks it, quickly followed by his other fist, which lands a solid punch to Henry's ribs. The crowd gasps. Henry clutches his side for a moment but shakes it off.

I look at the leader of the group, and he doesn't react. He watches closely, as though studying David's every move.

Henry's face hardens with determination as they face off again. David looks more confident now that he got a hit in. Where did David learn to do that?

Henry sweeps his leg toward David's heels and knocks David onto his back. But David rolls to the side and sweeps Henry's feet out, dropping him to the ground just as fast. They are both on their feet once more, staring each other down. Suddenly, as though a bell sounded that the true fight begins now, their fists start flying in every direction, but none of them hit their target as both boys are blocking and dodging perfectly. It almost looks as though they choreographed this. Sweat starts pouring down David's face as he blocks every punch thrown at him and continues to throw his own at Henry. My jaw drops as I watch David fight as though he's been training for years.

"Enough!" bellows the leader.

Henry immediately stops fighting, and David takes the hint. They both double over, hands on knees, as they struggle to catch their breath after the exertion. David's shirt is soaked with sweat, making it cling to his scrawny frame.

"Not bad," the leader says, as he walks around the two boys. "But it's still inconclusive. For now, you and the girl can sit by the fire while my people and I have a discussion on what to do with you," he says and then turns around. "Cassandra. Timothy. Get these two a jug of water and some food. I'd like you to keep an eye on 'em while the adults talk."

Immediately, the teenaged boy and the bushy-haired girl set off to fetch the stuff the leader said to bring. The adults head to their meeting, and the small children follow their mothers, playing a game of tag as they go. "Come on, Grandpa," I hear Henry say as he helps the old man up off the stump. He leads him to the large shelter made from small logs tied together with ropes and large tarps on the roof to keep out rain.

David walks over to me and unties my hands. He helps me off the ground, but suddenly he starts to sway back and forth looking like he's about to pass out.

"You okay?" I ask, worried.

"Yeah. I'm fine. Just tired and thirsty."

"That was amazing. What you did with Henry. How did you learn to fight like that?"

"I didn't. I have no idea what just happened. It was as though a fog started lifting out of my head; my hands were doing their own thing, and I was just along for the ride."

Cassandra and Timothy come jogging back with a basket of fruits and vegetables and a big plastic jug of water. We have a seat on stumps next to the fire, and they put the food between David and me. I grab an apple and wait my turn for the water, letting David have it first.

"That was pretty cool," Timothy says. "I've never seen anyone match Henry like that. He's the best fighter we got."

"Thanks, Timothy? That's your name, right?" David says.

"You can call me Tim. And this is Cass, my sister." He points to the bushy haired girl. "Only Matthias calls us by our full names."

Cass gives him a stern look and says quietly, "Don't tell them so much! We don't know if the adults are going to decide to let them stay or not."

We sit quietly as David and I eat our fill. I have about a million questions rolling around in my head. It has been at least twenty minutes since the adults left to go talk. Cass and Tim keep staring at us with curiosity as though we're aliens from another planet.

"What?" I finally blurt out, annoyed with the relentless staring.

"Nothing," Tim says, sitting up straight. "Well, it's just...I'm just so excited to meet a Rare."

"A 'Rare'? What's that?" I ask.

"Don't, Tim. You need to wait," Cass warns. I roll my eyes at Cass and stare off at the shelter, waiting for the adults to come back.

Tim leans down and picks a rock up off the ground as I'm finishing the last bite of my apple. Before I know it, my hand is in front of my face, stinging from catching the rock before it hit me in the eye.

"Did you see that?" Tim laughs, nudging Cass with his elbow.

"Wait... Why did you... How did I..." I start to ask, bewildered.

"You're a Rare," Tim says with a huge grin. "I could tell that you were different as soon as you came into camp."

"Cut the crap! How did you know that Olivia was going to catch the rock? And why would you throw it at her face?" David asks angrily. He glances at my hand and gives the red welt a gentle rub.

"Timothy. Cassandra. Don't bother answering 'em. They're leavin'," the leader, Matthias says. We were so distracted, we didn't see that the adults had come out of the shelter.

"Leaving? Wait! We want some answers too!" I say, finding myself not wanting to leave so quickly. I want to know what Tim was talking about.

The lady who was staring daggers at me earlier grips my arm tightly with one hand while holding a knife with the other. She stands me up, directing me out of their camp. "Didn't you hear him? He said you're leaving. Keep your mouth shut and go!"

"We said we came to the woods for answers! We think you could help us!" David pleads, struggling against Henry's death grip.

I stop moving my legs and lock them into place so the lady has to drag me toward the woods. David tries to wrench his arm out of Henry's grip, but his grip is too strong, and David is weak from the earlier fight.

I start to panic. I don't know who these people are, but I think they could help us. They at least have shelter and food and can defend themselves from beasts and other dangers that might be lurking in the woods.

Once they've walked us past the posts they tied us up to when we first got here, they give us a good shove, and I fall in the dirt. Henry and the cranky lady turn around and start heading back to the camp. Rage builds up inside of me, and I start yelling the first threat that comes to my mind.

"Just you wait! The soldiers will eventually find us and take us back to the city, and when they do, I'll tell my mother, Janice Sloane, a *Coalition* employee, that you're out here and where to find you! They'll come arrest you all!"

David helps me up off the ground. We start brushing ourselves off as Matthias comes marching over to us.

"What'd ya say?" Matthias asks, pointing the tip of his knife at my chest.

"I said that if you kick us out, the soldiers will find us, and I'll tell my mom, who works for the government, where you are," I say, immediately regretting it.

Matthias glares at me for a moment, and I'm worried he's going to kill me on the spot.

"Alexandrine! I'm overruling this decision. They stay!" he shouts, lowering the knife.

The dark-skinned lady gives Matthias a look of death, growls, and turns around to head back into camp.

"Timothy. Go grab our guests' supplies. They will bunk up with you and your sister for now," Matthias orders as he turns around and marches away.

"Yes, sir!" Tim says, grinning widely.

"What was that? Why did he suddenly change his mind? You don't think he's going to torture us and kill us now, do you?" I whisper hysterically to David.

David shrugs his shoulders.

"Come on, you two," Cass says. She leads us toward the shelter she shares with her brother.

I keep my head down and look carefully at the people in the camp. The old man—I overheard someone call him Saul—is back on his stump, whittling again. The little children are playing a game of hide-and-seek. The mothers are watching the kids closely and talking quietly among themselves, taking glances at David and me. The men and women are back around the fire, talking intently. Alexandrine and Matthias are standing outside the meeting shelter, having a heated argument. I slow my pace and listen to what they're saying.

"It was agreed that they were to leave our camp! You have no right going against what the group decides!"

"I've every right! Don't forget why we're out here. The only reason any of ya are still alive is because I brought ya here and have kept ya alive!"

"Oh, yes! Heroic Matthias. Our savior. Whoever would have thought that kidnapping would be such a..."

"Yo, Olivia! In here," Cass calls to me, drowning out what Alexandrine was saying. "You coming or what?"

I reluctantly turn and follow Cass's voice. What was she saying about kidnapping? I suddenly have a sick feeling in my stomach.

I walk into the shelter and see two piles of leaves and pine needles on the floor with blankets laid on top. Well-worn clothes and threadbare blankets are draped over a line of rope tied down the middle of the room, creating a makeshift wall between the rustic beds. Light streams in through gaps between the logs where they didn't quite match up right.

"I know it's not much to look at," Cass says sheepishly, "but it's all we got."

"No. It's fine." I give her a weak smile.

"You can have a seat anywhere you like," Tim offers, smiling. "Cass and I will go out and start gathering some leaves and stuff for your beds."

"Thanks, Tim," David says.

As soon as Tim and Cass leave the shelter, I start telling David what I just heard.

"David, I don't think we want to stay here. I just hear Alexandrine and Matthias talking, and she said something about 'kidnappings.'"

"Kidnappings?" David says, furrowing his eyebrows.

"What is this place? Who are these people?" I feel the familiar signs of a panic attack starting. I drop to the floor and bring my knees to my chest, rocking back and forth.

"Calm down, Liv. We're going to get some answers. This is why we came out to the woods. For answers. We can always sneak out of here if this place doesn't seem safe."

He sits next to me and puts his arm around my shoulder. He gives me a reassuring squeeze, and for the first time since becoming friends, I welcome his touch.

"Hey, you two," Tim announces his return. His arms are full of dried leaves. "I'm going to put your bed here, David, on my side of the shelter. We'll put the girls together over there on that side."

I watch Tim drop the leaves with a grin on his face as though this is fun, like he's having a sleepover with friends instead of complete strangers. Cass comes in with her load, and Tim explains where she should drop it. They both head back out to get another bunch.

"Tim seems nice," David comments.

"They both do," I agree. "They seem to be the only ones who really want us to be here."

"Well, the old guy who whittles sticks doesn't seem to care about anything but making wood shavings. I'm sure he doesn't care that we're here." He smiles.

I shake my head and give him a small smile back.

"I can't stop beating myself up for what I said to Matthias." I cover my face with my hands. "What do you think he's going to do to us?"

"I don't know, Liv."

"I have so many questions. I hope they are willing to answer them."

"We should probably take it slow. The group of people had decided that we shouldn't be allowed to stay here. I don't think very many of them are going to be forthcoming with answers right away. Perhaps we should keep our heads down and cooperate as best we can to earn their trust."

"Yeah. You're probably right. I'll try my best."

Tim and Cass come back with their second load of leaves.

"Just one more trip, and I think that should do it," Tim says cheerfully, patting Cass on the back.

"Did you want us to go get it?" David starts to stand up.

"Nah! It's no problem. You've had a rough day already, and you'll need your rest before tonight's reckoning. Be right back!" Tim heads back out for the rest of our beds.

David and I both look at each other with wide eyes.

"Reckoning? What do you think that is?" I ask.

"I have no clue. I hope they don't line us up and beat us with sticks to see if we're tough enough to stay in the group or something," David says.

"Matthias already said we're staying. What more do we have to do?"

David and I fall silent as we wait for Tim and Cass to come back. My mind is a whirl of questions and fear.

"That ought to do it!" Tim drops the leaves and wipes his clothes off. "Do you guys have blankets to use?"

"Yeah, in our bags, but mine was dumped out when they were looking for my gun," David says.

"That's right. Sorry about that. The guys can be a little rough sometimes. You want me to go get your things?" Tim offers.

"No. I can do it," David says.

Tim looks down at the floor, dejected.

"But...you can come with me if you want..." David adds slowly.

Tim's face lights right up like a dog who's been asked if they want to go for a walk. They both head out the door, and I call to David to bring my bag back too.

Cass is sitting on the floor next to her bed, looking at me, so I decide to make small talk.

"Your brother seems very...enthusiastic," I comment.

"Oh, yes. He is. Sometimes annoyingly so. He is just so happy to be alive."

"Did he almost die or something?"

"If Matthias hadn't brought us here to live, we would have," Cass says straightforwardly.

I wait for her to continue, but she doesn't offer any more of an explanation.

"Where were you living before that you feel you would have died had he not saved you?" I ask.

"The city."

"The city?" I say questioningly.

"Look. I want to answer all your questions. I really do. But I think you need to save your questions until after the reckoning."

"What is the 'reckoning'?"

Cass bites her lip as she decides whether she should keep talking or not. "All right, everyone who comes to stay with us has to go through a reckoning. You are going to be asked to give all your secrets and knowledge to the group through a series of questions. If they like what you say, then you can be in the group. If not, well..."

"What?" I ask.

"We've had some people go through the reckoning, and they didn't pass. Matthias took them back out into the woods, and we never saw them again. I thought maybe he was releasing them to go back to their lives, but then I saw blood splattered on Matthias's shirt. I didn't say anything, but from then on, I made extra sure I didn't step a toe out of line."

"He killed them?" I ask, horrified.

Cass nods.

"Holy crap! Why does Tim seem so excited about us going through this reckoning?" I ask, my voice shaking.

"Because he's not worried. He believes you two are Rare—"

"What is this 'Rare' you keep talking about?" I interrupt, getting more and more frustrated. But Cass doesn't answer because the boys return with the bags.

"Here ya go, Olivia." Tim hands me my bag. I set it next to me and stare at the floor. I feel like no matter where I go, my life is crap!

"Hey, are you okay?" David whispers in my ear as he takes the blanket out of his bag.

I shake my head slowly.

"You better hurry and finish making your beds. It looked like people were getting things ready for tonight's events," Tim says excitedly. Cass and Tim head outside.

"We're going to die, David," I whisper back.

22

"What? Why do you say that?" David says quietly.

"Cass just told me that they are going to question us, and if we somehow fail, we're going to be taken out into the woods and murdered!" I whisper hysterically. Sure, I tried to kill myself a few times, but the thought of someone else killing me terrifies me.

"David. Olivia. Please join me outside by the fire," Matthias says, peeking his head in the door of the shelter.

I start shaking as we both stand up. I reach in my pocket for my inhaler out of habit but stop when I realize that I don't really need it. This level of nerves usually makes me need at least two doses. I wish I understood what I was doing differently so I would never need an inhaler again.

The daylight is slowly fading as it turns to dusk. The campfire has been stoked, and the wood pops every now and then, causing me to jump a little. We make our way to two empty stumps next to the warm blaze. The group of people sits around the fire, their faces glowing in the soft light. Matthias stands by the stumps, holding two cups in his hands.

"Have a seat."

David and I carefully sit down. My heart is racing out of my chest. My face feels hot after only moments by the flames. I look over at David, wondering if he is as scared as I am. If he is, his expression doesn't show it. He looks at Matthias almost as though he's bored. How can he be so calm?

"Before we begin, I'd like you to drink this, please." Matthias hands us the cups.

"What is it?" David sniffs the contents.

I take a sniff too. It smells like sickly-sweet flowers and overripe, slightly fermented grapes mixed together.

"A little concoction I like to call 'rectitude wine.'"

"What did you say? Rectum wine?" David asks with a look of disgust.

Someone in the group starts to snicker until Matthias shoots a look at them, and they stop immediately.

"I said, 'rectitude.' As in honesty. Truth. You'll drink this wine before we begin the questions."

"What if I don't? Then what?" David asks.

I give him a look to try to tell him to knock it off. What happened to keeping our heads down and cooperating to earn their trust?

"If you don't, you'll be kicked out of our camp, and none of your questions'll be answered. You'll be on your own in the woods at night with the Havoc that like to prowl in the darkness. I suggest you do as I say."

David swallows hard. I don't like the idea of going back out there to try to find a place to stay in the dark. David looks at me and gives a little nod. We both raise the cups to our mouths and drink.

The wine feels thick like syrup, and I have a hard time swallowing it, it's so sweet. I start coughing and wish that I had some water to wash it down. My belly grows warm as it floods into my stomach. After a few moments, I feel a strange tingling sensation making its way up into my skull. It's not an unpleasant feeling; in fact, it's quite thrilling. I find myself suddenly wanting to share my life's story with these people. I sit up tall and wait eagerly for the questioning to begin. I take a quick look at David and see that he is also sitting up straight with a look of rapture on his face.

"All right. Let's begin."

Everyone around the fire grows silent as though they are all holding their breath. I glance over at Tim, and he gives me a big smile and two thumbs up.

"We'll start with somethin' easy. Olivia, what's your full name?"

"Olivia Rosette Sloane," I spew out automatically.

"And David, what's your full name?"

"David Allan Beckett," he answers immediately.

"How old are you, Olivia?"

"Sixteen."

Matthias pauses a moment before continuing, "And you, David?"

"Seventeen."

"What are your parents' names, Olivia?"

"My mom's name is Janice Eve Sloane. I do not know who my father is."

"Why's that?"

"My father died before I was born. My mother doesn't talk about him. She says it's because it hurts too much, but I think she's hiding something." The words flow out of my mouth without me even trying.

"What d'ya think she's hidin'?"

"I don't know. It is just a feeling I have. Something feels off about her and the way she likes her secrets."

"What does your mother do for a job?"

"I don't know what she does exactly, but she works at the United World Coalition for Peace building."

"And she won't tell ya what her job is?" Matthias asks, almost annoyed.

"No. It's just another secret she likes to keep from me."

"Does your mother ever tell you what the government's workin' on?"

"No, sir. She will only tell me when they are having a big important meeting, but she won't divulge any other information."

"I see. How 'bout you, David? Who're your parents?"

"Chloe Jill Beckett and Andrew Curtis Beckett."

"What do they do for a livin'?"

"My father is a mechanic at the Ace Auto Body Shop, and my mother works for Peace Pharmaceuticals, sir."

I hear a few murmurings among the group of people.

"Doin' what?"

"She oversees the sale and distribution of vitamins."

"So, she works for the government too?"

"I guess so, yes." David furrows his eyebrows as though he never realized this.

"Do ya love your mother, David?"

"Of course. She's my mother."

"What if I were to tell ya that anyone who works for the government isn't who ya think they are?"

"I know my mother. She is a good person," David says testily.

"I'm sure ya believe that. Most people who work for the Coalition are excellent liars."

"What is your problem, man?" David jumps to his feet.

"David!" I yell, worried he's going to get us in trouble.

"Have a seat, David. I don't wanna fight ya."

"No! Not until you start telling us what it is you're doing out here!"

"You'll get your answers, but I'm not done askin' the questions yet. Have a seat."

David slowly sits back down, staring daggers at Matthias.

"I'm interested in these vitamins. D'ya know what they do?"

"They're vitamins. They keep us healthy."

"Are ya healthy, David?"

"Well, no. I get sick a lot. But my mom tells me that if I didn't take the vitamins, I would be much worse off than I am."

"D'ya have any vitamins with ya?"

"No. Olivia and I forgot them."

"So, ya haven't taken any in a few days?"

95

"That's right."

"And how d'ya feel without 'em?"

David pauses with his forehead scrunched as he thinks about this question. "Well, I feel great, actually. The best I have ever felt in my life. But I can't say it's because of the vitamins or lack of vitamins—"

"How 'bout you, Olivia?" Matthias interrupts David. "What's your life been like up to this point?"

"My life is a joke. I am always sick and weak, and I have tried to kill myself on several occasions."

"And now?"

"I feel a lot better."

Matthias is silent for a moment and starts to pace in front of us. David and I wait quietly for him to ask the next question.

"Olivia, tell me what ya know 'bout your father."

"I already told you. I do not know much about him. My mom says he left to go fight in a war, and a bomb dropped on his location, and there was nothing left of him."

Matthias stops pacing and stands next to the fire, stroking his beard, listening intently. "Anythin' else?"

"She had another child with him, but the baby died before he was born."

"Go back to the shelter with Cassandra and Timothy," Matthias says abruptly, turning around and walking away.

"That's it? We're done?" I call out, worried about his sudden dismissal.

David and I both stand up and turn to head back to the shelter. Tim gives me a small smile, but that doesn't stop my legs from shaking uncontrollably.

23

I sit on my bed, picking up dead leaves and ripping them to pieces. Everyone is silent as we wait for Matthias to come back with the verdict on whether David and I passed the reckoning or not. I suddenly have a killer headache, and I no longer want to share my secrets anymore. The wine must be wearing off.

"Did we say something wrong?" I ask, my voice trembling slightly. I look at Cass for an answer. Her face is barely visible in the dim glow of the flashlight sitting in the middle of the floor.

"I don't think so. I really don't know what he was looking for. The adults never let us in on their deliberations," Cass answers.

David looks at me. His eyes reflect just exactly how I'm feeling. Fear. Unbridled fear that we are about to be kicked out or worse.

We wait for what feels like forever. Time only being measured by how many heartbeats I feel pounding in my chest. I start at Matthias's sudden presence in our shelter door.

"Ya two can stay. Rest up. Tomorrow we put ya to work."

And just that quickly, he's gone.

"Thank you!" I yell out but stop as my head feels like it's about to split.

Cass and Tim are on their feet, jumping up and down and smiling like loons.

"You did it! I knew you were going to be fine!" Tim says excitedly.

I breathe a great sigh of relief and smile as Cass and Tim spin each other in circles. David gets off his bed and sits next to me, smiling.

"We get to live for another day," David says quietly.

I lean my head against his shoulder and feel him rest his cheek against the top of my head. I'm suddenly exhausted and want nothing more than to curl up in a nice soft bed. I guess dried leaves and a blanket will have to do.

"Cass. Tim. I think Olivia and I need some sleep. I don't know about her, but I have a nasty headache, and I think I'm ready for bed."

"Yeah! Sure thing! We'll go back out by the fire and let you two get to sleep," Cass offers, shutting off the flashlight and handing it back to David.

I am so relieved that David spoke up first so I didn't have to stop their celebrating. I grab a sweatshirt out of my bag and wad it up to make a pillow. Now that the sun has gone down, there is a slight chill to the air. I fold my blanket in half and lie between the layers like it's a sleeping bag. I'm asleep in a matter of minutes.

I wake up to the sounds of birds singing and the small children giggling outside. The early morning light shines through the walls. I sit up and stretch out my sore muscles. Dried leaves do not give much support while sleeping.

"Good morning, Olivia." David says.

I look over at his bed and see him sitting with his back against the wall, facing me. I suddenly blush.

"Were you watching me sleep?" I ask, embarrassed at the thought.

"Only for a little bit. I just woke up too."

I look at Tim and Cass's beds and see that they're empty. I rub the sleep out of my eyes, and when I look over at David again, I suddenly realize that I can see every detail of his face. His acne seems to be clearing up, his eyes look more alert and hold my gaze confidently, and his jaw is darkening with stubble.

"David, I can see perfectly without my glasses!"

"That's great, Liv! See? I knew there was something to the woods," he says, holding his hearing aid on the palm of his hand, smiling wide.

Odd. His teeth are looking whiter and less crooked. I have to be imagining things.

"I didn't know we would start healing or anything, but I just had this feeling that there was something we needed to come out here for."

"Aha, you two are finally awake!" Tim says brightly, walking through the door. "You were allowed to sleep in this morning because Matthias knew you needed it."

"Why? What time do you usually get up?"

"At dawn. Everyone has chores they need to do in order to get breakfast ready. You'll catch on. Come on! We still have some breakfast for you to eat."

"I'm going to freshen up a bit first, David. Go on without me."

David nods and leaves the shelter. I take in a breath as deeply as I can and let it all out slowly. The lack of pain in my lungs makes me smile. I look around the shelter, taking in every single detail I can: pieces of bark chipping off the logs, a line of ants walking along the dirt floor, sunshine gleaming off an intricate spider web in the corner of the shelter. Out of curiosity, I grab my glasses out of my bag and put them on. I'm suddenly blind. I can't make out a single thing. I toss them back in my bag and get myself ready for the day with clean clothes and a thorough hair brushing.

Stepping out of the shelter, I look for David. He's sitting on a stump by the fire, eating food.

"You look nice." David smiles at me as I make my way over to him.

"Thanks. I wish I could take a shower. I'm starting to feel pretty dirty."

"There's a stream not far from here where we bathe," a voice says behind me. A woman with dark hair in a high ponytail steps up to my side and hands me a plate of food to match David's: scrambled eggs, a hunk of meat, and an apple.

"Thank you." I take the food from her. I do a double take when I see her. She looks familiar. I'm not sure where I've seen her before. Maybe not her specifically, but someone who looks like her. She gives me a small smile and walks back to where the children are playing a game of keep away with a weathered volleyball.

"Hmm, she looks familiar," I comment to David.

"Who?"

"The lady who just handed me this food," I say. David narrows his eyes and tilts his head as he looks at her for a moment but then shrugs his shoulders and goes back to eating.

I look down at my plate, trying to decide what kind of meat I'm about to eat.

"Try it. It's not bad. Could use a little salt, though," David says around his mouthful of food. Although his appearance might be changing, his manners are not.

I try the eggs first, wondering what kind of bird these eggs are from. They remind me of regular chicken eggs but are rather tasteless without salt. Once I start eating, though, I find it hard to stop. After I demolish the eggs, I stab my fork into the chunk of meat and take a bite. Warm juice floods my mouth, and I let out a moan.

David finishes his apple and turns toward me. "I don't know if I ever thanked you for running away with me. I'm glad you decided to come."

"Me too."

David is quiet for a moment before he asks weakly, "Do you think my mom is a bad person?"

"No! Of course not, David. She's one of the nicest ladies I have ever met. She's always been nice to me, way nicer than my mom."

"How come I never made the connection that she works for the government? Peace Pharmaceuticals. It was obvious once I said it during the reckoning."

"Maybe it was a truth that you kept hidden from yourself because you didn't want to believe it."

"Maybe, but it was pretty naïve of me. I just always thought she worked at a pharmacy that helped people, never once thinking about the link to the government."

"Look, just because she works at a Coalition pharmacy doesn't mean your mom is a bad person."

"I know she's always been nice, but I feel like she's somehow dirty now. Tainted by her loyalty to the president." David digs the toe of his shoe into the dirt.

"Maybe it's just a job to her. Maybe she just works there but isn't loyal—"

"Whatcha guys talking about?" Tim has a seat on one of the empty stumps.

David looks angry at the intrusion. I take his cue that he doesn't feel like sharing and make something up. "We were just trying to figure out where you got the eggs and meat from."

"Oh! We have chickens that we snuck out of the city. We usually wait until we've collected enough eggs for everyone to have some for breakfast. We also have goats that we get milk from. They live back behind the Commons shelter. The meat we're eating this morning is from some squirrels I shot and killed myself." Tim puffs out his chest a little with pride.

"Squirrel? I just ate squirrel?" I feel sick at the thought.

"Yup. You can't be picky when you live out in the wild. Meat is meat. I'm getting pretty good with my bow. Matthias has been giving me lessons and says it won't be long, and I can hunt Havoc with him," he says excitedly.

"What are Havoc?"

"That's what Alexandrine named the black beasts. I think she said it comes from a line in some old play, 'Cry Havoc and let slip the dogs of war,' or something like that."

"Are there a lot of them out here?"

"I wouldn't say a lot. They mostly stick close to the city's fence, but they wander out here from time to time. We have to stay on alert day in and day out, just in case. The adults take shifts at night, watching over the camp to keep everyone safe. Once I'm old enough, I will be able to take a shift too. That's why training is so important."

"What kind of training?" David chimes in.

"Weapons, hand to hand combat, stealth, balance, and control. Matthias takes it very seriously. And so should you."

"When do we start training?" David asks.

"Alexandrine handles the beginners, and she usually likes to do it in the morning or evenings. Since you guys slept in, it will be this evening," Tim says. "Anyway, it looks like you two are done eating. Come on. I'll show you where to clean your plates."

We follow him through the camp to a path that leads into the woods. I can hear the trickle of water through the trees before we see the river. We walk several yards until we come to a rocky river bank. Smooth stones cover the ground and gently slope down into a wide, slow-moving river. Giant boulders are scattered here and there, and I see articles of clothing laid out on them to dry in the sun.

"This is where we do all of our cleaning and get our drinking water. Wash rags for dishes are over there on that rock. Try to remember to lay them out flat to dry when you're done cleaning up," he adds as though to remind himself as well. "Also, if you are going to take a bath, make sure you tell someone first. I forgot to say something once, and now I can't look Rebecca in the eyes."

"Who's Rebecca?" I ask.

"One of the women with the little kids. She was Saul's live-in nurse back in the city before Matthias brought him out here. He went back and rescued her, and now she's our designated nurse."

"Why did Saul need a live-in nurse?" I ask curiously.

"I was told he had a stroke a long time ago. He couldn't care for himself, couldn't talk, couldn't even swallow food for the longest time, so he had to have Rebecca live with him. He's gotten better in some areas, but he still can't talk. It's a shame because he seems like a pretty cool guy."

I nod even though I don't know enough about him to really agree.

David grabs the plate and fork out of my hand and walks down to the water to clean up. Tim follows him. David looks over his shoulder at me to give me a look of annoyance at Tim's constant presence. I shrug and give him a little smile.

While the boys are washing up, I stand in the shade and look at the scenery. The sun is sparkling off the water. Birds fly overhead, singing beautiful songs. A fish splashes a little way down the river. A cool breeze blows my hair, tickling it against my neck. I stare out into the woods on the other side and wonder what kinds of animals are out there. I've only ever seen wild animals on the TV or in books.

"Aren't you worried about a Havoc coming from the other side of the river and attacking you?" I ask Tim as the boys make their way back over to me.

"Not really. Like I said, they stay close to the city for the most part, and Matthias says that Havoc seem to hate large bodies of water. They can't swim. He said they get most of their water from small puddles after it rains."

"How does he know so much about them?"

"He spends a lot of time studying them. 'Know your enemy' seems to be his mantra. You'll see once you start training with him. He says it at least twice every training session...if not more," Tim finishes with an eye roll.

"Ready to head back, Liv?" David asks.

I nod my head and sigh as we turn away from the beautiful river. I have a feeling I am going to spend a lot of my free time here, thinking. Seems to be a peaceful place for it.

"There you are. Matthias wanted me to take you two out to gather wood," Cass says as we step out of the woods back at camp.

"I was just showing them where to do their dishes."

"Good. You can take the dishes into the Commons shelter over there and then meet us by the fire pit." Cass points to a larger shelter in the middle of camp.

David and I walk together.

"Tim is really getting on my nerves. It seems like I can't do anything without him tagging along," David says quietly.

"Well, look around. Henry is the closest guy to his age, and he doesn't seem very friendly. He's probably lonely."

"I guess," David says reluctantly.

As we head to the Commons shelter, we see Saul sitting on the same stump as before, whittling away at a stick again. He looks up and smiles at me with a twinkle in his eye. I smile back and then look down at the stick in his hand. I see that he's not just whittling, he's carving something. Those symbols look oddly familiar, but before I can figure out where I've seen them before, David grabs my arm and leads me into the shelter.

We walk through the door and see baskets scattered all over the floor, filled with various fruits and vegetables. A few dead turkeys, relieved of their heads, hang upside-down from the rafters by ropes in the back corner. Bags of flour and rice lie in heaps by the walls. A round table made from a giant tree stump sits in the middle of the room with smaller stumps surrounding it. David and I spot a pile of clean dishes stacked on yet another tree stump that has been covered with a white towel. We stack our plates and forks on top and head back out.

"Where did all that food come from?" I ask David as we make our way back to the fire pit.

"I have no idea. Maybe it's time to see if Tim and Cass will answer some of our questions now that we get to stay."

Tim and Cass stand up as we walk toward them. "Ready?" Cass asks.

"We were wondering if you would answer some of our questions for us now?" David asks.

"We can talk while we walk," Tim suggests. He looks around nervously as I watch him slip David's gun into the back pocket of his jeans. Something about his sneakiness puts me on edge.

What if Tim isn't as friendly as we thought. I find myself suddenly worried about going out into the woods with him. What if he was instructed to take us out into the woods and kill us?

We make our way past our shelter and out into the forest on a narrow path before I call Tim out on it.

"What are you doing with David's gun, Tim?"

"Shh! Strictly speaking, I'm not supposed to have it. I snuck it out of Matthias's hut to bring with us for protection. The last time Cass and I went out to find wood, Matthias wouldn't allow us to bring any weapons, telling us we would be fine and that we needed our hands for carrying the wood. We wandered pretty far away from camp, and suddenly, we heard a few branches breaking in the distance and hurried the heck out of there. We never did see what it was, but I don't want to take any chances."

"Fair enough," David concedes.

I breathe a sigh of relief.

"So, you had some questions for us." Cass stoops down to pick up a few branches lying on the ground.

"I guess the first one on my mind is, where did all of that food come from? Like, where do you get bags of flour and rice out in the forest?" I ask, searching around for pieces of wood to bring back.

"Recon missions to the city. When Matthias goes to see if he can find another person to save from the city, they always swipe food and supplies for the group as well."

"But isn't that stealing?" I ask.

"Sure, it is. But they won't notice a few missing items," Tim says nonchalantly, like stealing is a normal thing around here.

"How does he get in and out of the city when there are guards posted by the fence?" David asks.

"Through the subway tunnels."

"What? What are subway tunnels?"

"Not really sure. I think that's what they brought me and Cass through when they saved us from the city, but I was so young then, I can't remember much about them. I overheard Matthias talking about the subway to Henry once. You'll have to ask him about it."

"Fine," I say, trying to remember some of the questions I had rolling around in my head. "What is the 'Rare' you mentioned?" I ask.

Tim's face brightens right up. "Oh! It's a special group of people who have enhanced abilities. Like how you caught that rock flying at your face, and you didn't even realize it. The Rare have better reflexes, heightened visual or hearing capabilities, and are far stronger than most people."

"So, like superheroes?" David asks skeptically.

"Eh, sort of but not really. The Rare have never been able to fly or have laser vision or shoot spider-webs out of their wrists and things like that. They're just better at all the things normal people can do. Their skills come naturally without much thought or practice. They are better fighters, hunters, scouts...you name it! I wish I were one," he says, childlike.

"You really think I'm a Rare?" I ask.

Tim stops walking and turns around to look at me with scrunched-up eyebrows. He grabs a piece of wood he was carrying and chucks it at me. Before I even give it any thought, I kick the wood out of the air with a perfectly executed roundhouse kick.

"Yup. I believe you are Rare," Tim says, smiling.

I look back at David, and he whistles. I roll my eyes at him and turn forward to continue our search for firewood. My cheeks blush slightly as a smile spreads across my face.

"I wonder what else I can do," I say dreamily.

"You'll find out at your training session," Cass says.

After we all have our arms loaded up with wood, we turn back around to take it to camp.

"So, what is everyone doing out here in the woods?" David asks.

"We are living free, away from the poisonous city," Tim says.

"Poisonous?" I ask.

"Haven't you noticed that there isn't any fog out here?"

"Well...yeah..." I start to say.

"The fog is only in the city," Tim says.

"How can that be true? Where does the fog come from?" I ask in disbelief. We step back into camp with the load of wood.

"Drop your piles over there and follow me."

We drop the wood on the small pile that is already stacked near the fire pit and follow Tim back out of the camp. Nobody calls for us to stop, so we keep walking out into the woods. The trees grow steadily taller and seem to loom overhead. Tim stops abruptly at a tree that has pieces of wood nailed to it all the way up to its branches.

"This is one of our lookout trees. You can see the city from up there. Go ahead. Climb up and see. There's enough room for both of you."

I reach up and grab hold of a makeshift step and start my ascent. I've never climbed a tree before, and I'm a little nervous of heights. After I'm a few steps up, David starts the climb. No turning back now. I make it past the wood steps and up to the branches. I pull myself onto a branch, holding onto the one above me, and feel the one I'm stepping on give a little, making a small cracking sound.

"Keep close to where the branch attaches to the tree!" Tim calls up to me.

I shimmy my way over closer to the tree and can feel that it is much sturdier.

"Thanks, Tim!" I call down to him.

I climb up to the next branch as David makes his way to where I just was. Slowly, I work my way up the tree, placing my hands and feet carefully on the branches. I can no longer see Cass and Tim at the bottom, and I start to shake as I realize just how high I am. I'm not quite to the top when I find a platform nailed up in the tree. I hoist myself onto it, relieved that I made it. There's just enough room for David to join me. I move over and grab his arms to help steady him as he pulls himself up onto the platform next to me.

There is a clearing through the branches that gives us the perfect view. We seem to be in a tree that's up on a hill. I can't believe how far I can see. A valley stretches out below us, filled with trees that come to a stop at the city's fence. Tim is right. The unceasing fog of the city doesn't go past the fence into the forest. I squint my eyes and see the sun shining off water past the city. The ocean. There isn't any fog there either.

"What the...?" I ask.

"How is the fog only in the city?" David asks.

"Better question is: why? Why is the fog only in the city?"

We stand together looking out at the scene in front of us for a few moments longer.

"Liv, there's something I was hoping to talk to you about," David says, shifting his weight back and forth.

"What?"

"Well, I was just, um, wondering if you noticed some chemistry going on between us? I couldn't help but notice you lay your head on my shoulder the other night and stuff like that."

"Oh, David. You never stop, do you? We're friends. Friends. Got it?"

"I just thought—"

"What? That I was suddenly going to want to be your girlfriend? How long have we known each other David?"

"Almost our whole lives."

"Exactly. I wouldn't want to ruin our friendship with a relationship that might not last. We are out here in the middle of nowhere, surrounded by people who hardly know us, trying our hardest to survive. I need you to be my friend, David."

Tears start forming in his eyes. He gives his head a little nod.

Suddenly, our conversation is interrupted by the sounds of a scream and a gunshot ringing out from the ground.

2 5

"Crap! What was that?" I ask frantically.

"Let's go find out!" David says, already lowering himself off the platform.

With thoughts of Cass in my head, I climb down that tree faster than I ever imagined I could. Once the ground is in sight, I let go of the bottom branch and fall ten feet, landing with a somersault. David does the same. I look around, desperate to find Tim and Cass. There's blood on the leaves at the base of the tree.

"Let's follow the blood and see if we can find where it came from," David suggests.

I follow closely behind David as he leads us farther into the woods. Splatters of blood can be found every few feet. As we keep going, the blood spots get further apart and harder to pick out. After we've walked about a half mile, I'm starting to feel nervous, being this far away from camp. We hear another gunshot and a whoop of celebration coming from up ahead.

"I did it! I killed one!" Tim yells to us as we run up to where he is standing. At his feet lies a large mass of black fur.

"Are you sure it's dead?" I stare at its body, watching for breathing.

"Yup! I followed its blood trail out here and found it. I shot it in the head to finish it off. I'm a hero! I can't wait to tell Matthias!" Tim beams.

"Good job, Tim," David congratulates him.

I walk slowly around the beast, looking closely at it. Its stench hits me, and I cover my nose with my shirt so I don't throw up. It reeks of sweat, wet dog, and rotting flesh. Its paws are slightly larger than my hands, with two-inch sharp claws. Its tail is bushy like a wolf's, and its fur is long and pitch-black. Even though its hair is long, I can see it has unnatural bulking muscles and an odd hump on its back. Its ears are pointed with long tufts of hair sticking off the tips. Its dead eyes are pools of black like I saw in my dream. Its long pink tongue hangs out of its mouth, past needle-sharp fangs. As I look at the lifeless creature, I feel a mix of relief that it's dead but sympathy also. It's clearly a creature made for hunting prey. Should we really punish an animal for doing what it's made to do?

"Where's Cass?" I ask, looking around.

"She went back to camp to get Matthias and tell him what happened. They should be here soon." Tim smiles.

"So, what happened? We heard a scream."

"Cass and I were standing at the base of the tree you guys were in, and we heard a crack of a branch. I pulled the gun out just as the Havoc jumped out of the woods toward us. Cass screamed and fell to the ground, and I aimed the gun at it, knowing I had to do something, or we were goners. I pulled the trigger and shot it right here." Tim points at the wound on its belly. "The Havoc yelped and turned to run away into the woods. I knew I needed to finish it off so it wouldn't suffer. I told Cass to head back to camp and get Matthias, and I took off into the woods, following the blood trail. I followed it here and shot it in the head to end its misery."

"You've got some balls, kid." We all start at Matthias's voice. He calmly walks toward the dead animal and stops; his facial expression is like stone. "However, if I ever catch ya sneakin' into my hut and takin' somethin' that's not yours again, you'll be livin' out here by yourself. Got it?"

Tim's smile slides off his face, and he looks down at the ground, deflated. "Yes, sir."

"Good. Now, give me the gun."

Tim hands the gun over to Matthias.

"It was stupid to use a weapon ya know nothin' about. What're ya out here in this part of the woods for in the first place?"

"We wanted to show Olivia and David the lookout tree so they could see that the neverending fog stays only inside the city."

"Why does it do that?" I ask.

"I'll answer your questions once we're back in camp," Matthias says.

After we silently make our way back into camp, Matthias sends Tim off to clean the animal pens as part of his punishment.

"Have a seat," Matthias points to the stumps by the fire pit. "So, what d'ya wanna ask?"

"What is the fog in the city? Why does it stop at the fence?" I ask first.

"From what we can tell, the fog's a manufactured poison that dampens the Rares' abilities, but we're not sure how it works...yet."

"If the fog is a 'poison,' then how does it not affect normal people?" David asks.

"As I said, we don't know how the fog works exactly. It seems like we're missin' a piece of the puzzle. Somehow, they've created a way to weaken the Rares and make 'em vulnerable."

"Why would they want to keep the Rares weak?" I ask.

"Do you know why Rares exist in the first place?" Matthias asks gruffly.

"No."

He sighs and pinches the bridge of his nose.

"What do they teach you guys in school?" he whispers to himself. "All right, I'll give you a little history lesson, so listen up. Long before we were born, scientists started messin' with genetic codes. They started tryin' to enhance human genes by pinpointin' the parts of DNA that are responsible for our senses and tweakin' 'em to make our senses better," Matthias says, looking directly at me.

"That's called 'genetic modification,'" David interjects.

Matthias glares at him for interrupting and then continues, "Well, it didn't work the way they thought it would. Instead of curin' problems like colorblindness or hearin' impairment, it created people with hyper senses. They pretty much created a form of superhumans. But not everyone got the changes. Only a small portion of the world got the benefits, and it became a case of immeasurable outrage and jealousy," he continues tensely, his fists balled up.

"There was an uprisin' of people who wanted the scientists to reverse the change, to take away what they'd given. Course, 'The Rare'—that's what they called themselves—didn't want to have their abilities taken away and started fightin' back. Across the globe, people were going crazy and huntin' down the Rares to kill 'em because they were different. It was a witch hunt!" Matthias pounds his fist on his thigh, causing David and me to jump.

"Other people got it in their heads to hide 'em. Well, rumors spread that the US had become a sanctuary for the Rares. Once that got out, the Rares started flockin' here, not understandin' what was gonna happen if they did. They knew that the United States was a powerful country with a strong military, and so they thought they'd be safe here. But the madness had spread throughout the world, makin' everyone believe that they needed to kill all the Rares. It was like Hitler with the Jews all over again, only on an even larger scale. They banded together to bomb the hell out of the US and all the sympathetic Americans. We're talkin' World War III here—"

"I knew there was a war. I just don't know the details. It seems like nobody wants to talk about it," I interrupt.

"People're still skittish 'bout the whole damned thing. But I think it's time we start educatin' ya young people, so ya don't make the same mistakes," Matthias says, pointing at David and me. "Anyway, the US didn't go down without a fight. We shot off a few missiles at China, Russia, Japan, and France. But in the end, we lost..."

"I'm done cleaning the pens," Tim says, walking up behind Matthias. As he gets closer to us, I start coughing at the stench of manure on the bottom of his shoes. I notice David scrunch his nose too.

"Good. Now ya can ask around camp for everyone's dirty clothes and go down to the river to wash it all."

Tim's eyes get wide, but he takes a deep breath to keep himself in check. "Yes, sir," he mumbles as he shuffles away.

"Now, where was I?"

"You said the war happened, and the US lost," David offers.

"Oh, yes. Well, a group of people here in the US got together to surrender and make peace with the other nations in hopes that they would call a ceasefire. They agreed on the terms that all the remainin' US population would be put into cities where they could be monitored, and if any Rares were discovered, they'd need to be 'taken care of.' The group of people agreed and called themselves 'The United Coalition for Peace.' They rounded up the survivors and stuck 'em in cities where they were fenced in and fed lies that the woods will kill ya, and you're not to leave the city at any time. Imprisonin' people and tellin' 'em it was for their own safety."

"Why did people believe them? Why would they allow themselves to be trapped inside the city?" I ask.

"Fear. Fear drives people to do stupid things. They were told that they'd be taken care of in the cities. After the war, people were shell-shocked, and they *wanted* to be taken care of. After a while, they were fed the lies about the dangers that lurked outside the city so often that they started to believe them."

"What made you come out here?" David asks.

"I found out what America was like before the war, that we were a free country once. People used to be able to live wherever they wanted to, own as many guns as they wanted to, and vote for the leaders they wanted instead of leaders bein' appointed to us by other countries. I left because I hate the Coalition and their dictatorship."

"How do you sneak back into the city to get supplies? Tim said something about subway tunnels, but I don't know what those are."

"Before the war, the city was about five times the size it is now. They had underground trains called subways that people used to get around to different parts of the city. After the war, the city as we know it is all that was salvageable. They fenced themselves in the livable part and fixed it up."

"Except for the bad part of town where they let the druggies and homeless people take over. That's still in ruins," I add.

"Correct," Matthias nods. "Well, they didn't think too much about the subway tunnels. They halfheartedly blocked up the entrances and forgot about them. Since the city downsized so drastically, some of those subway tunnels are outside of their fences, and I found one that leads from outside the city, into the 'bad' part of town."

"But going there is almost as bad as dealing with the guards, isn't it? You could get killed, no questions asked, on that side of town," David says.

"It's risky, but I haven't been bothered by any thugs yet. I never go in without a weapon, that's for sure. The tricky part is sneakin' into the better part of town without gettin' caught."

"Matthias! You're needed in the Commons," Alexandrine yells from the doorway.

Matthias stands up with a grunt.

"Wait! I have more questions," I plead.

"They'll have to wait 'til later."

David and I watch as Matthias walks away. After all that information he gave us, I feel like I have more questions than when we started.

"That was not satisfying," I say, frustrated.

"I want to know how all these people got out here. How the fog takes away the Rares' powers. Where the Havoc came from..." David says.

"What part my mom plays in the Coalition," I say darkly. "I can't believe how much my mother has been hiding from me. She's got a lot of explaining to do."

David stands and offers to help me up. I grab hold and feel the comforting warmth of his hand around mine. I look up into his eyes as I stand, and all I see is sadness. He lets go of my hand as soon as I'm on my feet and turns away from me.

"What should we do now?" he asks.

"We could go help Tim with the laundry," I say reluctantly.

"Nah. It's his punishment. Besides, I don't want to wash other people's underwear." He turns his head to give me a half smirk.

"Gross." I give him a shove on his arm.

"Look out!" David shouts, grabbing me and pulling me close to him just as a volleyball goes soaring through the space I just occupied. I look in the direction it came from, and a kid who looks to be about eight years old has his hand over his mouth, looking guilty.

"Sorry!" he shouts and runs after the ball to get it.

I suddenly realize that David is still holding me close, and my cheeks flush. I pull out of his grasp quickly.

"You okay?" David asks.

"Yeah, yeah. I'm fine," I answer, clearing my throat and fixing my hair.

"Hey guys, it's time to get lunch prepared," Cass says from behind us. "Do either of you know how to pluck a turkey?"

"Um...no," I say, slightly disgusted at the idea.

"Well, you're going to learn." She slaps David on the back. "Come on!"

We shuffle behind Cass as she leads us over to the Commons shelter. She ducks inside and comes out with the dead turkeys I saw hanging in the back corner as well as a couple of knives. She hands us the knives and leads us toward the river. We see Tim upstream, crouching down by the water, washing what looks like a bra with a scowl on his face.

We walk over to a long flat rock that stands waist high, and she lays the turkeys down. There are two empty metal buckets sitting on the ground next to the rock.

"What're the buckets for?" I ask.

"One's for feathers, and the other's for guts."

Stomach acid is creeping up my throat. I swallow hard and try to stay focused.

"What do we do first?" David asks.

"You two can work on that one, and I'll work on this one. Just grab a few feathers at a time and jerk them the opposite direction they're lying," she says as she demonstrates for us. "Put the feathers in the bucket as you go. Caroline wants to use the feathers to make a pillow." David grabs hold of the turkey's legs with one hand and pulls a few feathers out of the turkey's back. I watch him do it a couple more times as I work up the courage to make myself help. I grab hold of a few feathers and pull, but they don't come out. I try again, and only one breaks free.

"I can't do this," I say, hoping I can get away with not helping.

"Now's not the time to get squeamish. You wanna eat, right?" Cass chastises.

"Yes. I'm just not used to this. We buy meat from a grocery store. I've never had to pluck my own turkey."

"You'll get it. You just have to do it a few times. It took me a few tries my first time too. Of course, I was only seven when Matthias taught me."

I grab hold and pull again with no success.

"Here." David lays his hand on top of mine. "You have to pull up, against the grain."

The feathers come right out this time, and he gives me a smile. After a while, I've got the hang of it, and we take turns cleaning the bird, filling the bucket full of feathers.

"Now what?" I ask, relieved that we're done.

"Now we take the knives and gut them."

"No way! Nuh-uh. I'm not sticking my hands inside the turkey."

"Hey, you need to learn this stuff out here. This is survival stuff. It's gross, but you have to just shut your mind off to it and get it done." Cass hands me a knife.

I look at David, pleading him with my eyes to help me.

"I'll do it, and Olivia can watch." David takes the knife out of my hand.

"Thank you," I whisper.

I stand off to the side and watch as David mimics each of Cass moves, precisely. I cover my nose with my shirt once he cuts open the turkey. The stench of its insides is enough to make me gag.

His hands move deftly as though he's done this before. I'm amazed at how quickly David has taken to all this survival stuff. We never had to do anything like this in the city, but he's acting as though he's been doing it his whole life.

I follow David to the river's edge to wash our hands.

"Well, that was thoroughly disgusting," David says, washing the gore away.

"What other horrors do you think they have in store for us?"

"I don't want to know."

"Come on, you two. Let's get the turkeys back to camp so we can start roasting them." Cass pats her stomach. "I'm hungry!"

As we follow her, I glance back at Tim and see him violently whipping a shirt against a rock as though he's trying to kill it. I think I like the annoyingly upbeat Tim better.

Once we're back in camp, Cass hands the turkeys off to a man with a bushy red beard and bald head.

"Why don't you go with Frederick, David? You can learn how to properly cook a turkey," Cass suggests.

David gives me a small smile and takes off.

"Now what?" I ask.

"We can go into the Commons and see if they have more work for us to do," Cass suggests.

We turn to walk that way, but I stop short when I see Alexandrine standing next to the shelter, giving me a murderous glare as she spins a knife in her hand.

I grab Cass's elbow and whisper, "I don't think Alexandrine likes me."

"She doesn't. She hates you."

"What? Why?"

Cass shrugs her shoulders. "I don't know. I just overheard her telling Matthias that she refuses to teach you any lessons, and if it were up to her, you would be kicked out of camp."

I look up at Alexandrine and lock eyes with her. She turns her head, spits on the ground, and then walks out of sight.

I better make sure I'm never alone with her.

2|7

Once the food is ready, I tell David that I want to eat in our shelter, away from everyone. The look Alexandrine gave me put me on edge.

"Oh, this turkey is delicious," David moans as he devours his meal.

"I've never had wild turkey before. This is so good." I take a huge mouthful. I have to swallow a couple of times to get the dry white meat to slide down my throat.

"David, do you feel safe here?" I ask.

"I feel *safer*. These people know how to survive. I'm not sure what I would do if we came across one of the beasts in the woods on our own." He shoves a fork full of food in his mouth. "Why?"

"I don't know. I think Alexandrine is going to try to kill me," I say, paranoia creeping into my voice.

He gives me a quizzical look as he chews his overstuffed mouthful of food.

"After you left to go help cook the turkeys, she was standing outside her shelter, staring at me while spinning a knife in her hand. She had a look on her face that made it clear she doesn't want me here. Cass even confirmed that she doesn't," I say shakily. "Why do I always have enemies? Why does everyone hate me, David?" I start to cry as the all too familiar dark thoughts of suicide creep back up. It's been a while since I've contemplated death. But this time the thought doesn't stick. Things have been better out here, and I'm not ready to give that up.

"She's probably just jealous that she isn't the most beautiful person around here anymore," David says with a wink.

"Whatever." I shake my head at him.

"Look, I don't know why she would hate you. She doesn't know you. Maybe when we do our training tonight, we can ask her."

"Cass said that Alexandrine told Matthias that she refuses to teach me." I shove the food on my plate around with my fork.

"I guess we'll find out tonight, won't we?"

"I'm done!" Tim says, storming into the shelter and flopping onto his bed. He crosses his arms over his chest and stares at the ceiling. "I should just leave. Stupid Matthias and his stupid rules."

"Sorry you got in trouble, man," David says, "but I don't think leaving is the answer."

Tim just huffs and rolls onto his side toward the wall, making the dead leaves spread across the ground with a rustle.

"Is Matthias always harsh with his punishments?" I ask.

"Pretty much, yeah. He tries to keep everyone under control with threats of kicking them out. Most people listen because nobody wants to be kicked out of camp. But I'm close to just leaving and finding a different group to join. Screw Matthias and his dictatorship."

"Different group?"

"Yeah. We're not the only ones out here in the woods. There have to be other camps with other groups of people. I don't know where they would be, though, and that's where the problem comes in. It's dangerous to be out walking on your own in the woods, but I'm so angry right now I think I could kill a Havoc with my bare hands."

"How do you know there are other groups if you've never seen them?" David asks.

"Of course there are other groups. It would be illogical to think that we're the only people who refused to live under the Coalition's rule. Besides, sometimes Matthias and Henry leave for days, even weeks at a time, but they don't come back with stuff from the city. They won't tell anyone where they're going, but he leaves Alexandrine in charge, and she's just as bad as he is."

Just then, footsteps approach our shelter. I hope for Tim's sake it isn't Matthias or Alexandrine.

"Tim, Matthias wants to see you," Cass says, stepping through the door.

"What does he want now?"

"How should I know? He just told me to come fetch you."

He stands up, grumbling to himself. As he walks out of the shelter, David stands and offers to help me up.

"I'm done eating. Let's take our plates down to the river to clean, and maybe we can hear what Matthias is going to make Tim do now."

We walk out past the firepit, where Matthias is standing next to Tim, who's hanging his head like a child, awaiting his fate.

"I was a bit harsh. If ya really wanna learn to shoot a gun, then it would be best that I teach ya. Go get some empty cans from the Commons, and we'll target practice."

Tim's entire demeanor changes instantly. He is back to his bouncy, excited-to-be-alive self.

"Come on. Let's go get the dishes washed quickly so we can watch. Maybe we can pick up a few tips while we're at it," David says, hurrying down to the river.

By the time we're done washing up, Tim and Matthias are done setting up their target practice. There are four empty soup cans sitting on blocks of wood about ten yards away. David and I sit on stumps a safe distance to the left behind Matthias.

"Is it all right if we watch?" David asks.

"Yeah. Pay attention cause ya might learn somethin'," Matthias says gruffly.

"Now, you already know a thing or two 'bout guns, but since we got people watchin', I'll go over the safety tips for their sake."

"Yes, sir," Tim says.

"Your gun should always have the safety on until you're ready to shoot. Never point a gun at a person, even if you think the safety's on. Keep your finger off the trigger. Your finger should only be on the trigger when you're ready to shoot."

"Got it," Tim nods seriously, giving Matthias his full attention.

Matthias hands Tim the gun. "Ya wanna have a sturdy stance. Bend your knees slightly; ya don't want 'em locked."

"Like this?"

"Yup. Now, hold the grip, keep your trigger finger off the trigger, and keep your thumb away from the slide, or you'll be regrettin' it."

I glance at David, and he has his hands positioned like he's holding an imaginary gun, following Matthias's every instruction. Meanwhile, I have to force myself to pay attention. Guns hold no interest for me.

"Bring the gun up; arms should be straight but elbows slightly bent, not locked."

"Should I take the safety off?" Tim asks.

"Not yet. Are ya left-eye dominant or right-eye?"

"Right, I think," Tim answers.

"Ya think, or ya know?"

"I know. I did the test you showed me."

"Good. Close your dumb eye, and line up the sights just under where ya wanna shoot. Once you have it right, take the safety off."

Tim lowers the gun to locate the safety. I find myself yawning loudly, but David keeps watching them like a hawk as though this is the most interesting thing he has ever seen.

"Line it back up, and squeeze the trigger."

BAM!

I start from the noise and cover my now ringing ears. I don't remember the gun being that loud.

The soup can is still on the stump.

"I missed," Tim says disappointedly.

"Yeah, well, a soup can's a lot smaller than a Havoc. Try again."

"Aren't we going to run out of bullets?" David asks.

"Don't worry about that. We have ammunition." Matthias never looks away from his student. "Timothy, bring the gun back up like I showed ya. Focus down the barrel at your target. Hold steady when ya squeeze the trigger."

BAM!

I was ready for it this time. The can tipped over and rolled off the stump.

"Better, but ya just grazed it," Matthias grunts. "You need to work on holdin' still."

"Can I try?" David asks.

"I'm teachin' Timothy right now," Matthias scolds.

"No, it's all right. He can try." Tim puts the safety on and hands the gun over to Matthias. Tim walks over to me, looking slightly disheartened. "I thought I would be better at this since I can shoot squirrels. But a rifle and a bow are a lot different from a pistol." He plops down on David's empty seat.

David stands confidently next to Matthias.

"I assume you were payin' attention?"

"Yes, sir," David replies.

Matthias hands the gun to David, who is already standing the way Tim was taught. He brings the gun up and aims it at the targets.

"Good, now you'll wanna—" Matthias starts.

BAM!

The can goes flying backward.

David turns slightly to the can on the right. BAM! That can goes flying too.

I look at Matthias, and he seems just as surprised as I am. He's watching David with his eyebrows raised and his mouth slightly open.

David moves again to the next can. BAM! Direct hit. BAM! BAM! All five cans are now lying out in the woods.

David puts the safety on and turns to look at Matthias.

"Helluva good marksman. Let's see whatcha can do from back there."

I glance at Tim, expecting to see him jealous or mad at David, but I couldn't be more wrong. Tim is sitting on the edge of the stump, smiling like a goon with tears sparkling his eyes.

"I knew it!" Tim whispers excitedly.

I watch as Matthias and David put the cans back on the stumps and walk away to about twice the distance as the first round. Tim and I move to a safer spot.

"Do your thing, and I'll help if ya need it." Matthias steps off to the side.

David sets himself back up, takes a few deep breaths, and starts shooting them down, left to right. Every single can is hit dead center. Tim jumps off his seat and shouts in jubilation.

"Impressive." Matthias slaps David on the back.

David beams. "Liv's turn," he says, looking at me.

"Nah, you guys go ahead. I don't want to waste any bullets and have you laugh at me," I say dismissively.

"It's important to know how to use a gun properly. Get over here," Matthias says sternly.

I stand up and give David a death glare.

He winks at me in response.

I can feel my hands shaking from nerves. I really don't want to do this.

"Shouldn't I be closer for my first time?" I ask once I see how far away the cans are.

"Fine. Move up."

Once I'm in place, I start shifting my feet around until I'm standing how David was. Matthias hands me the gun. It feels heavier than I expected. I try to mimic everything David was doing, hoping I can avoid too much scrutiny. Matthias moves my thumbs around into position and takes the safety off for me. His hands feel rough and scratchy from the years of living out in the wild. I wonder if mine will eventually become like that.

"Remember what I told Timothy: aim down the barrel at the target, and squeeze the trigger," he says calmly, removing his hands from mine.

The gun shakes slightly in my hands. I take a couple of deep breaths and try to focus on the can. I let out my breath and squeeze the trigger.

BAM!

The can sits in exactly the same spot.

"Try again," Matthias says.

My heart is pounding so hard in my chest, my hands move slightly with each beat. I focus back on the can and take position. Deep breath in, out, and...

BAM!

The can on the stump next to the one I was aiming at falls over.

"What happened?" I ask.

"What do you mean? You hit the can," Tim pipes in.

"I wasn't aiming for that one. I was aiming for the one right in front of me," I say, embarrassed.

"What're ya lookin' at when ya pull the trigger?" Matthias asks.

"Nothing. I aim and then close my eyes as I pull the trigger..." I mumble.

"You should never close your eyes when shootin' a gun," Matthias scolds. "That's a good way to get somebody killed!"

"Okay, I'm sorry," I say bitterly. "I didn't even want to shoot a gun in the first place. I don't like guns."

"It's important to learn how to defend yourself, guns included. Since ya don't like guns, what weapon do ya like?" Matthias asks.

"I don't know. I didn't exactly train in combat when I was in and out of hospitals."

Matthias turns abruptly. "David, watch 'er while I go grab somethin'. Maybe ya can give 'er a few pointers." Then he turns back to me, "Keep practicin'. And for goodness' sake, keep your eyes open."

I huff as he strides away. David stands behind me and grabs my shoulders, turning me toward the cans.

"I thought for sure you were going to nail them like David did," Tim says contemplatively. "You know, being Rare and all."

"Not helpful," I mutter.

"Here, let me help you," David says. "Stand like this."

I copy his stance.

"Now, bring the gun up, and look through this sight with your right eye, and line it up with this sight on the end of the barrel. Move the gun until you have the sights aimed for a spot right beneath where you plan on shooting. Try not to move the gun when you squeeze the trigger." He steps back and to the left. "Okay, go—no, wait!"

BAM!

"Ow!" I scream as pain rips through my hand. I reflexively drop the gun and grab hold of my throbbing thumb. I can feel the warmth of blood wetting my palm.

David stoops down and picks up the gun, putting the safety on before handing it to Tim. He returns to me and wraps his arm around my shoulder. "I'm so sorry, Liv! I didn't see that your thumbs were wrong until the last second. Have a seat." He leads me to the stump.

"I'll go get Rebecca," Tim offers and runs off.

Hot tears are streaming down my cheeks. I hold my thumb tight, afraid to look. David squats down next to me, rubbing my back.

"Here, let me see it," David says, taking my hands gently in his own.

I squeeze my eyes tight, and little white dots dance beneath my eyelids. I feel lightheaded and take a deep breath, realizing I've been holding it in. I slowly let go of my thumb, and the air stings the wound.

"How bad is it?" I squeak.

"Well, you tore a good chunk of skin out, but I think you'll be okay," he says.

I feel his lips press gently against the back of my hand. I open my eyes and meet his apologetic gaze. I give him a small smile through my tears.

"I'm so sorry, Liv. I should have protected you."

"It's okay, David. But I never want to touch a gun ever again."

"What happened?" a voice says, followed by the crunch of footsteps on the gravel and dried leaves. I look up and see it's the same woman who brought us our breakfast the first morning. There's just something so familiar about her, but I still can't place it.

"The pistol bit her," Tim answers from behind her, breathing hard from running. "I don't like seeing people bleed. I'm gonna go find out what Cass is up to. Hope you feel better soon, Olivia."

"Thanks," I say as he runs off toward our shelter.

Rebecca takes my hand and pours a bottle of water over the wound. The blood washes away, and we see that I have about a one-inch cut on the side of my thumb.

"It's not too bad, but we'll need to get it bandaged tight to stop the bleeding."

She pulls her long black hair up into a high ponytail and sets to work wrapping the wound with gauze from her first-aid kit and then securing it with tape. I watch her as she's doing it, trying to figure out why she seems so familiar. I sense a sadness in her, a sort of sadness that's rooted deep in her pale blue eyes...

Then it hits me like a slap across the face. Pale blue eyes? Long black hair pulled into a ponytail? Cindy!

28

No, not Cindy...Joselyn. Yes, I can see it now. I stop myself from blurting out the question that is now stuck in my throat. I need to be careful how I word it.

"You're a mom, right?" I ask feebly. I'm such a moron.

"Yeah, why?"

"Oh, I was just wondering who your kids are."

She gives me a strange look but answers, "The twin boys over there." She points to two little boys wrestling on the ground, who look to be about four years old.

"They're cute," I say. Crap, she's almost done. Spit it out, Olivia! "Do you have any other children? Like, maybe ones that aren't here?"

She furrows her eyebrows, snaps the first-aid kit closed, and walks away. Smooth.

"Oh, and, um, thank you!" I say as she storms away.

"What was that about?" David asks me. "Why were you so interested in her kids? You came off as a weirdo."

I huff. "I know. I suddenly realized why she seemed so familiar to me. I think she might be Joselyn's mom. Or at least, related somehow. Her eyes are exactly the same."

"Joselyn? You mean like the girl in the loony bin you told me about?"

"Yup. That's the one," I answer. "But it can't be. Can it? Why would she be out here instead of in the city with her daughter?"

But before David can answer, Matthias comes back, holding a bundle of something wrapped in a blanket. He bends down and sets it on the ground carefully.

"Stand up," Matthias directs.

"What now? You're not going to make me shoot another gun, are you?" I ask worriedly.

I watch as Matthias starts unwrapping the blanket. He stands up, holding a sword. "Here, take this," he commands.

"I can't. I hurt myself on that stupid gun while you were gone," I answer.

"So what? Pain ain't an excuse for laziness. In a fight, you're gonna get hit once in a while, and you gotta learn to push through the pain if you wanna keep your life. Now stand up, and let's see whachya can do with a sword."

124

I reluctantly stand up and grab the sword hilt with both hands.

Matthias bends down and grabs another sword. He plants himself in front of me and looks at me expectantly. "You ready?"

"Um, no. You don't expect me to fight you with real swords, do you?" I ask, swallowing hard.

"You gotta learn somehow. Now turn sideways so there's less target for me to hit," he commands and waits for me to obey.

I reluctantly shift my body around.

"Good. Right foot forward, sword held up to protect your face, and remember to move your feet."

Matthias makes an exaggerated strike at my head with his sword. I awkwardly swing to block it. Our blades connect with a metallic clang that vibrates through my arms, making me almost lose my grip. He swings his sword around and tries to slice my stomach. I step backward and block it just in time. I take the chance and go for a blow to his neck, but he's too quick for me and knocks the sword out of my hands.

"Pick it up. Quickly," he says.

I bend down to pick up my sword, and he kicks me behind my knee. I topple to the ground and just barely catch myself before face planting.

"What the hell was that for?" I yell.

"Ya never turn your back on your opponent when in a fight. Ya need to be on guard at all times."

Rage from being humiliated is pumping through my veins now. I stand back up and face off with Matthias. I stare into his eyes, hoping he will feel my anger.

"Ya want to study your attacker. Learn his moves. Does he have a tell before he's gonna strike? Maybe he looks where he's gonna hit before swingin'. Maybe he steps to the side when he's gonna swing at your stomach. Ya need to know your enemy."

He goes to swing at my stomach, and I block it confidently. He picks up the pace and tries to strike at my head, but I duck and go for a knee shot. He moves just before I make contact. Something seems to click, and I can block every strike he makes and fluidly make my own attack on him. The clanging of our swords rings loudly throughout the camp.

I continue to concentrate on every move Matthias makes, mirroring much of what he does. Sweat starts dripping down my neck, tickling as it snakes its way along my back.

Block, strike, block, strike.

Our feet are in constant motion as though we are dancing: a warrior's dance. Matthias picks up the pace again, and I find that I'm not even thinking about my moves anymore; I'm just reacting. Adrenaline courses through my body, fueling me until I'm not holding back. A part of me wants to defeat Matthias, even if it means hurting him. As he pushes me harder with his attacks, I become more determined to end this with me as the victor. I crave to take him out.

It barely registers that we are surrounded by people. I'm so focused on what I'm doing, I don't even care that the sweat is dripping into my eyes, and my injured thumb is stinging with pain. I just keep pushing.

As Matthias makes a wide sweeping arc toward my neck, I shift my weight and block upward with all my might. His sword slips out of his hands and goes flying. That's when I make my move to end this. Dropping my sword, I close the gap between us, wrap my arms around his, and hip-toss him, dropping him on the ground. He lands with a thump. Before I know it, my right hand is wrapped around his throat. His eyes are wide with surprise. I quickly let go when I realize what I'm doing.

I hear a catcall from behind me, but I just keep staring at Matthias, afraid he is going to counter-attack and continue the sparring match. Or worse, he is embarrassed that I bested him, and he'll want me out of camp. He reaches his hand up to me, and I cautiously grab it to help him up.

"You're one helluva fighter, Olivia. I think ya could be better than any of us." Matthias gives me a slap on the back.

I smile at the compliment.

"Next time, ya fight David."

"Wait, what?"

"It's clear now that both of you are Rare. Nobody else in camp is, so you're gonna train against each other," he answers, turning abruptly and walking toward his hut.

I look at David, and he winks at me. My stomach drops as I remember when we first got here, and I watched David fight against Henry. He was good.

The group of onlookers starts to disband and head back to whatever it was they were doing. I start when I hear a voice behind my right shoulder.

"That was some fight," Henry says. "I've never known my dad to train one-on-one like that. He always delegates others to fight. There's something special he sees in you." And with that, he turns and stalks away.

David steps up to me and wraps his arm around my shoulder. "Good job, Liv!"

"I don't want to fight you, David," I whisper.

"What are you worried about? It's not a real fight."

"You don't understand. While I was sword fighting with Matthias, I had this sense of pleasure at the thought of besting him. In fact, I needed to win. And I remember seeing that kind of determination on your face when you first fought with Henry."

"True. But I would never hurt you, Liv," he says.

"I'm worried I'm going to hurt you," I say sheepishly.

"Ha! You can't hurt me." David smirks. I punch his arm playfully, and suddenly, I realize just how fatigued I am: my muscles ache from the sword fight, my thumb is throbbing, and my eyelids weigh about ten pounds. Plus, I'm dirty. I need a bath. I head back to our shelter and find Cass sitting on the floor, writing in a notebook.

"Hey, Cass. How come you didn't watch your brother shoot?" I ask, rummaging through my bag, looking for a clean change of clothes.

"I needed some alone time. Sometimes I need to write out my thoughts to keep my head straight." She closes the notebook. She sits there watching me with a hint of annoyance. I must have interrupted something important.

"I need to get cleaned up. What's the best way to get some privacy?"

"If you head up the river a little way, there's a spot where some branches hang down to the water. That's usually where I go."

"Thanks."

"You're welcome. Oh, and keep an eye out for the mukduks. They have a nest in that area, and I watch them whenever I take a bath."

"Mukduks? Will they attack me?"

"Nope, they're not menacing at all. They have shiny blue feathers, long bright orange beaks, and are about the size of an apple. They're so cute!"

"I'll see if I can spot them," I say with a quick smile.

I make it to the place Cass directed me to. The branches hang down low and gently touch the flowing river, creating a rustic wall. As I walk to the shore to lay my clean clothes down, I hear a small cheeping noise. There on a low branch of a pine tree is a nest with three baby birds. Cass wasn't joking; they are adorable. Their bright orange beaks are so long, it's almost comical. They are nearly the length of the bird's body. Even though the sun isn't shining on them directly, their feathers shimmer sky blue.

After watching them for a few moments, I force myself to get back to the task at hand. I lie down in the water and hold on to one of the branches so I don't float away. I shiver as the slow current of cold water flows around my aching body. A hot bath would feel so good right now, but I'll take what I can get. After lying in the water for about a minute, my skin prickles from goosebumps. I get washed up and grab my sweaty clothes to clean while I'm at it. Looking around to make sure nobody will see me, I stand up and walk to the river bank. I get dressed quickly and make my way back to camp, feeling refreshed but frozen.

After I hang my wet clothes up in some tree branches to dry by my shelter, I join David at the firepit. He's sitting alone, hunched over. As I sit down next to him, he turns his face away from me and rubs his eyes with the heels of his hands.

"Are you okay, David? What's wrong?"

"You weren't supposed to see that," he says, sniffing.

I reach my hand out to place on his arm but hesitate. I don't want him to read into my friendly gesture as an act of romance. But he looks so sad, I decide it's worth the risk. I lay my hand on his forearm and relish the warmth seeping into my frozen fingers. He looks at my hand touching his arm and grabs it with both of his hands, squeezing gently.

"What's wrong, David?"

"I miss my parents," he mumbles, staring at the ground.

I place my other frozen hand on top of his.

"I just hate the thought that they might be angry with me."

"What did you write in the letter you left them?"

"Not much. I just explained that I loved them, but I was tired of being a burden. I was going to go find some answers, and I would be back after I found what I was looking for." He sniffs. "I wish they could see me now."

He glances at me sideways, and I notice his eyes have changed. They used to be a muddy brown, but now I see flecks of green and a rich golden color surrounding his pupil. His skin has changed up too. His once ruddy, pimple covered face is now clear and slightly tan. Reddish brown stubble is growing along his jaw, making him look more like a man than a teenager.

"They love you, David. I'm sure they're sad, but I don't think they'll be mad at you. You're seventeen. You'll be an adult in just a couple of months. I think if they saw you, they would be happy that you left the city," I say with a small smile.

He lifts his hands up and kisses the back of my hand that's resting on top. A jolt shoots through me. I'm not sure if it's embarrassment, pleasure, or fear. I pull my hand away and pretend to scratch my nose.

"To be honest," I say, "I miss my mom too. I know we fight, but she's still my mom."

"Maybe we could talk Matthias into a recon mission to bring our parents out here. The city is a poisonous place to live. I would love to get my mom and dad out here where it's healthier."

"I doubt he'll agree to it, but I guess it wouldn't hurt to ask."

We hear the footsteps of someone walking up behind us, and I pull my hand out of David's grasp quickly. Frederick walks around to the fire pit and drops a bundle of sticks on the ground.

"Hey, kids. We're getting supper started. Go see what jobs are needed to be done," he commands as he starts breaking up sticks and putting them in the fire pit.

We stand up, and I grab David's bicep when my legs buckle, and I almost fall. His muscle feels well defined, not big by any means, but solid.

We start heading for the Commons when David grabs my elbow and stops me.

"What—"

"Shh!"

I stand there listening but hear nothing except some faint sounds of conversation coming from one of the buildings. I look at David, and he has his eyes closed and his head cocked to the side.

"Tell me what they're saying," I whisper.

He squeezes his eyes tighter as he concentrates and starts saying, "You need to tell her... No, I don't... If you don't tell her, I will... To hell, ya will.

129

Ya tell her, and I'll take ya out to the woods and make ya disappear... I'm not scared of you, Matthias..." and suddenly, David opens his eyes wide, and his mouth drops open. "Let's get out of here."

"What?"

"Quick! Get into the Commons, now!" David insists, pulling me.

Once we're in the Commons shelter, we see some of the women and their small children getting supper ready. One lady has her son and daughter peeling carrots as she chops up miscellaneous vegetables. Another woman has her little one help count out silverware. Rebecca watches her twin boys take turns stirring a big pot of boiling water. One of them scoops the spoon up and almost spills what looks like potatoes on his brother. She snatches the spoon away and scolds him. He furrows his brow at her but then lowers his chin to his chest at the reprimand, his bottom lip sticking out.

"Anything we can do to help, ma'am?" David asks the lady cutting vegetables, with a slight tremble in his voice.

"Don't bother with the ma'am stuff. My name's Caroline, but you can call me Carol. Those two women over there are Rebecca and Suzanne."

David and I look to where she's pointing, and both women give little waves in response to their names.

"Why don't you grab a bag of barley from the back corner and take it over to Rebecca?" She points with the knife.

Her two kids look up at us with shiny, curious eyes. I smile at them, but they just go back to peeling the carrots. I follow David to the back corner.

"What did you hear out there, David?" I whisper.

"Later, Liv. For now, let's just be as helpful as we can."

David heaves a large white bag labeled "barley" up onto his shoulder and carries it over to Rebecca.

"You can set it down right there," Rebecca directs.

David drops the bag gently. "Anything else we can help you ladies with?"

"Umm, it looks like we pretty much got things covered in here, thanks."

As David and I go to leave the Commons, Alexandrine storms in, holding a wet cloth on her face. The murderous look she's wearing makes the hairs on the back of my neck stand up. She looks at me, and her expression darkens even more. She turns to Rebecca and lifts the cloth off her face, saying something indistinguishable. David tugs on my shoulder and leads me out of the shelter and down to the river. The early evening sun is sparkling off the water, and a cool breeze picks up, giving me chills once again.

"So, are you going to tell me what's going on?" I ask.

"I wasn't a hundred percent sure I heard what I thought I did, but Alexandrine just confirmed it," David says. "He hit her."

"What? Are you serious? Is that why she had a cloth over her eye?"

"I think so," David says.

"So, Matthias is a woman beater? Maybe we shouldn't stay here."

"Maybe we shouldn't jump to conclusions. Perhaps she was trying to hit him first, and he was just defending himself—" David starts.

"What does that matter? He shouldn't be hitting women."

"Are you saying that a man should take a beating from a woman anytime, no questions asked, but a woman should never have a hand laid on her, even if she's the one who started attacking first? What if she pulled a knife on him? Or a gun?" David asks, eyebrows furrowed in angry confusion.

"I guess there are times when it would seem appropriate," I concede. "Do you think she attacked Matthias first? From what you were hearing, it sounded like Matthias was threatening *her*. Who do you think she was threatening to tell his secret to?"

"I guess we'll never know because I'm certainly not going to ask, and neither should you. I want you to watch yourself around him, Liv," David says, staring directly into my eyes.

I nod my head in response. The chilly air seems to have settled all the way in my bones now. I start shivering uncontrollably.

"Let's get you back up by the fire," David says.

I try to speak, but my teeth chatter instead. We shuffle our way back to camp. Frederick and another man are sitting next to the firepit, laughing.

"Is it all right if we sit by the fire?" David asks. "Olivia is frozen and needs to warm up."

"Help yourself," Frederick says. "Not sure if you've been introduced to my brother, yet. This is Markos."

I never would have guessed they were brothers by looking at them. Frederick reminds me of a Viking: bald, burly, and has a large red beard. Whereas, Markos is about half his size in body mass and has a short pointed red beard on his narrow chin. His eyes are sky blue, but Frederick's are dark brown. Looking at him closer, I can see the resemblance in their noses, broad with large nostrils. It fits Frederick's face but looks way too big on Markos.

"Hi, I'm Olivia," I say, lamely holding out my hand.

Frederick takes it in both of his and bows his head. "Brr, he wasn't kidding. You're like ice. Here let me move a stump closer to the pit so you can get warmed up," he offers.

"Thanks. Sorry for interrupting your conversation," I say, holding my hands out toward the fire.

"Not at all. Markos was just telling me that Alexandrine went and got herself in trouble again. She needs to learn when to quit, that one," Frederick says with a chuckle.

"Does she get hit a lot or something?" David asks.

"Matthias has to put her in her place from time to time."

Scandalized, my jaw drops, and I glare at Frederick.

"Look. She's a firecracker, that woman. Maybe if she would stop trying to kick us guys in the balls every time she disagrees with us, we wouldn't have to resort to hitting. She gets real physical real fast, and it takes a good lickin' to get her to stop."

"Why is she so violent and angry?" I ask.

"Well," Frederick says, shifting around uncomfortably, "She was 'attacked' by one of Turk's soldiers, if you get my drift. She ended up getting pregnant, and when the kid turned out to be a Rare, they took it away from her. If anyone has grounds to hate the president, the Coalition, or anyone who works for them, it's her."

My heart skips a beat as though it's breaking for her. How terrible! I guess I can see why she hates me now. I was quick to throw my mom's connections to the government at them when I thought they were going to kick us out. Not my finest moment.

A memory of the conversation I overheard after Matthias decided to let us stay slips into my brain. These guys seem pretty forthcoming with information; maybe they'll answer my question.

"I overheard Matthias and Alexandrine arguing once, and she said something about kidnapping. What was she talking about?"

"Well, first of all, kidnapping is a pretty strong word." Frederick shakes his head. "Leave it to her to make a rescue sound negative."

"Okay, what happened?"

"On one of the recon missions, Matthias came across Alexandrine fighting with a coalition guard. She had pulled a knife out and stabbed the guy in the neck while screaming, 'Give me back my daughter!' Matthias was drawn by her hatred of the Coalition and knew she was done for if he left her there in the city. So, he approached her while she continued to stab the guard and decided it would be safer for him and Henry to bring her out here unconscious."

"Once in camp, it took a very long time to convince her that it was for her own good; that had they left her in the city, she would either be in jail or dead," Markos adds.

"I can hear you idiots talking about me," Alexandrine says, startling us all. I was so involved in their story, I didn't notice her walking up behind them. She abandoned her wet cloth, and I can see the dark bruise forming around her right eye. "What do you think you're doing telling *her* information about me?"

"Sorry, Alex. We didn't mean nothing by it," Frederick says soberly.

"I want you guys to get lost. I'd like to have a little girl talk with Miss Priss here."

Markos and Frederick obey immediately. David stays where he is.

"Did I not make myself clear, boy? Get. Lost."

"I'm not leaving you here with Olivia alone. I've seen the way you look at her."

"If I were going to kill her, I would've done it already," she admits, stone-faced. "Now, give us a minute."

David stands up, gives me a worried look, and heads to our shelter.

My knees are visibly shaking, so I clench them together. We both watch David until he makes it inside. Then she turns to me with an ugly scowl on her otherwise beautiful face.

"I don't like you. I probably never will. I knew immediately who you were when you stepped foot into this camp." She points her finger at my chest.

"H-h-how do you know who I am?" I squeak.

"Just looking at you I could see it...the family resemblance."

"L-look, Alexandrine. I'm not my mother. I never—"

"I'm not talking about your filthy government-loving mother," she pauses, giving me a significant look. When I don't respond, she huffs, "Are you really this dense?"

My face grows hot as the rage starts bubbling up in my chest again. I'm getting real sick of her dancing around what she wants to say.

"Family resemblance? Are you going to tell me what you're talking about, or are you going to keep playing with me?" I ask, losing my temper.

"You moron," she mumbles to herself. Then looking straight into my eyes, she says, "Matthias is your dad."

30

"Bull." I shake my head at her. "That's impossible. My mom said my dad died in the war."

"Your mother is a liar," she spits out.

I continue to shake my head, glaring at her.

"Why do you think Matthias decided to let you stay here when you mentioned your mom's name? Did you actually think he was worried about Turk's disposable heroes coming out to get us?"

My head is buzzing. What is she trying to do? Why would she make this up? I'm not sure what to say to her, so I just keep staring in disbelief, hoping she shouts, "Gotcha!" or something. She stares right back.

"Whatever," she huffs. "I told Matthias I was going to tell you if he didn't. Now you know. Secret's out. Do us both a favor, and stay away from me. This will be the one and only civil conversation we have."

She stands up and stomps back to her shelter. I watch her, shell-shocked. What am I supposed to do with this? If it's true, if Matthias *is* my dad, then he better have a really good explanation for abandoning my mom and me. I stare at the fire as a mixed concoction of emotions is saturating my mind. I'm feeling so many things right now, my stomach starts to cramp, and I'm afraid I'm going to throw up. I'm relieved when David has a seat next to me by the fire.

I reach out and grab his hand to stabilize myself. I feel as though everything I thought I knew is suddenly fake. At least, David is a constant I can depend on. He squeezes my hand gently in return.

"She just told me Matthias is my dad," I whisper, still in shock at the thought. Tears are stinging my eyes.

"I heard," David says with a look of pity. "Why wouldn't he have told you as soon as he figured out who you are? And why would your mother lie?"

"Good questions. If you find out the answers, let me know," I snap. "Sorry."

"It's okay. I'm frustrated, and it has nothing to do with me," he says. "Are you going to confront Matthias with this? He didn't want Alexandrine to tell. He might get mad."

"I don't know." I cover my face with my hands. "I don't even know if it's true. But my mom has kept a lot of secrets from me, so I wouldn't be surprised if this is just another one."

My mind is filled with so many questions, I feel I could scream from frustration. Just as I'm about to lose it, David puts an arm around my shoulder. That calms my mind momentarily, at least, stops me from releasing the scream that is hanging in the back of my throat. We sit quietly by the fire, watching the flames dance and the smoke swirl. A slight wind blows and carries the smoke right in my face, stinging my eyes. I close them, waiting for it to move, but it's getting hard to breathe. The all too familiar feelings of my airways constricting forces me to get up. I soon find myself pacing, agitated once more.

How could he? How could Matthias have left my mom and me? How could he not tell me that he was my dad as soon as he found out? If I tell him that I know, will he be willing to rescue my mom and David's family? Will he be willing to right the wrong he made so many years ago? What if he's not my dad? What if Alexandrine is messing with me?

Before I know it, I'm marching toward Matthias's hut. Blood is pounding in my ears as I lose myself to rage. David calls my name, but I keep walking. Like an unfinished melody, this needs to be resolved.

"Is it true?" I ask, barging into his hut.

He spins around as he's pulling a shirt on. Before he tugs it down all the way, I see a number of scars etched across his well-defined abdomen.

"Ever heard of knockin'?" he growls.

"Is it true? Are you my father?" I ask loudly. My face is radiating heat from embarrassment and anger.

His face hardens, and he looks like he's about to start yelling, but he keeps his composure. "Yes. As soon as ya said your mother's name, I knew it."

My heart drops into my stomach. I liked it better when I thought Alexandrine might be lying to me. This is so much worse. Tears flood my eyes as my mind tries to make sense of this information.

"How could you? Why did you abandon my mom and me?" I ask as a lone tear runs down my cheek.

"I'm sorry, Olivia. I never meant to hurt ya. I never meant for your life to be hard like it was," he says, reaching out to touch my arm.

I reflexively pull away.

He makes his hand into a fist and drops it to his side. His face hardens a bit more as he looks into my eyes. "Look, I had to do what I had to do. The Coalition was gettin' too damn powerful. They took away our guns; they took away our rights; they took away our freedom; hell, they even took away the sun! It didn't sit right with me. Any of it. Every day I stayed there, it kept eatin' away at me 'til I thought I was gonna snap and kill someone. I knew we had to get out, but your mother was in too deep with the government."

He drops his gaze and starts pacing his hut. "I pleaded with her to come with us, but she refused. Stubborn woman! So, one day while she was at work, I packed up what I could carry and brought Henry and my dad out here to survive. It killed me to leave your mother pregnant and alone, but I knew she would never be swayed."

"Why didn't you come back for me?" I ask. "Didn't you care about my existence?"

"Of course, I cared. But it was too dangerous to go back and take ya away from your mother."

"Why? If you're not afraid of Turk's soldiers, why would you be afraid of Mom?"

"She's more powerful than ya think."

I give him a cocked eyebrow. "Is she a Rare too?"

"I'm not talkin' physically. She's Turk's right-hand woman."

"No way! What a bunch of bull!" I yell, my anger rising again. "First, I find out that you're my father, but you were keeping it a secret. And now you're trying to feed me lies about my mother to turn me against her? You're a real piece of work, aren't you?"

"Listen here!" Matthias steps closer to me, and for a moment, I'm afraid he's going to hit me, but I stand my ground. "I didn't tell ya I was your father because I was scared. That's right. Matthias, the fearless leader of a rebellion group, was afraid of a teenage girl. I knew I'd made a mistake, not comin' to get ya, and I was afraid of how you'd react. I figured it was better for me to just play the role of father figure as your leader. I didn't want your judgment and hatred, knowin' I'd abandoned ya."

A fresh tear leaks down my cheek. My thoughts are screaming inside my head. I've wanted to know who my father is for so long, and now I stand in front of a man I hardly know, who's claiming to be him. Things were easier when I thought my father was dead. At least, his absence from my life was for a reason. This is just painful. He's right about the judgment and hatred part. I feel nothing good toward the man in front of me.

"You're wrong about Mom," I growl. "She likes her secrets, but she's definitely not 'Turk's right-hand woman.'"

"What makes ya so sure? Ya told me yourself she never lets on what she does at the government building."

"I know my mother."

"Do ya?" He asks with a scowl. "I knew 'er once too. At least, I thought I did. Her love of secrets, long hours at work, and outright refusal to leave proved otherwise."

Confusion is taking over my senses. I don't want to believe a word Matthias says to me, but he has a point about me not really knowing what my mother does.

"Fine! Then, let's go rescue her now! Maybe if she left the city, she could change too."

"She's not a Rare. She won't change out here." Matthias shakes his head at me.

"Well, maybe knowing that you and Henry are alive will make a difference," I say, grasping at straws.

I don't know why I want my mom out here so badly. We fight all the time, but maybe we could patch things up and be a real family someday. Maybe.

"No! Now, I want ya to drop it!"

I hear a call from outside, "Supper's ready!"

I turn to storm out of his hut, but he steps in front of me. Pointing a finger at my chest, he says, "Nobody needs to know that you're my daughter. Not yet. Keep it to yourself for now."

"What...are you ashamed?" I ask, glaring.

"Not at all. But it might ruffle a few feathers from some other members of the group. Alexandrine knew that. Just keep quiet 'bout it, and I'll break the news on my own terms." And with that, he allows me to go.

I'm seething with anger, so I choose to go to my shelter instead of joining everyone for supper. I walk past Saul and take another glance at what he's carving. I manage to get a better look at the symbols, and suddenly, I know where I've seen them before.

My necklace.

The box marked "Dad's stuff" wasn't my mom's dad, but my dad's dad. Matthias's dad, Saul. It must have belonged to him. I wish I would have brought the necklace with me. It seems like it was important to him since he keeps carving these symbols. I wonder what they mean. Maybe I'll ask him or Matthias someday, but not right now. I'm too angry.

I march back into my shelter and flop down on my bed. After ten minutes of sitting there, trying to figure out what I'm going to do, David comes in carrying a plate of food for me. I grab it from him and eat quickly, hardly tasting anything.

"So, it's true, huh?" David asks, watching me stuff my face.

I nod my head in response. I swallow hard, almost choking on the mouthful of potatoes.

"I don't know who I'm madder at: my mom or Matthias."

David gives me a sympathetic look and has a seat next to me. "I know this situation sucks, but..." he grows quiet, hesitating to finish what he was going to say.

"But, what?"

"You just found out your Dad's alive! And you have a brother and a grandpa! You should be happier than this. Sure, he didn't tell you right away, but it was probably a shock that you suddenly showed up out of nowhere, and he didn't know what to do."

"He abandoned me! He took my brother and left me to live with my mom alone! I spent all these years thinking my father was so brave to go fight in a war and that he died with respect. Instead, I find out he was more of a coward than anything!" I yell.

"I blame your mom," David says matter-of-factly.

"What?" I ask incredulously.

"Your mom refused to go with your dad when trouble started. Then she lied to you and told you that your father was dead. She could have said he left her and that you had a brother."

I stay quiet, staring moodily at the opposite wall. He's right. I'm back to not knowing who I'm more pissed at. I wish my mom were out here so I could lay into her.

"I'm sorry. I don't mean to make things harder for you," he says calmly. "Here, let me take your plate. I'll leave you alone so you can think about things. If you need me, just let me know."

As I sit, thinking about how screwed up everything is, an unrelenting desire to confront my mom has taken hold of my mind. I need to talk to her. I need answers. I just hope I can sneak out without David noticing. And maybe I can grab the necklace while I'm back.

31

I decide the best time to leave would be in the middle of the night. I pretend to be asleep when David comes in to check on me. I hear him kneel next to me and whisper, "I'm sorry," as he runs his hand over my hair a couple of times. It takes everything I have in me to not move a muscle. He quietly stands back up and leaves the shelter.

I must doze off at some point, though, because now everyone is back in the shelter sleeping, and it's pitch-black outside. I sit up, cringing at every leaf that rustles under my weight. I grab my blanket and the sweatshirt I use as a pillow and stuff them in my bag. I sneak out the door, taking a look at David before I go. I know he's going to be mad at me, but I need to do this. If I told him I was going, he would only try to talk me out of it or insist that he goes with me. I can't risk his life by going back into the city. He's safer here.

I peek my head out of the shelter to make sure nobody is sitting by the fire. I blink a couple of times when I realize I am seeing perfectly in the darkness without any source of light helping me. It must be another benefit of my Rare abilities. I smile at how far I've come since stepping foot into the woods. I can breathe easier, see better, and even though we haven't been out here that long, I've actually started putting some meat on my bones. At least, something is going my way. I head to the Commons to see if I can find some food to take with me for the journey.

I grab as many apples as I can as well as some carrots and a few strips of dried meat. I think I still have a couple bottles of water at the bottom of my bag I never finished before Henry and Matthias found us, so I should be okay there. I spot a big filet knife in its sheath lying on the table and take that too. I'd rather have a sword, but Matthias keeps those in his hut.

Once my bag is full, I head to the river. I'm going to have to walk on the opposite side of it for a while to avoid the two people who are on guard duty for the night. Since Matthias believes the Havoc are afraid of water, they don't keep watch over the river, so this is the safest way out. I pull my socks and shoes off, stuff my socks in my pocket, and tie the shoelaces together so I can sling them over my shoulder to cross the river.

The water is frigid. I'm glad I don't have to walk in it for long. Once I'm on the other side, I sneak along the river bank, making as little noise as possible. I'm sure the water current would cover any sounds my feet make, but I can't take the risk. Once I'm confident I've made it far enough out of camp, I cross back over the river and find a fallen log to sit on so I can get my socks and shoes back on my frozen feet.

I keep going downriver, thinking it has to lead to the ocean by the city. I'll climb a tree once the sun starts to come up and get my directions right. I need to keep moving, and this seems like the logical choice.

Every owl hoot and cricket chirp draws my attention, and fear begins to needle its way into my brain. I listen closely for any signs of Havoc, praying hard I don't run into one. I feel so lonely and exposed without David by my side. Perhaps I should have brought him with me. He might have agreed to it if I explained how important it was for me to talk to my mom. I'm pretty sure David would do anything for me if I asked him, but I can't put him in danger just because I'm too chicken to be alone. This is for his own good.

I'm slowing down as I continually step over fallen logs and underbrush. After a couple of hours of plodding along, I sit down for a break. The night sounds are giving way to the sweet sounds of morning. Birds have become alert and are singing in the trees. The darkness is fading away to the soft light of dawn. I need to find a tree that's tall enough to allow me to see the city.

I climb a tree I think is tall enough, but once I make it to the top, I can't see past the other trees in the forest. I'll need to keep searching. I walk downriver until the sun is up fully, and the air is growing hot. I spot an oak that towers over all the surrounding trees. The problem is, the branches are about twelve feet from the ground. How am I going to reach those to climb?

Next to the giant oak is a smaller maple with branches closer to the ground. I pull myself up and climb until I'm level with the oak's branches. Taking a deep breath, I let go of the maple tree and jump to the oak. I manage to grab hold of a branch, but the rough bark skins the palms of my hands. Now my hands and injured thumb pulse with pain. I almost let go, but I keep my grip and swing my leg up on the branch. I straddle it and lean my back against the tree so I can take a look at my hands. Huge chunks of skin are peeled off, and blood has made its way to the surface. They sting bad enough to make my eyes water. That was a stupid thing to do!

I carefully pull my bag off my back and search for something I can use to wrap my hands with. I find a clean pair of socks and tie them around my injured palms, pulling the other end with my teeth. It's going to be much harder to climb the tree now, but I have to do it. I secure my bag on my back and carefully climb the rest of the way up. The socks make it harder to

141

grip the branches, but I manage to make it to the top. The sun shines down on me with blistering intensity. I hold on to the tree with one hand and use the other to shield my eyes from the blinding sun.

I can see that the river does, in fact, flow to the ocean, but it's miles away from the part of the city I'm trying to get to. I need to make my way to the far side where the subway tunnels are. Matthias never gave me an exact location of the entrance he uses, but I know the general area I need to be. By the looks of things, I still have at least a day and a half of hiking to go. I'm already feeling exhausted from hiking all night after such a short nap in the evening. I'll try to make it a little farther, but I'll need to find a place to camp out for the night soon.

I methodically work my way down the tree, supporting most of my weight with my legs to save my hands. Once I'm on the ground, I head east away from the river. I hate the idea of leaving the safety the river can give me from the Havoc, but I need to keep going.

After a few more hours of walking, I can barely lift my legs anymore. I come across a rock outcropping with a hole at the base big enough for me to lie down in. I'll be guarded on three sides, so it seems as good of a shelter as any. It's only early afternoon, but I can't walk anymore. I squeeze in the hole and stuff my bag in the opening I crawled through so I can at least feel somewhat hidden. Even though I'm hot, I cover up with my blanket out of habit and fall asleep almost instantly.

I snap awake when I hear a snuffling sound right outside. It's dark now, and I can't see anything other than the rock walls of my hiding spot. I don't know whether I should lie still and hope whatever it is goes away or try to sneak my way out. Not knowing exactly where it is makes the sneaking out part pretty much impossible.

A branch snaps not far from my bag, and I pray hard that it's not a Havoc. Adrenaline is coursing through my veins, and I try to keep my breathing shallow. I grab hold of my bag and slowly slide it to the side so I can get a glimpse of what's out there. I'm greeted with two glowing eyes only a foot away, and I stifle a scream with my sock wrapped hand. I lie still, gathering up the courage to look again. When I take a closer look, I realize it's far too small to be a Havoc. This creature is black with a stripe of white down its back and is about the size of a cat. It's sniffing at my bag and I realize it probably smells the food I brought.

I slowly spin my bag and take out an apple. I awkwardly toss it out past the critter, hoping he will chase after it. He takes the bait and follows the apple. I crawl out and stuff my blanket in my bag, watching the direction of the animal. Now that I can get a better look at the creature, I realize it's kind of cute. It has such a bushy tail, I almost want to pet it, but I know better than to touch a wild animal. As I swing my bag up to slide onto my arms, the animal gets spooked by my sudden motion. It lifts its tail, sprays something at me before running away, and I find myself covered in the most foul-smelling stench I have ever experienced.

I cover my mouth and nose with my hand, but that doesn't help one bit. My eyes are watering, and I fall to the ground, retching. I stand back up and try to run, hoping it didn't get too much on me, but the smell doesn't go away. I stop and start ripping my clothes off, anything to get away from this horrifying odor. Once stripped, I realize it's on my skin too. I start to cry at the ridiculousness of my situation. I'm standing alone in the middle of the forest at night, completely naked, and I smell horrendous. I need to find a way to wash this off.

I'm miles away from the river now, and I have no idea if there is any other water source to bathe in. I take the bottle of shampoo out of my bag and start rubbing it vigorously all over. My flowery shampoo does nothing to mask the stink. I keep scrubbing, scratching with my fingernails until my skin turns red and raw. I use a bottle of water as sparingly as I can since I will still need drinking water on this quest. The smell continues to permeate off my skin strongly. I yell out in frustration but clap my hand over my mouth when I hear it echoing throughout the woods. I'm going to have to just keep going and hope this stench fades away quickly.

I grab a clean outfit and get dressed. I decide to ditch the stinky clothes I tore off. I don't need them to make everything else in my bag reek.

Once I start walking again, I think about David and what he's doing. I wonder if he'll come out to try to find me. I hope not. I probably should have left a note or something. Too late now. I walk until the sun starts to show itself through the trees. I made it through another night alive. I go to yawn, and I realize I don't smell as bad as I did when I first got sprayed. Either that, or I'm getting used to it.

I hike for a few more hours, stopping to stretch every now and then. I'm not used to getting this much exercise, and my hips are aching with each step I take. Either I've pulled a muscle, or I'm not getting enough water. Probably both. But I need to keep going. If I continue walking, I should be able to make it back to the fence by nightfall.

By mid-afternoon, I'm exhausted. I wanted to ration my water so I would have enough to make it all the way home, but I couldn't help myself. I finished the last bottle about an hour ago when I felt like I was about to pass out from the heat. I would give anything to have a drink. I munch on an apple, sucking at the flesh to quench my thirst with as much juice as I can get. I can't keep going on in this heat. I'm going to have to make camp until it gets dark and cools off.

I look around for anything that might work to hide me. There aren't any rock outcroppings or caves, but I do find some underbrush that could work. I push my way through some thorns and branches until I'm in the center of it. I crouch down, and I can't see anything. This is as good a spot as any. Taking my knife out, I hack away at the plants to make a place big enough to lie down in. It's not going to be overly comfortable, but it'll do. I stretch out on my back, using my bag as a pillow. I hope I'm almost back to the city. I'm not sure how much longer I will make it without water.

I toss and turn, trying hard to adjust to a spot that will allow me to sleep. This is miserable! I don't know how I can be so physically and mentally tired, and yet I can't fall asleep. I lie there for hours, getting more and more angry. As the sky starts to darken, I can't take it anymore. I feel more sore and tired than when I started. I curse loudly as I grab my bag and start marching out of my hiding spot.

A low growl stops me dead in my tracks. I'm not quite all the way out of the bushes, so I crouch down as quietly as I can. My hands are shaking as I pull my bag in front of me and try to find my knife. I don't know what direction the sound came from. I slow my breathing so I can listen. I hear it again off to the right, not far from where I'm hiding.

I remember seeing a guy on one of the survivor shows make himself as big as he could when a black bear crossed his path. It scared the bear away, and he never had to hurt it. I weigh my options. I could try to do what the guy did and make myself as large and noisy as I can, but at a whopping height of five-foot-one, I doubt I would ever scare whatever is out there. More like annoy it enough to make it want to eat me as an hors d'oeuvre. Or I could continue to cower here in the bushes and hope it passes by quickly. I decide to continue crouching and hope it passes.

After a minute or two of sitting back on my heels, listening to where the creature went, my calf cramps so hard, I cry out in pain before I can stop myself. Out of reflex, I stand up and stretch my muscle out. I look over to where I last heard a noise, and there stands a Havoc about twenty feet away, staring at me.

32

I stand as still as I can, watching the Havoc slowly stalk closer to me, never taking its eyes off me. I want to run, but I don't think I could move even if I tried. Matthias isn't here to save me this time. I'm going to die, and I never said goodbye to David or to my mother. I inhale a shuddering breath, and a tear leaks down my cheek. My entire body trembles as the Havoc is now only a few steps away, moving slowly as though he's hunting me.

I can't take the suspense. I wish he would just get this over with quickly. Hopefully, he bites my throat and kills me instantly. I can't even fathom being eaten one leg or arm at a time—or worse yet, starting at my stomach and eating my insides first. I whimper as it takes the last step to close the distance between us. It stretches its neck out and sniffs at my pants. Exhaling hard and shaking its head as though it's trying to fend off a pesky bee, it turns around and trots away.

I collapse on the ground, crying tears of relief. I have never been more happy to smell bad in my life. I sit in the bushes for a moment, catching my breath and thinking about what just happened. It was looking right at me, so how come it didn't attack me? Perhaps it can only see movement. Maybe it saw me stand up, but since I stood still, it couldn't see me anymore? I guess it doesn't really matter. What matters is I'm alive.

I carefully stand up, looking around for any more threats. The coast is clear, so I step out of the underbrush, moving as quietly as I can. My calf is still hurting from the cramp, but I limp away from the area quickly. I've got to keep going while it's cool out.

Every single muscle and injury aches. I'm beginning to wish I had just stayed with David at camp, but the anger I have toward my mother's deceit drives me on. She has a lot of explaining to do. I hope she doesn't try to stick me in the looney bin for running off. I'll fight her tooth and nail to never enter that cursed place again. And now that I'm stronger and know how to handle myself, I bet I could win a fight with her if she tried to do that.

As I continue on, one thing becomes clear: I need water. My brain is sluggish. It's hard for me to even finish a thought. My muscles are shaky, weak, and keep cramping up. My tongue feels like sandpaper, and my lips have started to crack. I haven't peed since yesterday morning, and when I did, it was dark brown. If I don't get water soon, I think I'm going to die.

I keep trudging forward, one step at a time. I eat the last of my apples slowly, allowing the fruit to stay in my mouth longer than normal in hopes that I can produce saliva and alleviate this dryness, but there's no saliva left. I want to cry, but I would hate to waste any remaining fluid on tears.

As I try to step over a fallen tree, I trip and land on the ground. This is it. This is how I'm going to die. I think it would have been better to have been eaten by that Havoc. At least being eaten would have been quick. This is torture. I don't have enough energy to sit up, so I just lie here with my face pressed in the dirt.

I close my eyes. Once more, I find myself wishing for the sweet release of death. Anything to bring an end to this pain. And that's when I feel it. A drip. I open my eyes, wondering if I was just imagining it. And then another one hits me on the cheek. I hear the soft patter of raindrops falling on the leaves above me and all over the ground. I start to panic and force myself to get up, every muscle protesting and shaking from use. I need to find shelter somewhere away from the rain, or my flesh is going to melt off. A drop lands on my arm. I go to brush it away, but out of morbid curiosity, I lift my arm up to eye level to see if I can watch it melt through my skin.

Nothing.

The rain starts to pick up, and soon, drops are falling steadily through the trees. I hold my hand out in front of me and feel the rain tickle my skin as it lands. It doesn't hurt. In fact, it feels quite refreshing. I tilt my head back and open my mouth. A few drops fall on my tongue, and it tastes sweet, but there isn't enough landing in my mouth to quench my thirst. I look through my bag to see what I can use to catch some rain with. Other than the empty water bottles, I have no containers. The water bottles' openings are too small to catch anything.

It starts to pour, and I'm desperate to collect some of it to drink. I leave the bottles open on the ground anyway, but the fat raindrops keep knocking them over. I get frustrated as I keep standing them back up just to have them fall again. Soon, rain is dripping off my hair into my face, and my clothes are soaked. Then I get an idea.

I can suck the water out of my clothes.

It probably won't taste good, but water is water. I start sucking on my shirt, and I'm able to get a little out. I need more. I pull out every piece of fabric I brought with me and lay it out in the rain. I grab the bottom of my shirt and hold it out to catch more. Once my shirt's soaked, I bring it up to my mouth and suck every last drop out of it. I'm rewarded with two swallows of water. I grab my sweatshirt, which is lying in front of me, and draw every bit of moisture I can out of it as well. My head is starting to clear up a bit as I slowly rehydrate myself.

The rain continues to fall, and I keep drinking as much as I can, laying the pieces of clothing back out in the rain so they can get wet again. My muscles stop shaking, and my strength is returning to me. I've never really had much experience with God, but I lift my head up to the sky and thank him, anyway.

I realize that I should probably start trying to fill some of my bottles so I can have some water to keep going. I shouldn't be that far away from the city by now, but I don't ever want to be without something to drink again. I hold a bottle between my legs, and wring little sections of material over it, trying hard to not spill any. Once that shirt is wrung out, I lay it back down and grab another one. After I've gone through all the clothes and the blanket I have laid out, I start over again.

When the rain finally stops, I have two water bottles filled. I can't wring any more out of the material, so I suck out any moisture that might still be there and then pack it all back in my bag. I'm ready to find that subway tunnel and get back to my apartment.

The sun starts to come out once again, and I head in the direction of the sunrise. I walk at a slower pace, trying to keep myself from sweating as best I can. Two bottles of water are not going to last me long with how hot it has been lately. I'm so focused on watching the ground for tree roots sticking up or rocks that I might trip on that it takes me a little while to realize that it's starting to get foggy. I look up and see that the city fence is only about ten yards to the right from where I'm walking. I made it! I quickly get myself back into the shelter of the woods. I don't want a guard to see me. I must have passed where David and I came out of the city a while ago because where we exited, we went straight into the wilderness. Here, I'm finding city ruins I've never seen before.

Keeping a close eye on the city fence, I search for any sign of the subway tunnel. I have no idea what I'm looking for, though. I pick my way through overgrown piles of rubble from the war-strewn remains that once were part of the city. Half-erect buildings still stand, being swallowed up by nature. I pass between rows of dilapidated structures, assuming I must be walking on what was once a street. Now, it's covered in layers of dead leaves and dirt that plants have used to take root.

I get an eerie feeling from all this wreckage. People once lived here. Moms, dads, sons, daughters, brothers, sisters. It's surreal to think humans used to occupy this space. I pass by cars now rusted and covered in vines; a bicycle half-buried in bricks from a broken building; a baby stroller, turned onto its side, covered in dirt and mildew. I close my eyes and picture what this city must have been like filled with people. People driving, walking to work, going to school, hanging out with friends and family, having dinners and parties, shopping, kissing, fighting, yelling, laughing.

A tear rolls down my cheek as I think of the fear and loss that happened during the war. Loved ones being torn apart by death and destruction. Children crying for their mommies and daddies as bombs dropped on the city. People's homes being destroyed—all because of intolerance. I stand here now, weeping for the lives of the people who just wanted to give the Rare a chance at life, who wanted to give people like *me* a chance at being accepted.

I wipe my tears away and get ahold of myself. Until now, I have never truly thought about what sacrifice really is. What it means to stand up against the world to do what is right. I will never be able to thank the men and women who tried to fight for good. I hope one day, I will be able to repay them in some small way, but for now, I need to find that tunnel.

I walk up and down streets, completely guessing at where I should be going. Even though the fog here isn't nearly as thick as it is in the livable part of the city, it still makes me feel disoriented at times, losing track of where I've been and making me walk in circles. After at least an hour of winding my way around the fallen city, I finally find something promising: a stairway that leads down into the ground. Matthias said the subways ran under the city, so I think this might be it. A sign hangs above the stairway, but it's unreadable. I'm just going to have to take the chance.

I cautiously work my way down the stairs, worried about what I might find down here. I make it to the bottom and stand still while I allow my eyes to adjust to the darkness. The air is stale down here, and the dust my shoes kick up threatens to choke me. I look around in the dim light and see an area that looks like little gates. I walk over to them and try to lift one, but it won't budge, so I climb under it. Standing up and brushing the dirt off my jeans, I keep walking farther away from the stairs I came down. I sure hope I'm going the right way.

The walkway I was on suddenly disappears, and I stop just in time. Crouching down, I see the tiniest glint shine off something metal in the hole. I carefully lower myself down off the sidewalk. Running my hands along the metal that was on the ground, I feel that it's a long narrow strip. They told me subways were like underground trains. I bet this is the track! Now, which way should I go? I pull my bag off my back and grab the little waterproof capsule of matches I brought with me. I use the patch of sandpaper that's glued to the outside to light it. Holding it down by the railway, I search for footprints that Matthias would have left if this is the subway he uses. It takes three different matches, but I finally find what I'm looking for. I set off down the tunnel and wonder just how much longer this is going to take.

I continue down the dark track, occasionally stumbling on fallen bricks and rocks. The air down here is musty and unmoving. I imagine this must be what a tomb feels like. The thought makes me shiver. A constant drip echoes down the tunnel, putting my nerves on edge. I begin to feel panicked as the darkness closes in on me. I'm not sure how long I've been walking down here, but it feels like an eternity. Every step I take just leads to more blackness. I start to question whether I'm even moving at all. Are my eyes even open? I hold my hand up in front of my face, and I can't see anything. I was able to see in the darkness at camp, but down here, it's like I'm blind.

Just breathe, Olivia.

I stop walking for a moment and take a deep calming breath before a panic attack hits me. This would not be a good place to have one. I allow myself to drink a mouthful of water, to clear my head and some dust out of my throat.

Once my bag is settled back on my shoulders, I trudge on in hopes of finding the exit soon. Up ahead, I see a tiny pinprick of dim light come to life. It moves upward, holds still momentarily, and then is shaken out. I move cautiously, taking care to make as little noise as possible. As I get closer to where the little light was, I see a small red dot grow larger and then fade away to almost nothing. The air changes as I get closer to that glowing red dot. I take in a breath, and my lungs are filled with smoke. I cough involuntarily.

Suddenly, I'm blinded by a bright light shining directly in my eyes.

A guard found me!

33

I hold my hand out in front of my eyes to shield them from the headache-inducing beam.

"Who're you?" I hear a voice bark.

Should I lie? I don't know who they are or what they want. I wish David were here.

I stay silent.

"Wha'chu doin' down here, girlie?"

I squint at the source of light to see if I can spot the guy talking to me, but I can't see anything. He doesn't talk like I imagine a guard would.

"I got lost. I'm headed back into the city," I answer.

I hear him make a tsking sound.

"This ain't no place for playin' hide-'n'-seek. Why don'cha come closer, and I'll show ya why pretty little girls like you ain't 'spose to be down here."

He shuts the flashlight off, and I hear the swish of clothing as he comes toward me. I can't see a thing, but as soon as I feel his hand on my shoulder, instinct kicks in. I grab his hand and twist his arm behind his back into a wristlock. Now with just a small amount of pressure, I can lead him anywhere. I kick where I guess his knee would be, and he falls to the ground. I shove him forward and hear his head hit a rail. I stand over him, keeping pressure on his wrist.

"Ugh! You stink!" he says in disgust.

I guess the stench didn't wear off, I just got used to it. I bend his wrist harder, and he cries out in pain.

"Where's the exit? How do I get out of here?" I ask.

"Le' me up, an' I'll show you," he says.

He struggles to free his arm, but I step on his back and use both hands to apply force to his wrist. I can feel a bone crack and wonder if I've broken something.

"Ow! Ge' off me!"

"How much further until the exit!" I yell.

"A'ight, a'ight. You ain't that far. There's a hole in the wall up ahead. Go through, and then you at the platform to get out."

"How do I know you aren't going to try to attack me as soon as I let you go?"

"I guess you don't."

150

"Then I guess we're stuck here." I push as hard as I can on his wrist.

"Ow! You gonna break my damn wrist! Get off me, an' I'll let'cha go!"

"Give me your flashlight."

"Take it! Take wha'ever you want. Just stop breakin' my wrist!"

I reluctantly let go with one hand and grab the flashlight he's holding. I put some distance between us and turn on the flashlight, shining it right at the guy. The sight of him shocks me. His long stringy hair frames his gaunt face. His eyes are sunken and bloodshot. His ragged clothes hang loosely off his skeletal body. He cowers on the ground like a rat, no longer pretending to be a tough guy. He's still bigger than me, but I could easily take him down if he tried to hurt me. As he shifts his weight, he exposes his forearm momentarily, and I see a line of marks from the crook of his elbow, down his arm.

I momentarily shine the light toward the wall he mentioned and spot the hole. I point the light at him again and slowly back up toward the exit. He keeps his tired eyes on me but never makes a move in my direction. Being bested by a girl that he should easily have been able to subdue must have been sobering. Now he looks lost and defeated as he holds his injured wrist tightly against his abdomen. I scramble through the opening and use the flashlight to figure out where to go next. I see a platform up ahead, and I drop his flashlight, feeling guilty at the thought of stealing something from someone needier than me.

I pull myself up onto the platform and quietly walk toward the door, hoping to get out quickly. I crawl under the little gates just like the ones from where I entered the subway and climb the stairs slowly. The light streaming down the stairwell is the same hazy, half-light I've lived with my whole life. Once I'm almost to the top, I peek my head around the corner to make sure I'm not seen. I haven't been out in the woods for long, but I forgot how terrible it is to be surrounded by this thick fog. I can barely see anything.

I step out of the stairwell and start walking in what I hope is the right direction. The city is a little better here than it was on the other side of the subway, but I would hardly deem it livable. Most of the buildings have sections still standing, but I can't see a single one that is completely whole. It looks as though most of the windows are missing, and the walls that are still standing have been adorned with colorful graffiti.

I stride down the sidewalk, keeping a close eye out for guards—or any human for that matter. Anyone willing to live in this dump is probably just as much of a threat as a guard. I give a wide berth to a few people curled up in doorways who appear to be sleeping. A burly, unkempt man wearing a patched-up leather jacket over a stained white undershirt and camouflage pants stands in a doorway, looking in my direction. On the front of the door is a picture of a blonde woman holding a mug of beer, and I assume he must be in front of a tavern. He watches me as I get closer and blows a cloud of smoke in my face as I'm about to pass. From the smell of it, I don't think that was cigarette smoke. He guffaws as I run down the sidewalk away from him, coughing and hacking on the fumes.

The road up ahead is blocked by a fallen building, so I turn down a side street, feeling like I'm in some sort of messed up maze. I don't want to make too many turns, or I'm going to end up going in circles. I pass by a woman rummaging through a garbage can as her two little girls stand close to her, eyeing me with sullen, dead expressions. They look like they haven't had a decent meal in their entire lives. I stop walking, unstrap my bag, and dig out the dried meat strips I had grabbed from camp. I hold it out to them, and their eyes brighten, but they don't take it.

"Here you go," I offer. "Go ahead. Take it."

The older of the two girls slowly reaches out her dirt-crusted fingers, but just as she's about to grab the meat strips, her mom turns around and slaps her hand. The little girl recoils, and tears spring to her eyes.

"Don't you dare take food from some stranger! We ain't no beggars!"

"Excuse me, ma'am, but aren't you rummaging through the trash for food?" I ask in shock.

She quickly stuffs a little bag of white powder into her jeans pocket. "It ain't yo' business what I'm doin'. We ain't no charity case. You best keep walkin' if you know what's good for you." The mom's eyes are wild and threatening.

I give a sympathetic look to the little girls, who meet my eye for a second, and then I walk away. I turn my head and see that the mom has gone back to looking for whatever it is she's looking for. The girls glance in my direction, and while they're watching, I toss the meat strips behind me. I hope they will be able to sneak the food. A little dirty meat is better than no food at all.

I quicken my pace, but there is no way to tell if I'm even going in the right direction. My head starts to feel funny as though the fog is seeping into my brain. My thoughts are sluggish again, and I'm getting lightheaded. I need to get home. I spot an overweight woman with a head of bushy gray hair, shuffling her way down the sidewalk toward me, muttering to herself.

"Excuse me, ma'am. Do you know what direction the main part of the city is?"

She points to her right and continues shuffling along, having a one-sided conversation. I call out a thank you, but I don't think she heard me. I walk to the next block and turn the way she pointed. My feet ache from all this walking. I can feel the blisters forming, but I try to ignore it the best I can. I just hope I have enough to make it back to my apartment.

As I walk, I go over what I might say to my mom once I get home. I stop short when I hear a voice up ahead. It's garbled as though it's coming out of a TV or a radio.

A guard!

I scramble into an alleyway and hide behind a pile of bricks, listening to where the guard is.

"Hold on, Camden, I thought I heard something," the guard says.

I scoot down as low as I can and pray he doesn't find me. I hear his shoes scraping against the cement as he turns the corner into the alleyway. A beam of light cuts through the fog overhead, moving from side to side. My heart is pounding in my ears, but I can still hear his slow, calculated steps coming closer to my hiding spot. My sluggish brain is trying to come up with an escape plan. Other than chucking bricks at him, I'm not sure what else I can do. He's got a gun, and I can't dodge bullets. I chance a look to the side and see the barrel of his gun and the flashlight he's holding come past the brick pile. I rest my hand on a brick, ready to do what needs to be done in order to get away.

This is it. He's only one step away from finding me. Just as I'm about to draw the brick back, getting ready to throw it, a loud crash comes from down the alley, followed by a cat yowl.

"Damn cat!" The guard yells. I hear him slide his gun back in the holster and turn around to head back to the street. "Never mind. It was just a damn cat in the alleyway," he says. A staticky voice responds as his footsteps recede.

I let go of the brick and catch my breath. That was close. Too close. I stay hunkered down for a couple more minutes, trying to work up the courage to continue on. I must be getting close to the main part of the city if a guard is here. After I'm sure the coast is clear, I stand up with a groan. My muscles have seized up, and now, it's hard to move. I carefully make my way out of the alley, looking both ways down the street, but with the fog, I can't tell if there is anyone there anyway. I can't hear anyone, so I keep moving.

As the sun starts making its way to the horizon, I take notice in the dimming light that the buildings are starting to look nicer. I think I made it. Now, I just need to figure out where I am. Keeping an eye out for guards, I try to search for a street sign. I'm not entirely familiar with the streets of the city, but maybe I can figure it out. At the next intersection, I discover that I'm only a couple blocks away from my school. I'm almost home.

I start to get chilled as the sun is going down, and my clothes are damp from the fog. I pull out my sweatshirt and hide my face in my hood, hoping nobody will recognize me. As a couple of cars drive past me, I start to worry that this was a bad idea.

Finally, after another hour of cautiously making my way back home through the darkening fog that's intermittently lit with spotlights from the streetlamps, my apartment building stands before me. Keeping my head down so nobody can see my face, I walk up the stairs and to my front door. The ever-present smell of disinfectant and stale cigarettes that lingers in the hallway is even stronger than I can remember. I fumble with my keys and hope I can get inside before one of the neighbors spots me. I swing my door open and freeze when a gun barrel is shoved in my face.

3|4

I drop my bag and hold up my hands. I slowly move my right hand to my hood and pull it back.

"Olivia?" I hear my mom say in disbelief.

Before I know it, she's embracing me in an awkward hug. She lets go and tightly holds onto my shoulders at arm's length.

"Where have you been? Are you hurt? I was worried sick! Where are your glasses? Why didn't you leave a note? I thought you had finally succeeded in killing yourself! You have a lot of explaining to do!" She spits out, her concern turning to anger.

I take a deep breath and push her hands off me.

"I'm fine, Mom. But it's you who has a lot of explaining to do."

I step around her and walk into the living room. She follows close behind.

"What is that smell? Don't sit on my couch smelling like that. Go take a shower, and then we'll talk."

A shower sounds amazing right now, so I oblige. I relish the warmth of the water running over my sore muscles. I missed this. I open my mouth under the water, ignoring the taste, and drink until my belly feels full. After scrubbing three times with a loofa until my skin is bright red, I'm finally finished. Once I'm dressed in a change of clean clothes and fresh bandages, I go back to the living room where my mom has set out cold bottles of water and a bowl of chips. She looks at me with worry, but if I'm not mistaken, there seems to be a hint of contempt there too.

"So, explain yourself," she says.

"First, I want you to answer some questions. That's why I'm here." I sit down on the couch and grab a bottle of cold water. I have never been more grateful to have an endless supply of drinking water than I am right now.

"'That's why you're here?' You left without telling me where you were going. I've searched for you for over a week, trying to find you. I got the police involved! And you come back here as though you're perfectly innocent and demand answers from *me*?"

"I'll explain everything. Just let me start with some questions."

She glares at me, flips her long dark hair over her shoulder, and sits up straighter.

"Fine. Go ahead."

"Why did you lie to me about Dad?"

"I don't know what you're talking about," she starts to say, shifting in her seat.

"Cut the crap. You told me Dad died fighting in the war. That was a lie."

"What makes you so sure?"

"I met him," I say, watching her reaction closely.

Her eyes grow a little larger before she narrows them again, frowning. "I don't know who you met, but it wasn't your father. He died." She shakes her head at me.

"No, Mom. Matthias is alive. And so is your son, Henry."

Tears well up in her eyes. She looks down at her lap and picks a piece of lint off her pants as she gathers herself. "Where have you been, Olivia?"

"I'm still asking the questions. Why did you lie to me and let me believe my father was dead all this time?"

When she doesn't answer me, I lose control of my anger.

"Tell me!"

I can tell her patience is growing thin.

"I told you your father was dead, because by the time I had you, he was as good as dead. Especially to me. He left me! And he took *my* son with him!"

"He said you wouldn't run away with him. That you staked your allegiance with President Turk instead of him."

"Unbelievable. Of course, he would say that." She shakes her head in disbelief. "I was four months pregnant with you. Why would I want to go run out into the wilderness in my condition? I pleaded with him to just stay here, to try to make things work, for the safety of you and your brother. But that son-of-a—" She stops and collects herself before continuing. "He pretended to agree with me, but then, when I came home from work the next day, he was gone. He packed up and took Henry."

"So, why didn't you follow him? Or call the police and have him brought back?"

"I was going to call the police to find him and bring them back, but I still loved him." She pounds her fist on her leg in frustration.

I give her a quizzical look.

"I was afraid that if I got the police involved, they would kill him for being a traitor of the Coalition."

I grab a handful of chips and eat them while I let what she said sink in. Something about this seems off. Why wouldn't she go out of her way to get her child back? If she loved Matthias so much, why wouldn't she take a chance and join them? Then I remember my conversation with Matthias.

"Are you sure you weren't just trying to save face in front of President Turk, being his right-hand woman and all?"

"What are you talking about?"

"Matthias said you wouldn't go out in the woods with him, not because you were pregnant, but because you were in too deep with Turk."

She gives me a shocked look, but I can tell it isn't genuine.

"Are you part of the reason that the Rare are being kept weak?" I jump to my feet. Anger is rolling off me like waves.

Next thing I know, she's on her feet, pointing her finger in my face. "You've got a lot of nerve! You leave and don't tell me where you're going. You then come back and start accusing me of being a liar. And now, you think I'm Turk's right-hand woman, whatever that means."

"Answer the question!"

Her nostrils flare, and her chest is heaving as she breathes heavily. She stares into my eyes, hardly blinking, and I stare right back.

"You owe me," I say with as much anger as I can put into three words.

"Damn you, Matthias," she mutters under her breath and then sighs. "Sit down so we can talk."

Once we're sitting, she begins, "Fine. Yes. I play a part in the Coalition that keeps the Rare weak and monitored."

She pauses and takes a drink, never taking her eyes off me.

"I have never fully understood why the world freaked out like they did. Personally, I think it was amazing what the scientists had accomplished and what the Rare were able to do. With the heightened senses, there were some amazing detectives, scientists, athletes, musicians, you name it. But I guess that was part of the problem. Regular people were losing jobs and positions of power to the Rare because there was so much more that they could do, and it made people outraged and jealous."

"If you think we're so great, then why are you trying to keep us weak?"

She lets out another big sigh. "I take it you discovered you're one of them?"

I nod.

"Your grandmother told me that at the beginning of the peace deal, when the Coalition was first put into place, they didn't try to keep the Rare weak. Everyone just coexisted inside the city for a while. But foreign extremists were sneaking over here, hunting the Rare down, and killing them. Well, a couple of the extremists were killed by some of the Rare who found out what they were doing and fought back. Word got out about what happened, and the foreign countries demanded that something be done about it, or they were going to 'finish the job.'"

"'Finish the job'? They're the ones who kept starting it!" I interrupt.

"I know. Originally, the way they kept the Rare weak was to inject them with a DNA alteration, but it didn't always turn out right. Instead of dampening their heightened senses, it took them away completely."

"It took away their senses? You mean, they blinded people or caused them to be deaf?"

"Yes." She nods solemnly. "A lot of people had a psychotic break or died from it too."

"What?"

"The Coalition was in its early days, scrambling to find peace between the world and the United States. Over the years, we have been able to find a suppressant that does less damage. Of course, it comes with its downfalls too, but I have hope that we'll be able to create the perfect solution."

"The perfect solution would be for the world to stop being bigots and let us Rare exist without trying to kill us or control us!" I jump to my feet.

"Settle down, Olivia."

"The Coalition isn't any better. They set themselves up to keep the peace between the world and the US, and yet they give in to the demands that essentially wipe out the Rare; the very people the US was trying to protect in the first place."

"Lower your voice," she hisses.

"They are only looking out for themselves. They don't give a damn about the Rare. And you're in on it!" I spit out, marching off to my room. I slam my door, lock it, and then flop on my bed, seething with anger.

I hear my mother's footsteps stop outside my door. Her muffled voice says, "You don't understand anything. Nothing is black and white like you want to believe it to be. We have to do something, or they'll start up the war again, and there'll be nothing left!"

"Whatever. Leave me alone!" I yell into my pillow.

"Open this door so we can talk. I still have questions for you, young lady!" She rattles my doorknob. "You were gone for over a week. Where did you go?"

I say nothing.

"Where did you find your father? Did you leave the city?"

I lie on my side and stare at the door, wondering how long she's going to stand out there, asking questions.

"What...what did Henry look like?" she asks sadly.

This question tugs at my heart a bit. I'm about to stand up and let her in when I hear a sob, and her bedroom door thumps closed.

It was a mistake to come back here.

3|5

I lie on my bed, listening to my mom cry in the other room and then get herself ready for bed. I expect her to come talk to me, but she doesn't bother me again.

As I'm lying there, I suddenly remember the other reason I came back. I was going to grab the necklace. As I search my dresser for it, I see another letter addressed to me with no return address. I open it with a slight tremor in my hand, expecting it to be another threat from Cindy. I can just make out the water-splotched writing:

> Olivia,
> HELP ME!
> Joselyn

Come on! What does she expect me to do? There's nothing I *can* do.

I pace back and forth in my bedroom, holding the letter in my hand. I glance at those two words, crying out for help, and I start wondering what would happen if Joselyn escaped from the city. Would she get better like I did? How could she? I only got better because I'm a Rare.

I set the letter back down on my dresser and open my jewelry box. I pick up the necklace and smile. I was right. The symbols match Saul's carvings exactly, but I can't remember the pattern he made. I spin the different sections around, but nothing happens. I'll have to wait until I can look at Saul's carvings again. I stash the necklace in my bag where I won't lose it.

I continue pacing my room for a while, but exhaustion wins out, and I get myself ready for bed. Oh, sweet, comfortable bed. How I've missed you!

My mother wakes me up before she heads off to work in the morning.

"I suppose you think you're skipping out on school?"

"I'm never setting foot in that building again." I yawn.

She makes an exasperated sound. "Fine. I'll let it go this time, but you've got to promise me you're not going to leave again. I want to talk to you, but I have to go to work today. I can't miss."

"Mom, why don't you come with me?"

"I can't."

"You can't, or you won't? We could be a family again."

160

"Olivia, I don't have time to have this conversation right now. I promise we'll talk when I get back. I'll bring home some pizza tonight. See you later."

I hear the front door close, and her keys jangle as she locks it. I'm not waiting around for her to give me lame excuses for why she won't come out to the woods with me. If she wasn't willing to run away with Matthias when she was still in love with him, she's not going to be willing to go out there now after years of being devoted to the Coalition. I plan on getting out of here well before she gets home, but my bed is so warm and comfortable, I allow myself to sleep for a couple more hours.

Once awake, I take another long hot shower and then bandage up my hands with extra layers of gauze. I grab all the remaining bandages from the medicine cabinet, a bottle of vitamins, and the painkillers my mom hides in her room and stuff them in my bag. I fill all my empty bottles with water and grab extra unopened ones. My bag is getting so heavy, I'm afraid the straps are going to rip off. After I've stuffed a flashlight and as much food as I can fit into my bag, I search the apartment for some rope or bungee straps that will allow me to attach my pillow to my bag. I've decided I can't live without it. A wadded up sweatshirt just wasn't cutting it. I stuff my pillow in an empty garbage bag to keep water off and use an old bathrobe belt to strap it on.

I'm about to head out the door when a wave of guilt stops me. My mother hasn't been a very good mom, but she deserves to have some reassurance that I'll be okay. I drop my bag and sit down at the table with a sheet of paper.

> Mom,
>
> I know you're going to be pissed that I took off again, but I don't belong here. I found a group of people who have accepted me and are helping me to find my true potential. After leaving the city, I got so much healthier. The healthiest I have ever been in my entire life! I don't need my glasses or my inhalers anymore, and David has seen amazing improvements too.
>
> I really want you to come with me, but I know you would never agree to, so I'm making things easier on us both. I'm going back to where I was, and I want you to know that I'm okay. I'm sure I'll be back to see

you again someday. Please, don't try to find us. Just enjoy your life without all the hospital stays and fights we have.

I know I don't say this, like ever, but I love you. Thank you for taking care of me. Now, it's time for me to take care of myself.

Olivia

P.S. Henry is handsome and looks just like Matthias, but he has your smile.

I fold the letter and leave it on the table. The time is closing in on noon, so I grab a quick lunch of sandwich meat, a cheese stick, and an orange, and I head out. I throw my hooded sweatshirt back on so I can conceal my face, but once I step outside, I realize it's going to be too hot for it. I take it off and tie it around my waist. The fog seems thinner today, which means I'm going to have to be extra careful not to be seen.

I begin walking down the street, back the way I came when a car slows down as it gets near. I glance over my shoulder and recognize the car. I quicken my pace, keeping my head down and turned slightly away from the road.

"Olivia? Olivia, is that you?" I hear Mrs. Beckett call from her open window.

Crap!

Just as I'm about to turn down a side street and start running, she cries out, "Please! Just tell me David is okay. I'm not mad at you, Olivia. I just need to know my son's okay."

I stop walking, close my eyes, and take a deep breath, knowing I should just make a run for it, but I can't. She's always been so nice to me, I can't just run away without saying something.

"Yes, Mrs. Beckett. David is more than okay. He's the healthiest he's ever been," I say at my shoes, not wanting to make eye contact. "His seizures have stopped, and he doesn't need his hearing aids anymore." I chance a look at her and see tears rolling down her cheeks.

I turn and run down the alleyway to my right, making my way between foul-smelling garbage dumpsters and piles of wet cardboard boxes until I get to the next street. Glancing both ways before stepping out, I continue my way to the bad part of town. Every time I hear a car, I find a place to hide until they're out of sight. I'm afraid Mrs. Beckett is going to try to talk to me some more. I can't be seen and recognized again. I need to get out of here.

Walking as quickly as possible, I'm able to make good time. I can see the change in the buildings up ahead through the haze. I stop walking momentarily so I can listen for any guards. All I hear are some distant traffic behind me, the beating thump of some music being played loudly, and the wail of a baby. Everything seems to be okay, so I slip my way back to the dangers of the rundown part of the city.

I wind my way through the rubble-scattered roads, searching for the subway entrance. I stop when I get an uneasy feeling like I'm being watched. I look around but can't spot anyone through the mist. I decide to take a side street to try to shake the feeling. I really don't like being here. I wish I were back in camp now, but I have a long way to go.

I'm suddenly aware of how quiet it is. I no longer hear the baby crying, and the bass thumps from the music have faded away. All I can hear are my own breathing and the steady rhythm of my steps pounding on the concrete—that is, until I hear a brick clatter on the road behind me.

"Hello?" I squeak. I try to keep my breathing even. "Is someone there?"

No answer. I strain to hear any noise I can as I stare into the fog behind me. After a minute or two of hearing and seeing nothing, I continue on a little faster than before. That feeling of being watched comes back, and I whip my head around trying to spot the source of my uneasiness. I start to panic as the smell of the city's decay fills my nostrils with its unpleasantness: a mixture of rotting garbage, mold, and sewage. I don't remember things smelling this bad on my way through the first time. Then again, I smelled bad on the way through the first time.

I cover my nose with my shirt and take deep breaths to calm myself down. Up ahead, loud music and laughter flood the street and then muffle again. As I walk closer, I realize it's a tavern full of people. There's a picture on the door of a blonde lady holding a mug full of beer. I remember seeing that picture when that creepy guy blew smoke at me on my way to the apartment. I'm almost to the subway tunnel.

I run the rest of the way and stifle a cry of relief when I see the steps leading down to the subway. I pull out the flashlight that I remembered to pack and make my way into the darkness of the tunnel once again. I sure hope that nasty guy isn't still there.

Once I'm back on the railway, I push myself through the hole in the wall and shine my flashlight in every direction before I take any more steps.

A pair of eyes catch in my beam, and it startles me enough to almost drop my light. I shakily move my light back to where the eyes were. A mangy gray cat with bright yellow eyes stares at me, then hisses and runs away to hide in the darkness once again. I clasp my hand over my heart as I catch my breath. I continue to sweep the area with my light until I'm certain no one's there. The coast is clear, so I cautiously make my way back to the other entrance, keeping the flashlight shining toward my feet.

After trudging on for what feels like hours, I finally see the platform up ahead. Just as I'm about to climb up, a scuffling sound comes from down the tunnel behind me. I shine the flashlight around to search for the source of the noise, but nothing's there. It was probably that stupid cat again. I climb up the platform and head out of the subway tunnel, happy to be away from the dangers of people. Now, I just have to worry about the Havoc again.

By the time I get out of the ruins and back into the cover of the woods, the sun is setting. The fog is fading away, the farther I get from the fence. The scent of trees and dead leaves helps me to clear my head and feel calmer. I realize I feel more at home in the woods than I ever did in the city. The cool night breeze rustles the leaves above my head, making it sound like rain falling momentarily. A distant owl hoot reminds me that the night animals are on the prowl. I should probably find somewhere safe to spend the night.

I recall reading a book a couple of years back where a girl strapped herself to a branch up in a tree so she could sleep. I wonder if that would actually work?

I look around me and find a tree with thick branches. I climb my way up about fifteen feet until I find a branch that has enough room for me to get comfortable. There's a nub of a branch not far from where I'm sitting, so I hang my pack off it and untie my pillow. I try to use the bathrobe belt to tie myself to the branch, but it's not long enough. I pull a long sleeved shirt out of my bag and tie the belt to one of the sleeves, then wrap it around the branch and tie the other end to the other sleeve. It's long enough, but now I worry whether the knots will hold. I place the pillow behind my head and try to get some sleep.

I sleep lightly all night, waking up to every strange noise. I hear some odd howling in the distance and pray hard that Havocs can't climb trees. As soon as the sun comes up, I decide I've had enough and want to keep moving. My stiff muscles make it hard to climb back down the tree, but I manage to make it without falling. I eat a granola bar for breakfast and stretch out before continuing.

Excitement for getting back to camp makes me walk faster than I should. I force myself to keep my pace slow and steady so I can conserve as much energy and water as possible. I lose myself in thought as I look around at the beauty of the woods again. I wish I could have known about the healing powers of nature a long time ago. And not just healing for my body, but psychological healing as well. My thoughts were always so dark when I was living in the city. There wasn't a day that went by where I didn't contemplate dying. Those thoughts haven't gone away completely, but I feel more hope out here, more purpose. Maybe someday, I'll finally stop wanting to die and find some real joy in living.

Suddenly, a branch snaps behind me. I quickly hide behind a tree and peek around it to see if I can find the source of the noise.

Nothing.

The wind shifts the shadows around, making my eyes play tricks on me. Every little movement causes my breath to catch in my chest. I drop my bag on the ground and rummage around for the knife. Cautiously, I move on, holding the knife in my hand as I go. A sense of danger tickles the back of my mind. Is there a Havoc stalking me that I can't see?

As the sun makes its way across the sky, I'm grateful that the temperature is rather mild compared to my journey to the city. I stop occasionally for a drink of water, but otherwise, I move as quickly as I can. I want to be at camp, where I can be protected. I hope they'll let me back in. What will I do if Matthias is pissed at me and won't allow me in? What if he decides to punish me for leaving?

I can't worry about that right now. I snack on some dried mango as I work my way through the wilderness. I want to make it to the river before nightfall. The niggling in my brain that's telling me I'm in danger never goes away. I can't figure out what's causing it, but it feels like I'm being hunted.

Daylight is slowly fading away to dusk. My hair is dripping wet with sweat, and my backpack weighs a ton. I've rationed my water, only allowing myself a drink every half hour or so. I stop to take another drink and eat some cashews for supper when a flock of birds starts and flaps out of the trees behind me. I crouch behind a fallen log and watch to see what caused the sudden upheaval.

I can't see anything, but I hear the rustle of leaves in the distance. I stare at the spot I thought I heard the sound come from, watching for what

165

made the sound. After staring for about five solid minutes, my eyes start to lose focus, and my muscles cramp up from holding still. I slowly stand up and stretch out. The sun is close to setting, and I still haven't found the river yet. I change my direction and head northwest instead of heading straight west.

After another hour of walking, the sun is gone, and the woods are dark and ominous. I pull out my flashlight to keep myself from falling over branches. I occasionally stop and sweep the area around me with my light, trying to catch whatever it is putting my nerves on edge. I would almost welcome a fight at this point if it meant getting rid of the panic-inducing feeling of danger. But there is never anything there.

Finally, sweet relief fills me when I hear the sound of rushing water. I run the rest of the way, tripping occasionally on sticks and rocks. I stop at the water's edge and plunge my hands into it, scooping up handfuls of refreshing, cold water to wash my face with. I try hard not to drink any of the river water. I learned on one of the survival shows that you could get sick and die from drinking unclean water. The cool water is so tempting, but I'll just stick to my plastic-flavored bottled water.

I followed the river downstream when I left, so I make my way upriver to get back to camp. It shouldn't be too long now. I walk as fast as I safely can and finally start to recognize where I am. I see a dark figure stand up from a boulder as I work my way to the rocky riverbank.

"Olivia? Is that you?" I hear David call out in hushed tones.

"Yeah! It's me!" I call out and run the rest of the way to where David stands.

He stoops over to drop something from his hands, and we fall into an embrace, squeezing each other hard. Suddenly, David tenses and lets go.

"Did you bring someone with you?" he asks, quietly.

"No. Why?"

David bends over and picks up what it was he had dropped.

"Get down!"

I obey immediately and watch as he nocks an arrow and shoots toward a tree. I hear a voice yell out a curse and watch in horror as a man stumbles and runs away, holding his injured arm.

36

"Who was that?" I squeak.

"I don't know, but I'm going to go see if I can catch him. Wake Matthias!" he orders as he turns to run after the man.

"No, David! Don't..." I call helplessly after him, but he's already gone.

I run down the path to camp and barge into Matthias's hut. He's fast asleep on his back, gripping the handle of a knife lying on his chest. Thank goodness, it's sheathed. I drop to the ground next to his cot and shake him awake.

"Matthias! Matthias wake up!"

His eyes snap open. He pulls the knife out and has it up to my throat before I can utter another word. The cold, sharp edge of the blade rubs against my skin and cuts a line ever so slightly before Matthias realizes he's in no danger.

"Olivia? What are ya doin' in my hut? Never wake me up like that again. I could've hurt ya."

"David told me to come get you. He took off after some guy who followed me here."

"What?" Matthias jumps off his cot and throws a shirt on. He grabs his boots and pulls them on his bare feet. "Which way'd they go?"

"After he shot the guy in the arm, he took off downriver, and David ran after him. Please, you gotta help David."

"I'm on it. And when I get back, we're gonna have a long talk." He glares at me.

I watch as he runs to another hut to wake up Frederick and Markos and then heads off in the direction I mentioned. It takes only a minute before the brothers come rushing out of their hut and follow behind Matthias, carrying bows.

I go to my shelter to drop my backpack off. I move as quietly as my adrenaline-filled muscles will allow me so I don't wake up Cass and Tim. I don't need a barrage of questions at the moment.

I slip out and pace back and forth next to the fire pit. My neck stings where the knife cut me. That was a close call. I nervously pick at the dry skin around my nails. What was I thinking? Why did I feel the need to talk to my mom so badly? I hope the necklace was worth going back for.

My legs begin to get shaky as I keep walking the same track over and over again, searching every direction for any sign of their return. Maybe I should try to get some sleep. I'm not sure I will be able to sleep with David out there in potential danger, but I'm exhausted.

"Olivia. Get outside now. We need to talk," Matthias says sternly. I snap awake as soon as I remember the events of last night. I dig around in my bag until I find the necklace and slip it around my neck as I head outside.

"What happened? Did you catch him? Who was he?" I blink profusely in the bright sunlight. I look over to the fire pit and see Rebecca bandaging up a long gash on David's temple.

"David!" I cry. I try to check on him, but Matthias grabs my shoulder and spins me around.

"What the hell were ya thinkin'? Where'd ya go?" Matthias growls. He looms over me, making me feel like a small child.

"I-I needed to talk to Mom. I needed her to answer some questions. It was stupid, and I'm sorry," I say, staring at the ground.

"You're damn right it was stupid. You're a part of this group now. We look after each other. But if you're gonna be so damn foolish and run off to the city, maybe ya need to leave for good."

I glance to the right and see Alexandrine with a small smirk. I glower at her and turn my attention back to Matthias's angry face.

"Here." I remove the necklace and hand it to him. "I also went back to get this. I don't know what this is, but it has the same markings as the sticks Saul carves."

He grabs it from my hand and shoves it in his pocket without even looking at it.

"Did you catch the guy?" I ask.

"Not yet. We didn't know where David had run off to, and by the time we found 'im, he was unconscious, and the guard was gone."

"How do you know it was a guard?"

"David saw a tattoo on his forearm of the Coalition flag before he was knocked out."

"Well, what's the plan now?" I ask.

"We hope the guard either bleeds out before he can get back to the city, or Markos and Frederick find him. In the meantime, we prepare for battle."

"Do you really think they are going to come out here?"

"He knows where our camp is. If he makes it back to the city, they're comin', and we have you to thank for it."

"I said I was sorry, Matthias. I had to know why Mom didn't come with you. Why she lied."

"Yeah, well, your little honesty quest could mean a war for us. Ya didn't think. Ya only cared 'bout your hurt feelin's, and now we have to pay the price."

"Lay off, Pop. We've been found before, and we kicked their asses. We can do it again," Henry says, walking close to where we're squared off.

"Disrespect from you now too? Like two peas in a pod. I blame your mother for this."

"Well, I don't remember her so—" Henry starts to say.

"Animal pens. Both of you. Now!" Matthias storms off to his hut.

Henry huffs and swears under his breath. I look over at David, who now has white gauze wrapped around his head to keep the bandage in place, and give him a little apologetic wave as I turn to follow Henry to the animal pens.

"Thanks for sticking up for me back there," I say, breaking the silence.

"Don't mention it. Pop can be uptight, and sometimes he needs a reminder to cool it."

Silence falls between us again as we set to work. I watch as Henry grabs two shovels and hands me one, catching my eye. He looks so much like Matthias with the bushy facial hair, broad chin, straight nose, and muscular stature. However, his mouth is so much like my mother's, it makes me think of her just by looking at it.

"So, I guess you're my brother," I say lamely.

"Yup. Guess so." He scoops up a shovel full of manure and dumps it into one of the wheelbarrows.

"What's Matthias like as a dad?" I ask, trying to keep the tone light.

"Strict. Disciplined. Rigid. He wasn't exactly the perfect Dad, but he respects me, and he's taught me a lot."

I nod as we keep working.

"What's Mom like?" Henry asks hesitantly.

"Um, she likes her secrets. We don't exactly get along that well, but she tries to be a good mom, occasionally. Her taco making skills are excellent, though."

"Tacos? What are those?" Henry asks with a quizzical look.

"Oh, wow! I guess you probably wouldn't have had tacos out here in the woods. They're deliciousness wrapped up inside a soft flour tortilla."

"What's a tortilla?"

"It's like a really thin circle of bread," I start to say, but I can tell he still has no clue what I'm talking about. "You know what? Never mind."

The two wheelbarrows are full, so I follow Henry down a trail leading outside of the camp to dump it in the manure pile they save for fertilizer. I'm having a hard time coming to grips with the fact that this man in front of me is my brother. I'm not even sure how brothers and sisters are supposed to behave around each other. Henry seems too cool to be related to me. I feel the sudden urge to apologize to him.

"I'm sorry I left to go confront Mom. It was really stupid. I was just shocked when I found out Matthias was my father. I needed to know why Mom had lied to me my whole life."

"It's okay. Just don't do it again," he warns.

I nod.

I follow him back to the animal pens, and we finish cleaning up what's left. Henry makes a couple of noises as though he's going to say something but then stops. We work in the heat of the day, sweat glistening on our arms and faces. Henry seems to be troubled about something, but he doesn't speak. We take the rest of the filth out of camp to the dump pile, and that's when Henry finally says something.

"Hey, um, did Mom ever mention me?" Henry wipes the back of his neck nervously.

"No. I didn't know you existed until I found a picture of her pregnant, and it was dated five years before I was born. Her explanation for it was that she had a stillborn."

Henry narrows his eyes and shakes his head slightly.

"She did, however, ask me what you looked like when I was back in the city."

"What did you say?"

"That you're handsome like Matthias, but you have her smile."

He chuckles a bit at that. "Thanks."

As we take our wheelbarrows back to camp, Henry says, "I'm going to see if Pop will let me work with you and David for a while on your combat training."

"Okay."

"We should probably get started right away, so go get changed and meet me by the fire pit."

I throw on some sweatpants and a plain gray t-shirt and head back to the campfire. David is still sitting there, cradling his chin in his hands, staring down at the ground. I have a seat next to him, and he gives me a sad look.

"I'm sorry I didn't catch the guy. I feel so embarrassed about getting knocked out by him."

"It's okay, David."

"Why did you leave without me?" he asks. "You know I would have gone with you if you had asked me."

"No, you would have tried to talk me out of it."

"Probably." He nods. "We're not part of the city anymore, Liv. We belong out here."

"I know. I got confused with this whole Matthias thing, and I wasn't thinking rationally. It won't happen again, I promise."

"Good."

"I also grabbed the necklace from home that I'm pretty sure belonged to Saul."

"How do you know it belonged to him?"

"Saul carves symbols on the sticks he's always whittling, and I recognized them as the same ones that are on the pendant I once found in a box marked 'Dad's stuff.' 'Dad' meaning Matthias's dad, Saul."

"Cool! Can I see it?" David's eyes light up with intrigue.

"Nope. I gave it to Matthias."

"Why'd you do that? You probably won't get it back now."

"Maybe I can ask for it back once he's cooled off."

"Maybe," David says with disappointment. We fall into a moment of silence, and then I remember something else.

"Your mom spotted me while I was back."

"What? What did she say? Is she mad at me?"

"No. I told her how you're doing so much better, and it made her cry." David reaches out and puts his hand on top of mine.

"What did everyone do when they found out I was gone?" I ask.

"Nothing," David starts to say. I give him a shocked look, and he quickly adds, "Well, Tim, Cass, and I were dead set on going out there to search for you, but Matthias forbade it. He was pissed at you and said you deserved whatever you got."

"How fatherly," I mutter.

"He talked some sense into us that we probably wouldn't find you anyway since the woods are so big, and we didn't know which way you headed. I was so worried something bad was going to happen to you, I couldn't eat or sleep until you got back."

I give him a small smile just as Henry comes back with a bundle of weapons in his arms.

"He gave me the all clear. Let's get started."

We begin with sword fighting, but he isn't as good as Matthias, and I beat him within thirty seconds every time we start.

When it's David's turn, they seem to be a little more evenly matched as they fill the camp with metallic clangs from their blocking and striking. David taps out when his head injury starts to bleed through the bandages, and he almost throws up from the pain. I run to the shelter and get him some of the medicine I brought with me.

Tim and Cass join us as Henry and I are about to start hand to hand combat.

"Now, how much do you know about sparring?" Henry asks.

"She punched a bully in the nose and broke it," David says with a smirk.

"Nice," Henry chuckles. "Anything else?"

"Only what I saw you and David doing when we first got here. I don't know anything about it otherwise."

"All right, Tim and Cass, why don't you two pair up over here next to us and practice while I teach Olivia. You can show her how some of the moves look."

Tim and Cass quickly take their place next to us, and Cass whispers, "I'm glad you made it back, Olivia."

I smile at her.

"Okay, what you want to do is stand with your right foot forward. Your legs should be about shoulder-width apart. Hands up, protect your jaw. Tim, I want you to throw a slow punch at Cass's head. Cass, block, and punch to his ribs."

I watch as they do what Henry says with exaggerated movements. Looks simple enough.

"All right, good. Olivia, your turn."

Henry throws a slow punch at my head. I block it and land a punch to his ribs.

"Perfect. Now Cass, I want you to come at Tim with both hands toward his neck. Tim, you're going to block her hands and knee her in the groin."

They both nod, and Cass starts toward Tim with both hands. He steps forward, brings both hands up with a circular motion and blocks them outward, then lifts his knee up to her groin without making contact.

"Yup. Now you try, Olivia."

Henry comes at me, and I mimic everything I just saw Tim do. It feels so natural like I've been doing it my whole life.

"Great. Now we're going to try—"

"Enough!" I hear a voice yell. I look up just as Alexandrine steps behind Henry. "Stop babying her. It's time to show her what real combat is like."

My heart starts to race as I look at the anger that borderlines insanity in her dark brown eyes. Her hands are up, and she's bouncing back and forth on her feet, itching to fight. Henry steps off to the side with concern on his face. I bring my hands up and shuffle my feet, trying to stay light on my toes. She throws a fast punch and lands it right in my stomach. All the air is knocked out of my lungs, and I drop to my knees as I gasp for breath.

"Come on! You're gonna have to do better than that!" Alexandrine goads.

Once I manage to breathe again, I stand back up and get ready for the next blow. She throws a punch toward my head, but I block it and punch her in the stomach. My fist hits solid abs, and I think my hand hurts more than her stomach does. She seems angered by the punch I got through, and she starts throwing strikes at me rapidly. I block and dodge the best I can, but some of them land their mark, and I'm momentarily stunned. She takes advantage of this and continues to punch me in the ribs or the stomach.

I'm having a hard time staying on my feet each time she lands a punch, but I'm determined to not let her win. My body feels like it's being tenderized. I can already feel bruises forming on my ribs. I start to tighten my muscles every time she throws a punch, and it helps.

"Show me what you've got, oh, great Rare one!" She takes a break from punching me and instead dances around me.

I decide to make a move and lunge at her, but she's too quick, and I'm suddenly lying flat in the dirt. My head swims from the sudden fall, but I stand up and wait for her next attack with renewed determination.

She stares me down for a while as we stand off, and I begin to wonder if maybe she's ready to be done, but then she charges at me. It's like a slow-motion movie playing before my eyes. I watch as she cocks her right arm back, takes a step forward with her right foot, and then brings her fist toward my head. I easily block it and sweep her leg out from under her, knocking her on the ground. Before I know what I'm doing, I drop to the ground too, wrap my legs around her torso, lock my feet together, and squeeze her ribcage. Her eyes bulge as the breath is being squeezed out of her body. She taps my leg with her one free arm, but I keep squeezing. It isn't until I hear everyone around us telling me to stop that I snap out of it and let her up.

"Where'd you learn that take-down?" Alexandrine asks, bent over as she tries to regain her breath. She doesn't seem at all angry that I almost killed her.

"I didn't learn it. It just felt right," I answer truthfully.

"You need to learn to block punches."

"Maybe if you hadn't insisted that I take you on without proper training, I could be working on that," I say, getting angry.

"You wouldn't have known that was something you needed to work on unless we had a sparring match. Now you know."

"What is your problem? Why do you hate me so much?"

"I don't have time for this. I need to go help Matthias get ready for when the guards come out here because of you."

I watch as she storms away. I want to pick up a rock and throw it at her head, but I keep my cool and mutter curse words at her instead.

"Don't let her get to you," Henry says. "She's not an easy person to get along with."

I smile a little at him.

"She is right about you learning to block better, though. That was kind of brutal."

"So, teach me."

3|7,

We spend a good portion of the afternoon learning combat moves and strategies. I teach everyone the take-down I used on Alexandrine. When David performs it on me, he loses his balance, and his face comes within inches of mine. He pauses a moment as though he's considering kissing me, his breath hot on my face, but I roll away from him to stand back up before he has the chance.

We are all sweaty and tired by the time Caroline tells us it's time to prepare supper. Once we're eating, I can't help but notice everyone seems to be on edge. Markos and Frederick haven't returned yet, and I can only hope that's because they've caught the guard's trail and are close to finding him. Nobody else asks me where I went or why I left, and I'm grateful for it. The young children whisper to each other while eyeing me once in a while, but they never say anything to me. I'm happy to be back out here, and I hope to never set foot in the city again.

I go to bed before the sun even sets. It's been a long day, and I'm exhausted. I wake up to Cass shaking my shoulder.

"Olivia, you need to get up. We have to get breakfast ready. You and I are on food prep duty."

I groggily roll off my leaf bed and feel as though I were hit by a truck. Yesterday's sparring match with Alexandrine has taken its toll. I can barely lift my arms without pain ripping through my ribs and stomach. I gently lift my shirt up and see dark purple bruises dotted across my torso.

"Ouch! Alexandrine wasn't pulling her punches with you. Maybe you should take another soak in the river to help with the swelling."

"No, I'll be all right. As long as we don't have to do any more training today."

I'm not so lucky. Henry insists that we keep on it. Injured or not, we need to prepare. I take some medicine, and it helps take the edge off, but the bruises make me slow. We do some target practice with the bows, and David is a natural with it.

"I practiced while you were away," he admits.

I take a shot at it, and I manage to hit most of the cans. At least, I'm better at shooting bows than I am at shooting guns. Maybe I can get even better at this once my bruises heal, and I'm feeling good again.

Alexandrine hasn't said a word to me since our sparring match, but she isn't giving me death glares either. She seems to have moved to ignoring me. I'm okay with that.

Another day of physical training has exhausted me, and I sleep like a rock. It's just before dawn when everyone in my shelter wakes up to the sound of Frederick's voice calling out for Rebecca. We all rush out to see what's going on.

"Frederick, what happened to Markos?" Rebecca asks as she runs to his side. Markos is slung over Frederick's meaty shoulder, unconscious.

Matthias runs out of the woods from where he was keeping watch over camp. He helps Frederick get Markos off his shoulder and down on the ground.

"What happened?" Matthias asks, staring down at the bloody wound in Markos's chest. Rebecca lifts his shirt, and we can see a two-inch stab mark close to his heart. Markos's skin is pale, and his chest is just barely rising as he breathes.

"We were hot on his trail, tracking his bootprints and the blood streaks on the trees where he rubbed up against them. But then we lost sight of any traces, so we decided to split up and search the area. I hear Markos yell, and I run to where I heard him, thinking he had picked up the trail. Instead, I come to find him lying on the ground, bleeding. I hear the snap of a branch and just catch sight of the guard running again toward the city. I had to make the choice of hunting him down or helping my brother before he dies. I couldn't just leave him. I'm sorry, Matthias!" Frederick wipes snot off his nose with the back of his hand.

Matthias sighs deeply. "Ya did the right thing, Frederick. But this means we need to relocate camp. We can't stay here."

"What? How are we going to move everything?" I ask, bewildered.

"We're not. We take the essentials and find a new place to build a camp."

Everyone is quiet as we all watch Rebecca clean Markos's wound and hold pressure to stop the bleeding. Frederick pulls a stump over from the fire to sit on and watches helplessly, exhausted from carrying his brother back to camp. His shirt is soaked in Markos's blood, but he doesn't seem to notice.

"What do you think, Becky? Is he going to make it?" Frederick asks.

"I don't know. He needs a hospital," she says, worry etched on her brow.

"Do what ya can," Matthias grunts, and then turns to address everyone else. "Y'all should be preparin' for the move. Rebecca's got this under control. Get to work!"

Guilt weighs heavily on my mind. I did this. I got Markos stabbed. I made it so everyone has to abandon their home. I look around at the group, and they all look sad or worried. David and Cass give me small sympathetic smiles.

Tim leans in and whispers, "It's okay, Olivia. We've had to move camps before."

"Really?" I ask, slightly relieved.

"Yeah. Alexandrine tried to go find her daughter once, and she had a group of guards after her. They followed her, and we managed to kill the guards, but we changed locations before people came out looking for the missing men."

"I just hate that it's my fault."

"We all make mistakes." Tim pats my shoulder.

David and I follow Cass and Tim to our shelter. I haven't taken much out of my bag since I've been back at camp, so it doesn't take me long to pack. I search around for anything more I can do.

I walk past Rebecca as she's stitching the hole in Markos's chest.

"I don't know if this is going to work. If the knife cut something on the inside, he's going to die from internal bleeding," Rebecca frets.

Frederick covers his face with grimy hands. I'm not sure I will ever be able to look him in the eyes again if Markos doesn't make it.

I step into the Commons shelter, where two other women are gathering up cooking supplies and food.

"What can I do to help?" I ask feebly.

"We're going to need the wheelbarrows to move all this stuff, but you guys used them to haul manure. Take them down to the river and wash them out as best you can," Suzanne says.

I don't let on how disgusted I am. It's payment for the mess I got us all in. I just nod and set to work. I pull the two wheelbarrows down to the river and tip them on their sides so the current can do most of the work. Meanwhile, I look around at the morning sun shining on the trees across the wide river. It's so peaceful here. I close my eyes for a moment and listen to the Mukduks up river chirping their happy song, the trickle of water over rocks, the creaking of trees swaying in the wind.

I grab a cloth off the boulder that is supposed to be for dishes, but I've got nothing else to use. I start scrubbing the smelly remains of animal waste out of the wheelbarrow when I hear a sorrowful cry from camp.

"*No!* No, please, God! Don't die, Markos! Don't leave me!" Frederick cries.

Tears spring to my eyes, and I start weeping with him. I want to run back to camp and tell Frederick how sorry I am, but he needs this moment to himself. I'm not sure he's ever going to forgive me. I wouldn't if I were him. Markos seemed like such a nice guy, and I killed him. I killed his brother.

My sadness turns to anger toward myself. I'm an idiot. Maybe I should be kicked out and eaten by a Havoc. Maybe I should have died a long time ago. Maybe I should die now. I focus my anger toward the cleaning job. I start scrubbing the wheelbarrow so hard, I rip one of the scabs open on my hand, and it starts bleeding. I relish the pain. I deserve pain.

The sound of Frederick's sobbing continues. I finish one wheelbarrow and start on the other. David joins me by the river bank and crouches next to me.

"It's not your fault, Liv."

"Yes, it is. It is entirely my fault. I'm the one who ran back to the city. I'm the one who was followed. I'm the one who got Markos killed!" I know David is trying to make me feel better, but that just makes me angry. Denying the fact that it is all my fault is foolishness.

"All right. It was your fault," David says. "What are you going to do about it?

"I don't know. Stop breathing?"

David slaps me on the shoulder. "Knock it off, Liv. I'll tell you what we're going to do. We're going to honor Markos's death by helping the group in any way we can, and we're going to keep training. We'll pour ourselves into our lessons and make ourselves useful. You and I are Rare. If we focus on becoming the best versions of ourselves we can be, I don't think we'll have to worry about the stupid guards anymore. They won't stand a chance against us."

I stare at the cloth in my hand, waiting for David to finish his lecture. I feel like crawling into a hole and never coming out again, and here he is, full of enthusiasm, making it sound like we are prized members of the group. Like I didn't just get a fellow member killed. Like I deserve to be here. Alive.

David puts his hand on my shoulder. "Hey," he says calmly, "I know you're upset, and I can't say I wouldn't be if the roles were reversed, but you are not in control of other people's actions. You didn't make Markos run after the guard and get himself stabbed. It sucks what happened, but none of that was in your control." David stands back up and walks to a boulder nearby to have a seat.

I really wish he would leave me alone.

"You can go back to camp, David. I'm almost done."

"I'm not leaving you here by yourself, Liv. I know how you can get when something bad happens, and you feel guilty. So, I'm going to stay right here until you're done cleaning those wheelbarrows, and then I'll help you take them back."

I huff angrily at him and get back to scrubbing. Suddenly, David starts singing, and I stop to listen. He's been tone deaf ever since I've known him, and it's always been painful to listen to him try to sing songs. He was so bad, most of the time you couldn't tell what song he was trying to sing unless you listened to the lyrics. But now his voice is so clear and beautiful, goosebumps pop up on my arms and the back of my neck. I close my eyes as I listen to the lilting beauty of his melancholy song that echoes through the trees. His voice is rich and deep as he sings the haunting lyrics of love and loss. I've never heard the song before, and I'm not sure I will ever hear it's equal again.

"How was that?" he asks once he's finished.

A tear runs down my cheek. I clear my throat, and all I can say is, "Wow."

"All right, all right. I'll stop distracting you. Get back to work," he says with a wink.

I turn my attention back on the wheelbarrow and hurry up to finish. It suddenly seems so quiet, and it takes me a moment to realize I don't hear Frederick crying anymore. I pull the wheelbarrow out of the water and scrub my hands extra hard, wishing I had my soap with me, but it's all packed up. I don't feel like going back to get it.

David and I take the wheelbarrows back to the Commons and help the ladies load it up with supplies. Cooking utensils, dishes, and tools go in one, and the bags of food go in the other. They use ropes to strap it all down, and David helps to get it tight. Carol's son comes walking over to us, leading two of the camp's goats, and Carol places something across their backs that looks like two bags attached by a strip of cloth in the middle. She then proceeds to fill the bags up with loose foods like apples, onions, and carrots.

"I had no idea you could use goats to haul stuff," I comment.

"Yup. They're smart animals. You just have to train them up a little bit," Carol answers.

"Do we really have to leave, Momma?" the boy asks with sad eyes.

"Yes, Noah, we do," she answers calmly, ruffling his hair.

"How is Daddy going to find us if we move?"

I suddenly feel uncomfortable listening to their conversation, but I can't seem to walk away either. I know very little about these people, what their stories are, and I'm curious.

"Baby, he isn't coming. I know you miss your Daddy, but he signed up to work for the bad man," she says gently, wiping a tear off his cheek. "Now I need you to be strong for your sister and me. You're the man of our family. A little bit of crying is okay, but then you wipe those tears away, and you get back to doing what needs to be done."

"Yes, Momma." Noah sniffles. He tries hard to wipe the tears away and stand a little taller, but his chin quivers, and it makes me want to cry along with him.

"Go help your sister get her stuff packed up. I think we'll be leaving pretty soon."

Noah turns around and shuffles back to their shelter.

"He seems like a good boy," I comment.

"Most of the time," Carol says. "He's only eight, but he's had to grow up really quick living out here."

"You said your husband works for the 'bad man.' Do you mean Turk?"

"That's right. He signed up to be a guard, even though he knew how I felt about it all. I want nothing to do with Turk and what he's doing to people."

Just then, Rebecca staggers by, looking shell-shocked and covered in blood.

"Excuse me." Carol runs over to Rebecca to help her down to the river to get washed up.

The other women are finishing up with the rest of the food, so David and I head back toward our shelter. As we walk past the fire pit, we see Frederick walking into the woods, carrying Markos's body. Matthias is walking next to him, carrying a shovel with one hand, and his other hand is on Frederick's shoulder. My heart drops again, and I feel like I'm going to be sick.

Tim and Cass have the shelter emptied of their things, and we all sit by the firepit, waiting for the rest of camp to be ready. Henry leads Saul out to the firepit and has him sit down. He looks at me and smiles with a twinkle in his eye. I wish I could have gotten to know him better before he got to be this way.

Everyone waits by the firepit for Frederick and Matthias to return. The chickens have been caught and put in cages made from sticks and twine. They voice their displeasure at being trapped by clucking frantically and flapping their wings. The goats don't seem to care what's going on as they munch on apples that Noah gave to them.

Nobody talks as we wait patiently for the men to return. It feels like we are paying our respects to Markos with a long moment of silence. Even the young children sit quietly with their mothers. Finally, Frederick and Matthias come back to camp, arms and clothes covered in dirt, and walk solemnly down to the river to clean up. We wait some more as the men go back to their shelters to change clothes and gather up their things. Nobody dared go into Matthias's hut to grab the weapons, so it takes a little while for Matthias to get everything together.

Matthias hands out the weapons to everyone, except the children. I'm given a sword, and I strap it to my back and then put my bag over the top so it's mostly hidden, but I can reach it easily if needed. It's not very comfortable, but my safety is more important.

Frederick joins the group, and the women take turns hugging him and expressing their condolences. I feel like I should say something, but I also feel like I should just keep my mouth shut and never talk to him again. I don't deserve to even look at him. A tear slides down my cheek, and I feel about one inch tall right now.

"All right, group," Matthias says. "I'll lead. Saul will stay by me. Henry, ya take the back, and everyone else can fall in line. Let's go!"

I take one last look around at our camp, and a feeling of loss hits me. I haven't been here that long, but I feel like I'm leaving home and never going to see it again. It must be so much worse for everyone else. With a heavy sigh, I follow behind David as we head off into the unknown once more.

3│8

Our pace is set at the speed of Saul, which is about as slow as you can get. We are heading northwest from our camp, putting as much distance as we can between us and the city. We walk in the water up the river for a little while, so we can hide our footprints, but the current gets to be too strong for Saul and the children, so we move back to dry ground.

We stop periodically for water breaks and snacks. Suzanne's little girl, Sonya, has had enough already, and she falls asleep in her mother's arms. Suzanne asks for the other women to help by taking turns carrying her. The weight of their bags, plus a sleeping child, is a bit too much for hiking out in the woods, and they have to pass her around before someone accidentally drops her from fatigue.

The sky is cloudy today, which keeps the temperature mild in the forest. There isn't much wind, so the woods seem extra quiet. Other than goat bleats, chicken clucks, and the occasional whispers and giggles from the children, our group moves as silently as we can through the woods.

David glances back at me occasionally to give me a small smile or an eye roll from our turtle like speed. It's going to take forever to make it a safe distance, but I don't complain. We find a small clearing and stop for the night. After a supper of dried venison, apples, and raw carrots, Matthias and a few men set to work hanging all the bags that have food up in trees a safe distance outside of our camp so they don't attract bears. The rest of us set up the sleeping arrangements. We put the small children together in the middle, their mothers and Saul around them, then the rest of us on the outside perimeter. Matthias tells Frederick to take the night off and that he and a few others will take turns keeping watch.

I lie awake for a while, listening to Frederick quietly crying himself to sleep. The only other sounds we hear that night are the sounds of the nighttime animals looking for food. Hopefully, none of them will have a taste for goat or chicken. By sunrise, Alexandrine is waking the group up so we can get started on the day.

"This is kind of exciting, isn't it?" David asks quietly as we eat breakfast away from the rest of the group.

"It would be if it weren't my fault we're doing this."

"You're going to have to forgive yourself, Liv."

"I can't, David. Markos is dead because of my actions."

"I think you should talk to Frederick. At least, tell him you're sorry. Distancing yourself and staying quiet isn't helping anyone."

"I will. I'm just waiting until the time is right."

"Don't wait too long."

After everyone is finished eating, we gather up our things and burden ourselves with our heavy bags once again. I hear the bottle of vitamins I grabbed from the apartment rattle. I should probably give them to Matthias sometime since he seemed so interested in them. I'm curious to know what he thinks is wrong with them.

The walk is rather uneventful, other than the constant potty breaks the kids keep having to make. Who knew children needed to go to the bathroom so often?

We stop a little early to set up camp because Saul's feet are swelling from all the walking. Matthias sends Tim and three men out to hunt for some meat. Cass and I set to work collecting wood so we can cook the meat once they're back. Wood isn't hard to find, and soon, we have a nice pile.

I look over and see David talking with Frederick. Frederick is nodding his head somberly, and then they both look over at me. My cheeks turn red, and I quickly look away.

"Olivia, come here," David calls.

I give him a quick death glare but make my way over to them. How dare he put me on the spot like this.

David whispers, "Now's the time."

I take a quick glance at Frederick, and he's looking right at me. I gaze back down at the ground, and tears start to well up in my eyes.

"Frederick, I am so sorry for what happened to your brother. It's all my fault!" I say as I start ugly crying. "I never should have gone back to the city. I'm an idiot. Please, forgive me."

I feel his big hand rest gently on the back of my head, and he starts stroking my hair. That makes me cry even harder.

"Markos died with honor. He gave his life to protect those he loved. And since he was always willing to give people a second chance, I think he would want me to forgive you. And I do. Don't be too hard on yourself, Olivia. Markos is in a better place, and one day, I will be with him again."

With that, he puts his big arm around me and pulls me into a hug. I hug him in return but hold my breath because he smells like BO after a long day of hiking.

"Touching. Now let's get camp finished up," Alexandrine cuts in.

"She's right. It will be dark before we know it," Frederick comments with a small smile.

I feel like a weight has been lifted off my shoulders. It feels so good to have apologized and made things right with Frederick. Now, I need to work on forgiving myself.

After another hour, the hunters come back with a big doe and a few squirrels. The men set out to clean it away from camp, taking the shovel along to bury the entrails, and Cass works on starting a fire. The little children are playing a game of hide-and-seek in the trees around camp. Their laughter helps lighten the mood a bit. Everyone is still mourning the loss of Markos, and I think it will be a while before people get back to normal.

It's well after dark by the time we finish cooking the meat and eating. As we start to lay out blankets, David stops and shushes everyone.

"There's something out there. I can hear it breathing."

We're all quiet, and everyone jumps a little when we hear leaves rustling.

"It could just be a squirrel," Tim offers.

David pulls the flashlight out of his bag and shines it in the direction of the noises. Two eyes glow from close to the ground, and that's when I see it: a white stripe down its black body.

"Nobody move," I whisper frantically.

Everyone stands still. Suzanne scoops Sonya off the ground and holds her tightly.

"I don't know what they're called, but they spray stinky stuff out of their butt that's hard to wash off," I say, and I hear Noah giggle.

"It's a skunk," Matthias says. "Henry, fetch me the bow, will ya?"

Henry carefully shuffles his way to the back of the group to find the bow. David keeps the flashlight shining on the skunk.

"You're not going to kill it, are you?" Noah's little sister, Emily, asks.

"Yes, I am."

Emily starts to whimper, and Caroline slowly drops to her knees to hug her. Henry returns with the bow and hands it to Matthias. The skunk has moved farther away from camp, but we can still see it with the flashlight. He takes aim, careful with his movements, and fires. He misses but spooks the skunk enough that it takes off into the dark woods. We all relax and start getting back to what we were doing, and then the smell sets in. Not again!

Pandemonium erupts as the kids start squealing about the stench, jumping up and down with their noses pinched.

"The skunk must have sprayed as it ran away," Henry says, covering his nose with his shirt.

Everyone is coughing and complaining all at once. Let's hope there aren't any Havoc nearby to hear us. And then I remember my first run-in with a skunk.

"Well, one good thing about this is we're less likely to be attacked by a Havoc," I say and tell them my encounter with the skunk.

"Great. We'll just all die from the stench instead of being eaten." Alexandrine scowls.

"We're not gonna die from the smell. Now, everybody, settle down, and get some sleep," Matthias orders.

It's a restless night for everyone. Once we get the kids settled down, we all try to get some sleep, but the smell is just too much. By morning, everyone is cranky and ready to move out.

For four more days, we plod along through the woods. Luckily, we found a small pond yesterday, and everyone took turns bathing in it, in hopes of washing the lingering smell of the skunk off. Thank God, nobody was directly sprayed by the skunk this time.

After walking all morning, we come to a large clearing, and Matthias has everyone rest while he, Frederick, and Henry scout the area. They climb trees to see what they can find. About forty-five minutes later, they come back to the clearing.

"This is as good a place as any to set up camp. There's a small stream not far from here for our water needs. Let's begin," Matthias announces.

We spend the first day clearing the area of rocks, sticks, and other debris. We let the chickens out of their cages, and they happily strut around the place, letting us know they're here. The children run around, keeping them near camp. Everyone seems to be in a better mood knowing that we finally found a place to make home.

The next day, the men go out to the forest to find wood for making shelters. The women build a nice-sized fire pit that will allow everyone to fit around it comfortably. The kids run around having sword fights with branches, and Saul has found a fallen log to sit on to whittle sticks again. I asked Matthias if I could have my necklace back, but he was too busy to dig it out of his bag at the time. I didn't dare ask him if I could look for it.

As I help the women plan out our camp, I start to feel a sense of hope and belonging. The sadness of Markos's death is still there, but I'm slowly letting go of the guilt. I'm not sure if I will ever let go of it entirely, but starting somewhere fresh will be helpful. Alexandrine gives me the cold shoulder now and again, but she seems to enjoy having something to do, and I catch her smiling occasionally.

I sleep soundly after a hard day of work. I'm feeling so much closer to everyone in the group. Matthias, Henry, and Saul may be my family by blood, but everyone in this camp is my family by choice. Even Alexandrine.

The next day, the men head back out to find more building materials. Rebecca, Caroline, and Alexandrine are discussing where gardens should be planted while Suzanne keeps an eye on the kids. On one of the last recon missions, Matthias was able to get his hands on some seed packets. According to the packages, we will be able to grow radishes, spinach, broccoli, green onions, and baby carrots in about a month. In the meantime, we have to scavenge for food so our supply doesn't run out too quickly. That's what I'm doing today.

I head out with some bags to find anything that might be considered food. Suzanne gave me a book with pictures of edible plants. Let's hope I can identify them correctly.

After walking only five minutes away from camp, I come across a bush with thorns and fat berries. I open the book and flip through the pages until I find a picture of it. The book says it's safe to eat, so I pull one off and smell it. It smells sweet and makes my mouth water. As I bite into it, the berry bursts in my mouth, flooding my taste buds with sweet juice. I have never tasted something so good. Being careful of the thorns, I set to work filling the bags full of them.

We have a tasty supper of berries and venison from another deer Tim was able to shoot. Everyone seems content with a full stomach, and we start to get settled in for the night. I can't wait to have shelters built again. I don't like feeling exposed while sleeping.

Tim pleads to take first watch, telling Matthias that he's gotten so good with the bow now, he feels like he should be able to keep watch like all the other adults. Reluctantly, Matthias agrees to it, and we all settle in for a good night's sleep. I stare up at the stars contentedly and say a little prayer to ask God for forgiveness for Markos and to thank him that I'm here—stronger, healthier—and that my life is better than I ever could have imagined it. Then I close my eyes and drift off to sleep.

I wake up in the middle of the night, needing to go to the bathroom. I look over at Tim, who's supposed to be keeping watch, but he's fast asleep. I'll wake him up when I come back. I carefully step over people and walk a good distance away from camp for privacy. The night is still and peaceful, and I can see stars shining through the forest canopy. As I'm finishing, I hear footsteps coming from the direction of camp. I wonder who's up. I start to head back, but I'm stopped in my tracks by a gunshot ringing out through the forest.

I start to panic, wondering what's going on. I run a short distance but quickly hide behind a tree when I see a group of government soldiers surrounding the camp. They're wearing gas masks and pointing guns at everyone, who are now awake and on their feet. How did they find us so quickly?

"Which one of you is Olivia?" A soldier says through his mask, making his voice muffled.

My heart is racing out of my chest. What do they want with me? I carefully look past the tree to see if anyone was shot, but everyone seems to be okay. Nobody in camp moves. They all stay quiet except for small sobs from the children. A huge soldier has his arm wrapped around Tim's neck and a gun pointed at his head. Tim looks scared out of his mind with tears streaming down his face.

"Maybe you didn't hear me. Which one of you is Olivia?" The soldier yells. "Give her to us, and maybe we'll let you live."

I stay hidden behind the tree, terrified to move. I watch as Matthias slowly reaches behind his back to grab the handgun he has stashed in a holster on his belt, but a soldier notices and marches up to him, pointing his gun in Matthias's face.

"Give me the gun."

Matthias glares at him but puts his hands in the air. While the soldier reaches around Matthias's back to grab it, Matthias locks eyes on Henry and gives a nod ever so slightly. Henry gets the message, and they start fighting with the soldiers to disarm them. All hell breaks loose as every able-bodied adult in our group starts fighting tooth and nail to disarm the soldiers. Suzanne yells for Cass to gather up the children and run for cover, but Cass gets pulled into the fray.

I hear guns firing, and I can't just leave everyone to fight these soldiers just to save me. I race to the nearest one and pray that I don't get shot. I kick his legs out from under him, and he falls to the ground. I rip his gas mask upward and punch him in the nose as, hard as I can, feeling the bones crack under my knuckles just like Victoria's did. He points the gun at me, and I grab the barrel, shoving it away as I kick him in the ribcage. Finally, his gun falls on the ground when I stomp on his male parts. He curls up in a ball and I search around for the next opponent.

I look over at Cass, who's biting the hand of the soldier she's fighting. I watch as another soldier grabs her hair and rips her head backward, bringing a knife to her throat. Without thinking about it, I dive at the soldier who's about to kill my friend and send his knife flying.

I start hand-to-hand combat with this guy who appears to be only a few years older than me. He knocks me to the ground and before I can stand back up, he lifts his mask and shouts, "I found her!"

I watch in horror as a few soldiers pull canisters from their belts and drop them on the ground. Smoke spills out of the canisters, filling the camp quickly. I try to cover my nose and mouth with my shirt, but it doesn't do any good. I see my friends dropping to the ground like flies. David gives me a fearful look just before his eyes roll back, and he falls to the ground.

God, my friends need me! Please, don't let me die!

I land on the ground with a thump, and everything goes black.

A continuous rhythmic beeping pulls me from my dreamless slumber.

Oh, thank God! I'm not dead.

SUICIDE PREVENTION

If you are feeling suicidal or an urge to harm yourself,
please, find someone to talk to.

You are not alone.

If you can't talk to a family member or a friend, reach out to
the National Suicide Prevention Lifeline:

1-800-273-8255
or
www.suicidepreventionlifeline.org

You have a purpose.
Don't ever give up.

ACKNOWLEDGMENTS

First and foremost, to God be the glory!

I would like to thank my husband, Sage, for the support you've given me through the good times and the bad. It has been a long road, but I'm grateful to have Jeeped it with you.

Thank you to my best friend, Lydia, for reading my manuscript and giving me tips along the way. You are the best!

Thank you to my parents for everything you do for me. I love you.

Thank you to the lovely ladies at Authors 4 Authors Publishing Cooperative for giving me a chance. You have been so great to work with. I am truly blessed.

ABOUT THE AUTHOR

Diane lives in central Wisconsin with her husband and three boys. When not reading or writing, she likes to go hiking as often as she can. Her favorite trail—so far—is the Ice Age Trail with Skunk Foster Lake being her favorite section of it.

Diane's fascination with superheroes sparked the idea for her first novel, *Supernova*, taking some inspiration from X-Men.

Diane can also be found serving as an Awana leader at her local church. She has been serving there for ten years.

Follow her online:

www.dianeanthony.info
Twitter: @DianeMAnthony
Facebook: @DianeMAnthony

Also by Diane Anthony
SUPERNOVA

When librarian Madeline Hayes wakes up in the front yard with no memory of why she's there, her simple life in a small town becomes more complicated than she ever imagined. Strange things start happening: her father heals an injury with a touch, her elderly neighbor seems to become younger, and everyone starts getting this strange blue light in their eyes—and in their veins.

And then people start dying.

Can Madeline unravel this mystery and stop the strange transformations before it's too late?

books2read.com/supernova

AUTHORS 4 AUTHORS PUBLISHING

A publishing company for authors, run by authors, blending the best of traditional and independent publishing

We specialize in speculative fiction: science fiction, fantasy, paranormal, and romance. Get lost in another world!

Check out our collection at https://books2read.com/rl/a4a
or visit Authors4AuthorsPublishing.com/books

For updates, scan the QR code or visit our website to join our semi-monthly newsletter!

Want more YA Science-Fiction? We recommend:

Hard as Stone
by Beatrice B. Morgan

Seventeen-year-old Raven Thane wants an adventure...and she's going to get one. Just not the way that she expected. Bored and disinterested with a routine life in her remote underground community, she fails to notice a thief during her turn at guard duty. Zander, a charming sharpshooter, tasks her with helping him retrieve the mysterious stolen item. Can Raven fix her mistake and prove herself more than a simple country girl? Or will she create even more chaos?

books2read.com/hardstone